Johanna Bell is a freelance journalist living in Surrey with her husband, daughter and dog. She developed a passion for learning about the wars after chatting to her granddad about his experiences in World War II. She is the author of the Bobby Girls series, about the first policewomen in London, also published by Hodder & Stoughton.

To hear more from Johanna, follow her on Twitter: @JoBellAuthor

The Blitz Girls

Book One in the Blitz Girls Series

JOHANNA BELL

HODDER &
STOUGHTON

First published in Great Britain in 2023 by Hodder & Stoughton
An Hachette UK company

1

Copyright © Johanna Bell 2023

A CIP catalogue record for this title is available from the British Library

Paperback ISBN 978 1 399 70876 0
eBook ISBN 978 1 399 70877 7

Typeset in Plantin Light by Manipal Technologies Limited

Printed and bound in Great Britain by Clays Ltd, Elcograf S.p.A.

Hodder & Stoughton policy is to use papers that are natural, renewable
and recyclable products and made from wood grown in sustainable forests.
The logging and manufacturing processes are expected to conform to the
environmental regulations of the country of origin.

Hodder & Stoughton Ltd
Carmelite House
50 Victoria Embankment
London EC4Y 0DZ

www.hodder.co.uk

For Gary,

Who was always so interested in what I was writing.

Dear reader,

I'm so excited to share this first book in the Blitz Girls series with you.

Whatever led you here (whether you stopped by after reading my Bobby Girls series or you've discovered this series afresh), I hope you enjoy what I have created.

I was so excited to start work on a new series, but it was bittersweet as it meant leaving my beloved Bobby Girls behind. However, as soon as I started writing and developing the main Blitz Girls characters, I fell in love with Viv, Dot, and Peggy.

Switching my research from World War I to World War II, I was struck by how much more the Second War affected everybody back home in Britain. Innocent civilians, who hadn't chosen to sign up and fight, were being targeted regardless. People of all ages and classes were affected. I found it difficult reading about young children being killed in such a violent, senseless way. The research was hard going at times, but I chose to include some of the tougher details in the book as I think it's important that we don't sugar-coat what our relatives went through in order for us to live with the freedoms that we enjoy today.

I lost my wonderful father-in-law while my agent was negotiating the deal for *The Blitz Girls*. I'd told Gary about the book, and he was so excited for me and proud of what I was doing. He was always genuinely interested in what I was writing – even the projects I thought he would find dull seemed to spark a light in his eyes as he listened.

I'm devastated that he passed before I got to tell him the deal had gone ahead and that he never got to see the finished product. I've dedicated this book to him, and I will donate a percentage of my earnings to the MND Association in his memory.

I really hope you enjoy reading *The Blitz Girls* as much as I enjoyed writing it, and if you do, then please keep an eye on my social media for details of the next book in the series.

Love,
Jo

The Blitz Girls

Prologue

The sickening wail of a falling bomb filled the air as the ambulance driver carefully negotiated her vehicle around the wreckage. The noise was becoming far too familiar. The air-raid sirens had sounded just twenty minutes before, and already the streets of Chelsea were full of destruction. She closed her eyes briefly and took a deep breath when she spotted some poor soul's severed leg at the side of the road. She kept her eyes fixed forward, then, not keen on discovering the rest of the body. There was no point in stopping here to help – she knew from experience that there was nothing to be done.

Making her way towards her destination, she was momentarily grateful for the fact she had some help to guide her on her way. She had grown accustomed to driving through the streets of London in the dark since the blackout had been imposed, but tonight there was light to guide her – only it was coming from the burning caused by incendiary bombs and explosions. A red glow filled the sky. She suddenly wished it was pitch black again, and that her route wasn't being lit up by the bonfire caused by people's homes and businesses – and lives – being destroyed. But as everyone around her scrambled for safety and shelter, she kept driving towards the danger that the city's nightly visitors were inflicting. It's what she had done most evenings since the Germans had started their relentless attacks on London a week before. To block out the terror that she felt, she tried to focus on how many people she and her partner could help get to medical aid.

Turning into Upper Cheyne Row, she felt bile rising in her throat. When the call had come in, they had only been given the street name. She had hoped all the way here that the public shelter hadn't been hit, but there was no denying now that she was here that the Catholic Church of our Most Holy Redeemer and St Thomas More had taken a direct hit. She felt sick thinking about how many innocent people would have been sheltering in the crypt when the bomb had ripped through it. The one place they would have felt safe.

Searching around for an ARP warden, she spotted Dot and Peggy waving her over. She parked up a few houses down from the church – as close as she could get without shredding the tyres to pieces – and took a moment to digest the rubble and flames before leaping into action.

'What a night to work your first shift,' she said as lightly as she could manage to Dot as they all made their way towards the smouldering wreckage. She tried to block out the groaning and wailing that she could already hear coming from trapped survivors.

'I don't think there was ever going to be a good night to start,' Dot replied, fixing her hat and smiling weakly. Suddenly, a worrying thought popped into Vivian's head. She had run into this woman on her way home recently – and it hadn't been far from here. She didn't want to ask the question – too afraid of the answer. But she had to.

'Do you know anybody who was in there tonight?'

Tears filled the warden's eyes despite her obvious attempts to stop them. Peggy, who hadn't yet taken her eyes off the flames licking the sky, took hold of Dot's hand as they both continued to stare at the horror in front of them, and when she spoke her voice was shaking.

'We both do.'

I

Two weeks earlier

London, 1 September 1940

D ot Simmonds fiddled with the pages of her ration book as she waited in line at Woolton and Son greengrocer's. She could hear Mrs Parker striking up a conversation with Mrs Woolton as she rang up her shopping, and there was an audible sigh of frustration from further down the queue. Everybody in their little corner of Chelsea knew that once Mrs Parker got started it was difficult to end the exchange. They could be stuck here for another ten minutes while the lonely old dear regaled Mrs Woolton with all the gory details of her latest ailments. When she had cut her finger making a vegetable stew, she'd spent so long telling Mr Wyatt at the butcher's next door about it that he'd been forced to shut up shop an hour later than usual.

Dot smiled to herself, grateful to her neighbour for adding time to her trip. Most people Dot knew groaned about the queues for groceries these days. It had grown gradually worse since rationing had been introduced at the beginning of the year. Back then they were only rationing butter, bacon and sugar. These days, meat, tea and even margarine had been added to the list. It seemed that you couldn't pop out for anything without getting caught up in a long wait. But while everybody else seemed to get upset about anything that delayed their onward journey – like Mrs Parker holding up the queue as she nattered – Dot welcomed the hindrance. In fact, she quite enjoyed it.

Dot's weekly trip to Woolton and Son for the household shopping was the highlight of her week, because it gave her a break from Beryl. Dot had been stuck at home alone with her mother-in-law since her husband Tommy had joined the Royal Engineers in April. Dot had never quite hit it off with Beryl. Tommy was the older woman's only son and she had leaned on him for support ever since his father died five years before. Tommy had even left a well-paid job in the north of the country to move in with his mother after his father's death. Dot hadn't thought there'd been anything wrong with them being so close – in fact she'd believed a strong bond between mother and son suggested a good, reliable and caring man. And, besides, Dot would probably have never met Tommy if he had stayed up north instead of moving to London to look after his mother. She had all but given up on finding love after years of loneliness – all the men in Chelsea had seemed to either be taken or downright awful.

So, Tommy had walked into her life like a breath of fresh air just when she had decided she needed to come to terms with living out the rest of her days as a spinster. Dot could still picture the way he'd grinned at her when he'd first come to her father's garage to work for him – how romantic he'd been then. Thinking back now, she realised she had been so desperate to settle down and get married that she had made it quite easy for Tommy to sweep her off her feet. But sweep her off her feet he had done, and they had been happy for a time. She smiled as she remembered how good he had been at making her laugh in the early days of their relationship. And how he'd made her feel so special. But that was before she'd known what married life was really like.

After losing her own mother when she'd been a teenager, Dot had been desperate to form a close bond with Tommy's mother when they'd first met. But every effort she made seemed to be thrown back in her face; Dot felt as if she couldn't do anything right in Beryl's eyes. The older woman had been unwilling to let go when Tommy had met Dot, and just refused to accept her no matter how hard she tried. To make matters worse, Tommy appeared to be completely oblivious to the tension between the women. Instead of trying to help his mother understand there was room enough for the two of them in his life, Tommy ignored Beryl's possessive behaviour and appeared to suffer bouts of blindness and deafness whenever his mother said anything out of turn to his wife – which she often did.

When Tommy and Dot had first started courting, Dot had tried on occasion to talk to him about it, but he'd been so protective of his mother that the conversation had never ended well. Then he would say something to make Dot laugh and her heart would soften and she would forget why she had felt so upset. When she had complained about it to her friends all those years ago, they had asked why she put up with it and that was when Dot had realised she was in love with Tommy.

'When you fall in love with somebody, you fall in love with every part of them – faults and all,' she'd said with a shrug. They had wed soon after and, suddenly, putting up with Beryl had seemed bearable if it meant Dot had Tommy's devotion.

Mrs Parker finally finished her monologue and a tired-looking Mrs Woolton waved forward the next customer. Dot noticed the woman's blue air-raid-warden overalls and felt a wave of sadness sweep over her. Dot was desperate to do her bit for the war effort but, instead, she was stuck at home all day every day with Beryl. Tommy had never wanted Dot to work. When they'd married, she had been excited about finding work as a receptionist – she had spent many years helping out on the reception at her father's garage, after all. But as soon as they were living under the same roof, Tommy had insisted she focus on starting a family. She had planned on asking her father for support in convincing Tommy that she was capable of manning the reception at the garage at least, but her beloved daddy had died a few months after their wedding. Tommy had taken over the business and Dot's dreams of a career had died along with her father.

As the queue shuffled forward again, Dot noticed a poster in the window. She was pulled in at once by the picture across the top of women walking together with purpose, and the striking photograph of a woman in a gas mask. Dot read the text with interest:

ARP
It's the women we need . . .
Women ambulance drivers, women wardens,
women for first aid and casualty stations.
ENROL AT ONCE!

Of course, when women had started signing up to help keep the country running as the men went off to fight, Dot had been keen to get involved. But she hadn't mentioned it to

Tommy. He'd made it clear that Dot getting a job was out of the question, and he'd been so relieved that she was going to be at home to look after his mother while he was away that she couldn't bring herself to say anything. How could she tell him that she'd much rather be out on the streets putting her life at risk to help others than sitting at home with Beryl? It would break his heart and she couldn't do that to the man she loved. Her 'job' these days seemed to be making sure Beryl was fed and watered and that her house was clean and tidy, when Dot knew full well that her mother-in-law was capable of taking care of all of that herself.

'Are you thinking of volunteering?' A voice cut into Dot's thoughts, making her jump. She'd been so caught up in imagining herself out on the streets, rounding people up and guiding them to safety, that she hadn't even noticed the queue ahead moving forward again, much less the ARP warden paying for her shopping and walking back towards her. Dot took in her overalls now, as she tried to come up with a response that didn't make her sound terribly pathetic. *My husband won't let me* was the truth, but there was no question of her admitting that – especially not to someone who was clearly very brave and selfless. This warden was also younger than Dot – she must only have been in her early twenties while Dot was almost thirty. The realisation made her feel even more wretched.

'Oh, erm . . . I have a lot on, caring for my mother-in-law, and looking after the house,' Dot stuttered, avoiding eye contact. She was ashamed of her lie, and she knew it sounded pitiful – but it was better than being honest.

'That's a shame. We could do with some more plucky women on our side. You look like you know how to stand up for yourself.' Dot could feel her cheeks flaming red as she smiled apologetically and shrugged her shoulders. As the woman walked away, Dot wondered what had given her the idea that she could stand up for herself. She might have thought that about herself many years ago, but married life and a nit-picking mother-in-law had drained all the fight out of her.

Walking home with her shopping, Dot couldn't stop thinking about the friendly air-raid warden and the exciting life that could open up to her if she signed up to volunteer. Of course, it would be dangerous – but war in itself was dangerous. She was at risk just by being in London. What more peril would she put herself in by trying to help those around her? Besides, despite all the talk of air raids, and all the preparations the country had gone to, nothing much had happened so far. There had been some bombs dropped on the East End a week or so before, but, after the initial panic and Churchill's orders to retaliate on Berlin, nothing had come of it all. The city had emptied out following France's surrender to Germany back in June but, even then, none of the feared aerial bombardments had followed. People who'd fled to the countryside had now started returning, and even some of the children evacuated at the start of the war were being sent home to their families.

Would it be so bad if she volunteered to help make sure people stuck to the blackout and got to shelters safely when the regular false alarms sounded? Dot wondered. When she turned the corner into Lawrence Street and the Simmonds' terraced house came into view, Dot's heart did its usual drop. Shaking her head and laughing lightly, she pushed all thoughts of signing up to volunteer to the back of her mind. What had she been thinking? Clearly, she wasn't going to become an air-raid warden. Tommy wouldn't even let her get a job in an office, for goodness' sake! But then, Tommy wasn't here . . .

Stop! She scolded the naughty little voice in her head. Yes, she was frustrated with her life, but it was no reason to rock the boat and cause problems with Tommy. There was absolutely no way she would be able to keep it from him, anyway, not with Beryl breathing down her neck. Dot had to admit, though, that it had been fun to entertain the idea – even if it had been very briefly.

With a long sigh, Dot opened the front door and waited for Beryl's tedious voice to ring out. When she was met with silence, she walked quietly along the hallway and peered into the living room, hopeful that her mother-in-law had fallen asleep in her armchair after eating the breakfast Dot had left out for her. Beryl was never up before 9 a.m. and yet she regularly dozed in her favourite chair after stuffing her face. Dot had made the mistake of sitting in the seat one afternoon shortly after she and Tommy had started courting. The old woman had let out a shriek so loud it had probably woken the baby five doors down. Such was the fuss that Beryl had made, Dot had worried she'd failed to spot a cherished pet on the chair and managed to sit on a cat and squash it without realising. But after jumping back to her feet and checking, she'd found the spot empty.

'Didn't your parents teach you any manners?' Beryl had roared as she'd shoved Dot out of the way and plonked herself down on the chair. 'You'd think she'd check before making herself at home,' she added as a quiet aside to Tommy, tutting as she picked up a newspaper and turned all her attention to that. Dot looked to Tommy for backup; surely, he wasn't going to let his mother talk to her like that just because she'd sat in her chair? But he simply gave Dot the cheeky wink that always made her knees go weak and waved her through to the kitchen where he proceeded to make a pot of tea as if nothing had happened. She went to protest but he leaned over and kissed her so passionately that she thought she was going to lose her balance. She couldn't be upset with him after that.

Dot often thought back to that first encounter with Beryl and wondered why she hadn't run a mile. Well, she had a pretty good idea – it was Tommy's charm that had won her over every time. But she should have known then that Tommy would always put his mother first, no matter how awful the woman was being to her. Maybe she had overlooked the negative signs in her desperation to settle down before she was too old, and with no other prospects in sight. She'd felt so relieved when Tommy had shown interest in her that she'd been worried about messing things up. Of course, she felt guilty for thinking that way – she did love Tommy. But they had certainly faced a lot of obstacles during their time together, and his mother was one of the biggest. Dot felt a pang of longing when she thought back to the early days with Tommy – things had been so fun and easy between them. Where had it all gone wrong? Had he turned off the charm, or was she just blind to it now?

'You took your time,' Beryl snapped. Dot took a deep breath and walked through the living room to the kitchen to unpack the shopping. *This is where it all went wrong*, she thought bitterly, looking at Beryl. But then she scolded herself. She couldn't put all the blame on her mother-in-law. Tommy had changed, too.

'It was busy at Woolton's. I got stuck behind Mrs Parker again. She burned her finger this week.'

'Silly old fool. They should have sent 'er off to the countryside when they got rid of 'er grandchildren. 'Ere, that egg you left me was too runny. You know they make me sick if they're too runny.'

Dot bit her tongue. She couldn't remember a time when Beryl had thanked her for doing anything. She was often left wishing she hadn't bothered. But, as awful as Beryl was to her, Dot just wasn't the kind of person who would do – or not do – something to spite somebody. She'd been making an egg for herself that morning so it had been no bother to do an extra one for her mother-in-law, although she wondered now if she would have been met with less criticism if she had only looked after herself.

'Maybe it's not your cooking, though,' Beryl continued. 'June at number thirty says eggs lose their quality the further they travel.' Dot stopped what she was doing. Was Beryl being *nice* to her? Maybe the runny egg really had made her sick. 'Of course, if you'd managed to give me a grandchild by now, then we wouldn't have this problem, would we? We'd 'ave been packed off to a lovely little country cottage with the little 'un when the war had started, where we'd be able to get eggs straight from the hen.' Dot turned to look at Beryl, who put on her glasses and picked up her newspaper. 'Just imagine the quality of *those* eggs!' she exclaimed as she shook out the newspaper and started to read intently. Shame rushed through Dot. She hated how other women judged her because she hadn't been able to give her husband a child yet. On her worst days, she feared it was the cause of Tommy's coldness towards her. And she hated how Beryl constantly used the fact to put her down.

'Make us a cuppa while you're up, would you, Dorothy?' And that was another thing. Beryl insisted on calling her

Dorothy even though she knew full well that she didn't like people using her full name. She much preferred Dot – it was fun, young and friendly. And her own mother had always called her by the shortened version. But she'd given up asking Beryl to stop using her full name. She suspected she did it out of spite now, so she tried her hardest not to bristle when Beryl addressed her. A knock at the door made both women jump. Dot wiped the tears of anger and frustration that had formed in the corners of her eyes and she stomped past Beryl to the front door. She knew that the lazy so-and-so wouldn't even consider getting up to answer it herself.

Dot was surprised to find the air-raid warden from Woolton's standing on the street outside. The sun behind her seemed to glisten off the strands of dark hair which had escaped from the ponytail hidden beneath her tin hat. Dot could see her own face reflected back in the woman's big brown eyes.

'Hello again,' the warden said with a laugh. 'I'm Peggy Miller. I'm just doing the rounds to check on blackout preparations. Are you getting on all right with it all so far?'

'Dot Simmonds. And we're doing just fine, thank you.' Dot smiled. 'There's no light coming out of these windows after dark.'

'For what good it's doing!' Beryl bellowed from the living room. Dot flushed crimson and gave Peggy an apologetic look. 'Waste of time, all this blackout nonsense! The shelter they made my Tommy build in the garden was a waste of effort, too! And you lot – you're just busybodies – everyone knows ARP stands for 'anging round pubs!' Embarrassed, Dot stepped out of the house and pulled the door to behind her.

'I'm so sorry about that. My mother-in-law's convinced the bombs are never coming but I keep telling her we need to be prepared. Especially now Churchill has retaliated on Berlin.' She wasn't convinced herself that more bombs were on the way – surely, they would have landed by now. But this Peggy seemed like a lovely girl, and she admired what she was doing, even if it did appear to be in vain.

'Don't worry, I come across the same kind of resistance every day. But they'll all be grateful of us when the proper bombing starts up.' Dot nodded meekly. She hoped Peggy was wrong – on the bomb front, at least. 'Are you sure you won't sign up? She doesn't seem like she needs much looking after, if you don't mind my saying,' Peggy added quietly, nodding towards the door. Dot cleared her throat awkwardly.

'I'm not sure I'm cut out for it. I can't even stand up to my mother-in-law. I'm not sure I'd cope with everything you have to put up with.'

'I think you might surprise yourself,' Peggy said confidently. 'If you can deal with an old battle-axe like that, then I reckon you can deal with anything.' Dot couldn't help but laugh. 'Sorry,' Peggy added hastily. 'I know she's your family.'

'Oh, goodness, don't apologise.' Dot smiled. 'I'll think about it, all right?'

'Make sure you do,' Peggy sang out as she made her way along the street. Watching her go, Dot allowed herself once more to imagine what it would be like to volunteer as a warden and finally have a sense of purpose.

'I'm dying of thirst here, Dorothy!' Beryl's voice screeched through the gap in the door, and she was pulled back into her mundane, miserable life once more.

2

As she poured out tea into the mismatched row of mugs, Peggy took a deep breath and whispered to herself, 'Please keep the bombs away for another night.'

'What was that, Pegs? You doing your praying business again?' Stan called out from across the dining hall and into the kitchen. Peggy ignored her colleague and continued making the round of teas. She often volunteered to make the hot drinks when she was on duty and waiting for a possible call-out at their ARP base at Cook's Ground School in Old Church Street. She didn't particularly enjoy the task, but it gave her space from Stan – the only air-raid warden at the base who didn't seem to be able to accept a woman in the same role as him. He put her down at every opportunity and, although the rest of her male colleagues showed her respect and were kind to her, they rarely stuck up for her in front of Stan. She could understand why – he was a nasty piece of work and nobody wanted to get on the wrong side of him. Whenever they interacted, he was downright hostile towards her. And if he wasn't being mean, then he was acting creepy. She wasn't sure which one she disliked more.

Peggy knew Stan picked on her because, as well as being an easy target, she was a woman in a 'man's job' – although that phrase annoyed her because the Air Raid Wardens'

Service was actively looking for women to join the ranks now. She deserved to be there just as much as he did. And she had done all the same training as him. But there were still a lot of men around who just couldn't accept women stepping up to help where they could – and trust her to get stuck with one of them. Sometimes she wished the elusive bombs would drop on Chelsea so that she would get a chance to prove herself, but then she told herself off for hoping for such a dreadful thing.

'Hitler's not gonna listen to you, love – you just keep on doing what you're good at,' Stan called from the doorway, nodding towards the teapot and laughing to himself. Peggy rolled her eyes at the plump, balding lump of a man – he always seemed to be hanging around when she was having a rest break. As usual, there was no backup from any of her other colleagues.

There were warden posts every five or six hundred yards in London, with a maximum of ten posts per square mile. It meant that nobody was ever more than a half-mile walk from a post. There were six of them based at the school post: Peggy, Stan, Charles, Roy, Bill, and their senior warden, Victor. There were also a couple of messengers ready to cycle around the streets they covered when the bombs dropped and inform Victor of their locations and casualties so that he could phone it in.

Peggy was desperate for some female company on her air-raid-warden shifts – and the support that would bring. She was certain that a coward like Stan wouldn't pick on her or letch over her if she had another woman with her. Men like that were only brave when a woman was on her own and vulnerable. What made things worse was that Stan was Victor's brother-in-law. So, as much as she longed to tell him to bog off, she couldn't very well do so without getting herself into bother with their senior warden. She suspected this was also one of the reasons her colleagues never stuck up for her.

Thinking about having another female on duty with her reminded Peggy of Dot Simmonds again. She seemed as though she would be perfect. She was older than Peggy, and she was married, which Peggy always felt made a person more worldly-wise. Dot could be somebody to look up to as well as an ally against Stan. And she had definitely been looking at the recruitment poster in Woolton's longingly. Lawrence Street wasn't on Peggy's usual patch, but she had had some extra time that afternoon and decided to do some blackout prep check-ups in the wider area. It felt like fate that she had bumped into Dot so soon after talking to her about volunteering at the shop.

'Please keep the bombs away for another night,' Peggy whispered to herself again, more quietly this time so that Stan didn't hear her. She didn't like to be disturbed when she made the plea. She wasn't entirely sure who she was pleading with. She certainly wasn't religious, and she wasn't praying as her colleagues always assumed. It was just a habit she had got into when she'd first started her rounds as an air-raid warden that had sort of stuck. They hadn't had any raids so far although everybody had been certain they were coming when the war had started. Peggy knew it wasn't anything to do with her little mantra every evening, but now she got panicky if she didn't go through the ritual properly. As long as she did it the same way every time then she wouldn't be able to blame herself if a raid finally took place on her shift.

After her cup of tea, Peggy made her way around the local streets on her usual rounds. She took her role of warden very seriously despite the lack of raids, and she did her best to make sure she knew as much about the residents on her patch as possible. A lot of people thought she and her colleagues were just nosey, but the true reason was more heartbreaking than they imagined. When she had done her training, the importance of knowing everything possible about everybody on her patch had been drummed into Peggy. She had been taught that a good warden knew the habits of the people who lived in their sector so that when the bombs dropped, the emergency services could be directed straight to where the survivors were likely to be found. Her knowledge could make the difference between life and death. Knocking on Mr and Mrs Young's door in Old Church Street, just down the road from the ARP base, she smiled when the old lady answered with her usual bluster.

'Yes, yes, dear – Harold's over at his brother's for his evening dram. Just like he is every night. Now, can I help you with anything else?' Poor Mrs Young sighed and looked like she couldn't wait to get rid of her unwanted visitor. Peggy knew that the pensioner found her regular call-ins a hassle. She didn't like being disturbed on her nights off from her husband as she didn't get to enjoy a lot of peace and quiet when he was around. But it was vital that Peggy was certain Mr Young was at his brother's house around the corner – because if a bomb dropped on this part of Chelsea tonight, then she wanted to make sure the rescue teams were digging in the right place to find him. She knew that he wandered over to his brother's for a drink and a break from his wife most evenings. But what if he didn't go one night and she directed the search teams to the wrong house without realising? Mrs Young might find her tiresome, but Peggy's constant checking in could end up saving her husband's life.

Peggy also knew the shift patterns of all the factory workers in the street, as well as who was sneaking around with who when they shouldn't be. Brenda at number twenty-five was carrying on with Philip across the road while her husband was fighting in France. Peggy had seen him surreptitiously letting her in after dark one evening when they'd thought nobody had been watching, and when she had knocked to do her daily rounds he had claimed to be in on his own. The encounter had angered Peggy. Not the affair – that was none of her business, although she did feel it was particularly off of Brenda to do the dirty on her husband while he was away fighting for her freedom. But it was the disregard for the rescue workers that really got to Peggy. What if a bomb dropped while they were up to no good? If she hadn't rumbled their secret and had spent the last few weeks believing their lies, then she could end up sending the search teams into Brenda's house to look for a body that wasn't there. The two of them rarely made it to the local shelter when the siren sounded, and none of the gardens in this street had room for Anderson shelters, so she suspected they took the opportunities to cavort in the comfort of one of their homes.

Peggy waved Mrs Young goodbye and retrieved her list from her jacket pocket. She carried the log of all the residents on her patch with her whenever she was on duty. When the sirens sounded and everybody gathered at the public shelter in the crypt at the Catholic Church of the Most Holy Redeemer in Upper Cheyne Row, Peggy would tick them all off the list. And if anybody was missing, then she knew if it was because they were at work or if she needed to scramble back out and round them up. Some of the older residents insisted on staying at home, especially now there had been so many false alarms. She could understand them not wanting to spend all night cramped up in the crypt getting no sleep, but she was terrified about what might become of them when the bombs finally did fall. There wasn't a lot she could do for them if they dug their heels in though – apart from direct the search teams to them if it ever came to that.

After another quiet shift, Peggy returned to her boarding house on Bramerton Street the following morning. She changed out of her overalls and sat down at her dressing table, picking up the framed photo of her siblings. Peggy had taken the picture just before she and the oldest of her brothers and sisters had gone their separate ways when war had been declared. She was the middle child of seven, and she missed her family desperately.

Growing up in Sussex, they had all been very close. Peggy would have loved nothing more than to have bunkered down at home with them for the duration of the fighting, but everyone had been keen to do their bit when war had broken out. Peggy had signed up for air-raid training in London immediately, while her older brothers, Lee and Jamie, had joined the forces along with their father. Joan – who at nineteen was the closest to Peggy in age – was working as a land girl now, and their three younger sisters – Lucy, six, Martha, four, and Annie, three – were all still at home with their mother, who had recently taken in evacuees. Peggy had thought it ironic that as she had left the countryside for London, younger children had been ferried into the safety of her childhood home. But she was glad that her mother and sisters had the distraction of the city youngsters to keep their minds from wandering to the dangers Peggy, Joan, their brothers and their father were in.

Sitting down after a shift and taking time to think about her family and wonder what they were up to and hope they were all right was another little ritual Peggy had slipped into recently. But this one brought her comfort. She felt like they were all close when she did this. She often wondered if any of them were thinking about her at the same time. She hoped so. A knock at the door forced Peggy to set the photo back down. She was pleased to find Lilli on the other side of her door, holding out a cup of tea and a slice of toast.

'Good morning.' Lilli smiled as Peggy took the mug gratefully and retreated back inside, gesturing for her to follow. Lilli was a refugee from Austria whom Peggy had taken under her wing when she had moved into the room next to hers at the boarding house. Poor Lilli had arrived with nothing and knowing nobody after losing her parents back home. Peggy had done everything she could for her – she couldn't stand to sit by and watch anybody struggle, especially somebody so young. Lilli was still in her teens and Peggy couldn't comprehend somebody so young going through what her new friend was having to deal with. Despite this, Lilli was always cheerful and bright. The two girls had grown close. Peggy had soon realised that Lilli was filling the void left by Joan's absence, and she had become a bit of a surrogate sister to her. Lilli brought Peggy a cup of tea and a slice of toast after every shift, and the small but generous gesture made her heart burst every time. Not least because Lilli did it despite being well aware that Peggy had a gas ring in her room and was more than able to rustle up breakfast for herself.

They sat on Peggy's bed together while she ate the toast and drank her tea. This was their usual routine and Peggy always looked forward to it. She told Lilli about her evening and watched as her long blonde hair bobbed up and down while she nodded along and took in the details. Her hazel eyes always showed such interest in what Peggy had been up to, even on the quietest of evenings. She knew Lilli looked up to her and it made her feel even more responsible for the young woman.

'So, what did you do with your evening?' Peggy asked now.

'Some of the older gentlemen taught me some card games in the living area.' Lilli beamed. 'It was much fun. I even won a game!' She launched into details about the various tricks she had picked up, talking too fast as her eyes shone with glee. Peggy couldn't help but get caught up in her enthusiasm despite the heavy tiredness that was descending on her limbs.

'Maybe we can show the others when we go over later,' Peggy suggested. 'Let's remember to take a pack of cards with us.' Lilli nodded her agreement.

Helping Lilli had opened Peggy's eyes to the plight of refugees – many of whom were now being housed in Chelsea. At first, she had simply donated what clothes and kitchen equipment she could spare, as a lot of locals seemed to be doing in response to the borough's appeal for help. But after doing some research she had joined a Committee of Women, which had been set up to look after the refugees. They met regularly at the artist James Whistler's former house in Cheyne Walk to discuss all that needed doing. All the women had adopted several houses each and become godmothers to the refugees living in them.

Peggy had only taken on one house because her work with the ARP took up a lot of her time. Lilli had become her unofficial assistant as her impressive English made her a very helpful interpreter for Peggy.

'You sleep now,' Lilli said warmly. She got up off the bed and took Peggy's plate and mug from her before leaving the room. It always amazed Peggy how caring and nurturing Lilli was towards her, despite the fact she was the youngest of the two of them. Sinking under the bedcovers, Peggy looked forward to getting some rest. She needed to be up in time to go and see her refugees with Lilli ahead of her next shift that evening. All her volunteer work kept her very busy, and she sometimes felt exhausted, but she knew that it was nothing compared to what so many men were going through in order to protect her and everybody else still enjoying their freedom in Britain. She closed her eyes and sent safe wishes to her father and brothers before falling into a deep slumber.

3

Making her way down to the dance floor, Vivian Howe searched around for her friend's face in the crowded room. She should probably call William Carter more than a friend by now – they had been stepping out together for a little while, and she could tell just by the way that he looked at her that he was besotted. If she was being honest with herself, then she had to admit that she was besotted with him, too. But she wasn't ready to declare that to him – or to anybody, for that matter. As the band started up a lively number, Viv – as she liked to be called – smiled and continued down the stairs to search for William. The band had set up in the space in the middle of the two staircases that swept down to the dance floor, and Viv watched the musicians dancing away as she made her way down the steps.

Viv was a regular at the Café de Paris in Coventry Street, Soho. She was a regular at most of the London nightspots that had reopened their doors since the government had relented on their silly ban on entertainment in 1939. She had experienced quite the panic when all her favourite haunts had been forced to shut up shop immediately after war had been declared. Viv had always used dancing as a way of helping her deal with whatever stresses she was having to face. Letting loose to some good music was a sure-fire way of melting away her worries. She had thrown herself into training to become an ambulance driver as soon as all the entertainment venues had closed – she was desperate to do something to help and she also needed a distraction from what was going on in the world without her beloved dancing to take her mind off it.

It had been easier than Viv had expected to become a London County Council ambulance driver when she had arrived in London a year ago. She had already known how to drive: growing up in the Surrey countryside she'd been taught by her father when she was just twelve. But being asked to transport a very old and rusting bus around the streets of London had somewhat thrown her. To her relief, the streets around County Hall in Waterloo that she had been asked to negotiate had been quiet, and she had found the vehicle easy to manoeuvre. She'd also had to steer the bus around obstacles in a yard and had done her best not to spill the water in a bucket sitting in the footwell while doing so.

Once she had officially become a member of the London Auxiliary Ambulance Service, she had discovered that standards for the tests had been dropped dramatically due to a shortage of ambulance drivers in the city, but she hadn't let that dampen her spirit or quell her pride at what she had achieved. She also hadn't mentioned it to her father when he had written to congratulate her.

Soon after she had joined the service, most of the restaurants and dance halls that Viv loved had seen sense and started up again. The management at The Berkeley, which had a particularly lovely dance floor, had even declared: 'Dancing will make people forget their worries,' when they'd reopened their doors the previous September. Viv couldn't have agreed more. She couldn't understand these people who sat cowering at home, listening to the news bulletins and just waiting for the bombs to drop.

Viv tended to lean towards Café de Paris for a good dance these days. As much as she hated to admit it out loud, the fact that it was two floors beneath the pavement tended to make her feel that much safer. She loved the feeling of leaving the blacked-out, eerie streets of London and emerging twenty feet below ground to be surrounded by glitz and glamour. And she loved the music of the resident band: the West Indian Orchestra. Their frontman, Ken 'Snakehips' Johnson, was such a joy to watch and listen to. Viv could pretend she wasn't living in the midst of a war while she was down here, dancing the night away. Or at least, she could, if she wasn't surrounded by so many uniforms and casual frocks.

There seemed to have been an unspoken change in dress rules since the outbreak of war; while Viv still made sure to dress her very best for a night out in the West End, it was suddenly acceptable for women to arrive straight from the factory in a boiler suit to sip cocktails and dance. Uniform, daytime dresses and workwear were all acceptable in the fanciest of venues, along, of course, with soldiers in their kit. Viv didn't think any less of the women who had stopped going to any effort, but she certainly wasn't ready to drop her own standards just yet.

As she reached the dance floor, Viv felt a hand on her shoulder, and she knew immediately that it was William. He was tall, broad, and strong, but he had such a gentle touch. She spun around and grinned up into his bright blue eyes as his hand went down to her waist and he peered longingly into her own eyes. Viv was tall, but

William was even taller. When a strand of blonde hair fell forwards across his forehead, Viv couldn't help herself – she reached up and swept it away at which point William leaned down towards her and planted a soft kiss on her cheek. Her body tingled with the sensation and for those few moments it felt as though they were the only two people on the crowded dance floor.

The band started up with a livelier number, which snapped both Viv and William back into the room. Suddenly, couples were twirling and swirling around them as they jostled to keep from being knocked into.

'If you can't beat them, join them, darling?' William said, a grin spreading across his face and reaching those beautiful eyes as he held his hand out to Viv. She took his hand and nodded gratefully. William had driven down from his RAF base in Sussex for the evening to see her before she clocked on for her night shift, and, while she knew they should take the opportunity to catch up, she found she would much rather dance the night away with him. William had been so much fun when they had first met at one of these dances at the beginning of the year, but lately he had started trying to get all deep and meaningful with her. Viv really liked him and she didn't want to ruin things by pushing him away. So, she was trying to keep the fun going between them by avoiding situations that allowed him to get too heavy. If she could keep him on the dance floor until her shift started, then she would be happy.

But, after an hour of dancing, Viv couldn't avoid it any longer. She finally agreed to William's fifth offer of a drink, and she did her best to keep the conversation light as they sat at a table on the edge of the dance floor.

'I got a letter from my mother today,' she said brightly as she swished the straw around in her lemonade. William nodded and raised his eyebrows, indicating that he wanted her to tell him more. As she rambled on about her mother's latest drama as head of the local WI in the Surrey village where Viv had grown up, she could sense from William's expression that he was only half listening while waiting for his chance to change the subject. She carried on regardless – if she could just make it to the end of her drink, then they could enjoy another dance and finish the evening on a high. But when the band broke off for a break, William took his chance to lead the conversation.

'I have something serious to talk to you about, my darling,' he said. He pulled his chair closer to Viv's and her heart flipped. Having him so close gave her goosebumps but at the same time terrified her. He leaned in closer, so he was able to whisper into her ear while the room bustled around them. 'There's a rumour that Hitler is turning his sights to London and civilian targets. I haven't been able to stop thinking about you since it started circulating.' He paused, closed his eyes briefly and sighed, and then looked at her again. 'I don't stop thinking about you, anyway. But now I can't stop worrying. I don't think you're safe here anymore, Viv.'

'Oh, I'll be just fine,' she said with a laugh, feeling slightly relieved that he hadn't said anything too soppy, as she had feared he might.

'No, Viv. Please listen to what I'm saying. The bombs are finally coming. I think you should go to your parents' as soon as you can. You'll be safe in the country.'

'But I don't want to leave London. I love my life here! Have you any idea how many dance halls there are in my little village?'

William's serious demeanour broke, and he started laughing. He ran his fingers through his thick hair and sighed, shaking his head. Then he took her hand and stared into her eyes again. 'It's not all about the dancing, my dear,' he said lightly. 'I don't want to lose you.' He was serious again now.

'I don't want to lose you, either, but – even if these rumours are true – you're still going back to the RAF this evening, aren't you? You're not running scared, so why should I? If Hitler really is coming for London, then that is all the more reason for me to stay put and help. Maybe I can finally be of some use, driving the ambulances. All these months on duty and I've hardly seen any action. I can't scarper as soon as they actually need me.'

William sighed again and reached across to take her other hand in his. 'Marry me?' he asked.

Viv was – for once – lost for words. 'It's no use trying to make an honest woman of me just because the bombs are coming,' she said as lightly as she could manage. She tried her best to ignore the obvious hurt on his face as she turned his proposal down. But, she told herself, it was better this way – for both of them, no matter how much it pained her to do it. 'Oh, come on, my love. You're only asking me to marry you because everybody else is suddenly rushing to the altar, scared that time is running out.' Relief swept over her when William smiled again.

'You've got me there.' He laughed. 'You certainly know how to keep a man wanting more, Vivian Howe,' he added jokingly. 'I'll tell you what, though. I think I'll ask you again once this blasted war is over. How about that?' Viv was debating how to respond when the wail of an air-raid siren burst through the room. A few revellers panicked and dashed to the stairs, but everybody else stayed put. Viv couldn't blame them for preferring to stay safe down here rather than cramped up in a public shelter or rammed in an Anderson shelter in their garden. Especially when all they had experienced so far were false alarms. She would have stayed too, if it wasn't for the fact that she was due on duty later that night. It was better that she went straight to the ambulance station from here while the warning was still going rather than waiting until later. William knew that, too. The West Indian Orchestra started up again – this time a definite notch or two louder than before, to compete with the siren.

'Good timing!' William shouted over the racket, rolling his eyes playfully as they both got to their feet. She smiled back. She knew he had planned to stay on for a drink with some of his friends after she left for her shift, as he wasn't due back in Sussex until the following morning. He had driven all that way to spend such a short amount of time with her, and now she was having to cut their evening short as well as turning down his marriage proposal. She felt a deep ache in her heart as he pulled her to him in an embrace.

'I'll see you again soon,' he whispered into her ear. She only just heard him over all the background noise. 'You go do your bit.'

Viv pulled away and reached up on her tiptoes to plant a kiss on his cheek. How she wished tonight could have gone another way. A few seconds later, she was taking the stairs two at a time before rushing out into the cold night. She pulled her lipstick from her clutch bag and expertly applied it despite the lack of a mirror and the darkness. She was just pursing her lips together when a car approached. She had to squint through the blackness to check and as soon as she was certain it was a taxi, she held out her hand to hail it. She had learned early on that it was silly to walk the streets of London during the blackout. More people were coming to harm from falling over in the dark streets than they were at the hands of the Germans in London! Once she was safely sitting in the back of the taxi, Viv popped her lipstick back into her bag and smiled.

'Danvers Street Ambulance Station, please.'

4

Scrubbing the bathroom floor, Dot closed her eyes and longed for more of a sense of purpose to her life. The floor wasn't dirty – in fact, the whole room was gleaming due to the fact Dot had cleaned it from top to bottom the previous day. But she continued to scrub regardless, because if she was doing that, then she wasn't having to listen to Beryl's moaning and griping. Dot had taken to vigorous bouts of cleaning as a way of avoiding Beryl over the last few days. Since the visit from Peggy, the older woman's sniping seemed to have escalated, and Dot found that cleaning was the perfect way to steer clear of her. She laughed to herself. It really came to something when you would rather scrub a toilet than spend time with your mother-in-law. She couldn't wait for the war to end so Tommy could come home and life could go back to normal. At least when he was around, Beryl went a little easier on her.

Dot sighed and shook her head. She couldn't believe it had been almost a whole week since she had bumped into Peggy the ARP warden at Woolton's. She had been shocked when she'd checked the calendar that morning and seen that it was 6th September already. She sometimes felt as if her life was slipping away from her. What had she done since that day at the greengrocer's, apart from clean and daydream about becoming an ARP warden? She paused to rack her brains. No – that really was all she had achieved over the last six days.

Oh well, at least she didn't need to worry about the state of the house upsetting Tommy if he unexpectedly came home on leave. He liked to have everything clean, tidy, and *as it should be* for his arrival. It would help, of course, if she knew when he was due home to spend time with them. But he never wrote ahead to tell her like other husbands, instead turning up out of the blue. Dot's friends thought it lovely that he liked to surprise her, but for some reason the fact that he could walk through the door unannounced at any minute put Dot on edge. She wasn't quite sure why because she was always happy to see him.

After finishing up in the bathroom, Dot decided to head out for a walk. She always found the fresh air helped clear her head when she was feeling low like this. She crept down the stairs as quietly as she could and was relieved to find Beryl asleep in her armchair in the living room. At least she wouldn't have to explain herself before leaving the house.

Wandering along the King's Road, Dot enjoyed the hustle and bustle of people going in and out of the shops around her. She browsed some of the clothes aisles, longing for a time when she would have somewhere to wear a new dress, and before she knew it she was walking along the bank of the Thames. She always felt a calmness sweep over her when she was near the water. Her walks always seemed to end up at the river, no matter what she had planned when she set out. It was unseasonably warm for September, and the path next to the river was busy with others relishing in the sunshine.

Dot stopped to enjoy the reflections in the water and, as she watched the river rippling, she wondered when the next air-raid warning would sound. There had been an increase in false alarms over the last few weeks and she wasn't sure if she could stand another night cooped up in the Anderson shelter with Beryl. At least in the house she could escape to her cleaning. But in that tiny six-feet-by-four-feet area, she was forced to listen to her mother-in-law as she criticised her and everybody and everything else in Chelsea. It was so uncomfortable down there that she couldn't even go to sleep to block out Beryl. And the lack of rest then seemed to make Beryl even more scathing the following day.

Starting her walk home, Dot decided she would try to convince Beryl to take shelter in the crypt at the local church the next time the sirens went off. It was only a stone's throw away from their house, after all. Dot knew a lot of people from their area had been going to the Catholic Church of our Most Holy Redeemer and St Thomas More when the air-raid warnings went off because they felt safer there than in the shelters in their gardens. Many others had stopped seeking shelter at all, they were so fed up with the false alarms. But Dot wasn't ready to take that risk. And if there was one thing that she and Beryl agreed on, it was that they should listen to the government's advice to protect themselves when there was even the slightest risk of an attack from the skies. They had also promised Tommy they would be careful while he was away.

'What's for dinner, Dorothy?' Beryl's voice called out before Dot had even managed to take off her shoes. She sounded in a good mood, so Dot decided to broach the public shelter idea with her.

'I managed to get a nice piece of chicken today, so I'll boil that with some vegetables for us,' she replied, as happily as she could manage.

'Hmm . . . your chicken's always a little dry, but I do fancy something different,' Beryl muttered from her chair.

Dot smiled through the comment and continued. 'I was talking to some of the women in the shop about the shelter at the crypt, actually.'

Beryl sniffed. 'I don't understand why people are cramming into these public shelters when they have perfectly adequate shelters in their gardens.'

Dot took a deep breath. She had known this wouldn't be easy and she was prepared. Women like Beryl were very set in their ways, and difficult to convince that there might be a way better than their own. 'Sally takes her knitting down with her. She said Mrs Jones from across the road has given her some great tips.'

'Well, Sally never was very good with her hands.'

'She's knitted a whole jumper for the first time now. She always gave up before. Looks really good, too.' Beryl opened her mouth to respond but Dot forged on before she had a chance. 'It took her eight nights in the crypt. Can you believe that? I told them you could knit a jumper in just one night!'

'Course I could. It doesn't take any time at all when you know what you're doing. I used to knit all our Tommy's clothes. I'd do the same for your little 'un if you ever got around to 'aving one.' Dot bit her tongue. She was trying to build the woman up to get her onside and she still managed to put her down in the most savage way. But she was learning to stop her comments from upsetting her. And getting her own way here was too important – she had to ignore the hurtful statement and persevere. It would be worth it if it meant getting down to the crypt and being surrounded by others instead of having to put up with Beryl on her own during air raids.

'Well, they didn't believe me,' Dot said quietly, turning away and starting to walk into the kitchen.

'What do you mean they didn't believe you? What did they say about my knitting, Dorothy? You come back here and tell me!'

Dot smiled before turning back round to face Beryl with a serious look on her face. 'Sally said she'd never heard of anybody knitting a jumper in one evening, and Mrs Jones said the same. I tried to stick up for you but I'm afraid they weren't having any of it.' Beryl's face screwed up in rage. Dot's plan was working but she stopped herself from grinning. Before she could say anything else, Beryl was on her feet, gathering up her knitting needles and a bundle of wool.

'That's it, Dorothy,' she raged. 'No more being cramped up in that flimsy shelter with you at night. Next time those sirens go off, we're off to the crypt. I'll show those two nay-sayers what a proper knitter can get done in an evening.'

'Oh, but I quite like it being just the two of us,' Dot replied quietly, trying to look sad. She knew she was pushing it, but she had definitely played the right card with Beryl and now she was just having some fun.

'You really must learn to stand on your own two feet, Dorothy. With Tommy away you can't lean on me for support all the time. You need to make more effort with finding some friends. This will be good for you.'

Dot smiled and retreated to the kitchen to make a pot of tea. Her mother-in-law really didn't know her at all despite all the time they spent together. Dot had a lovely group of friends and Beryl would know that if she ever took the time to talk to her properly instead of talking *at* her and constantly complaining. But that didn't matter right now, as Dot was too busy feeling relief that the next time the air-raid sirens sounded, she wasn't going to be stuck in a hole in the ground with Beryl. She didn't even feel bad for manipulating her into wanting to go to the public shelter.

After their dinner, which Beryl declared to be 'not as dry as I had been expecting' and Dot decided to take as a compliment, both women retired early to bed. The nights in the Anderson shelter had certainly caught up with Dot and she was keen to catch up on some sleep before any more restless nights. She wasn't quite sure how she would cope as an ARP warden like Peggy. She found it impressive that a lot of the volunteer workers also held down jobs during the daytime. It made her feel quite ashamed to be in such desperate need of some sleep. But then, she supposed, if she was going to be losing sleep in a shelter, then she may as well be losing sleep because she was out and about helping people get to shelters. It didn't matter anyway, she thought sadly as she snuggled into her pillow, because she was never going to get the chance to volunteer like Peggy.

The following morning, Dot got out of bed feeling much more positive. When Beryl finally came downstairs, she immediately started on some knitting while muttering to herself about proving silly women wrong and making the best jumper of her life. Dot giggled to herself, glad to have given her mother-in-law such a useful distraction, as she popped a few doors down to Sally's house. Sally was one of only a few of Dot's friends who understood just how difficult her relationship with Beryl was. Dot knew that Sally wouldn't mind her using her in her ploy to get Beryl to the public shelter, but she needed to warn her because the older woman was sure to make a big deal of the whole jumper-knitting debacle. She wasn't too worried about

Mrs Jones – she was in her late eighties, her hearing was going, and she was always forgetting what day it was let alone what she had said to anybody about anybody else.

Later that afternoon, at about 4 p.m., Dot was starting to think about what to make for dinner when the familiar wail of the air-raid siren started ringing out. She went through to the living room and found Beryl standing by her chair, knitting paraphernalia under her arm and an overnight bag in her hand, ready to go. Dot wasn't sure she had ever seen her move so fast. She was just about to go and grab her own bag when a loud, low growl took over the room. She looked at Beryl in shock before they both headed for the front door. They stepped out on to the street, eyes to the sky, at the same time as most of their neighbours. Dot's previously rumbling stomach suddenly flipped, making her feel queasy. She stared up in horror as masses of planes soared through the sky. They were so far away they looked like big black birds, but even so it was obvious what was happening. Everybody was transfixed. Children started running around excitedly in the street, pointing at the planes. There must have been a hundred or more.

'Best stop gawping at them and get to safety,' Dot shouted over the booming engines. She watched as her neighbours snapped back to the reality of what was happening.

''Ere, who put you in charge?' Beryl demanded as Dot rushed back into the house to fetch her bag.

'Let's get to the crypt before it gets too busy,' Dot said firmly, pushing her way back through the front door and past her mother-in-law. She had a feeling that many of the people who had stopped taking shelter would be seeking it this afternoon and she didn't have time to put up with Beryl's comments.

'Get to your shelter,' she said urgently to anybody they passed who was still on the doorstep in a daze. She was worried that the bombers were headed to the Port of London and the East End docks – the Germans would be keen to destroy the supply chains to the rest of the country. But that didn't mean they weren't all in danger here in Chelsea, too. Suddenly, a warden rushed past them blowing on her whistle. Dot recognised the messy dark hair unfurling from the ponytail under her tin hat straight away. She heard Peggy ushering stragglers to the church, and she found herself feeling foolish for having done the same thing moments before when she had no authority to do anything of the sort. She waited for a sarcastic comment from Beryl on the subject, but none came. She was grateful, although she wished she hadn't had to wait for an enemy attack to get some respite from her mother-in-law's caustic comments.

They were soon at the church, where they found a tall and plump male warden outside, guiding shelterers in. They joined the queue of people waiting. Dot jumped when another load of planes roared overhead and shortly afterwards gunfire started up in the distance. The sky had started turning a strange yellow-orange colour, almost like a sunrise. She shuddered when she thought about how many fires must be blazing across the city to light the sky up in such a way. Once inside the church, Dot and Beryl fell into line, filing past all the pews and the impressive statues and paintings. Dot had never been particularly religious but, being here, she found a sense of calm sweeping over her, despite what was going on outside.

Down in the crypt, people were clamouring to get space for themselves and their companions to settle in. There were bodies everywhere and the sound of people shouting for each other through the crowds filled the air. Suddenly feeling protective of Beryl, Dot grabbed her arm and gently guided her to the far end of the room where she could see a bit more space had opened up since a family had rushed over to an elderly gentleman who had arrived alone. Beryl, who was normally so fiercely independent, submitted and went with Dot readily.

'It's going to be all right,' Dot whispered as she helped her ease her way to the cold stone floor. Beryl clutched her bag of knitting to her and looked around warily. Dot was just about to go in search of a blanket when she heard a familiar voice.

'That's it, there's more room over this way. Just mind this lady's feet. That's better. Yes, it's busier than usual tonight; I think the planes have got everybody spooked. We knew they'd come sooner or later, though.' Peggy didn't seem to stop as she switched from helping one person to another. 'There are blankets near the entrance; if you get yourselves settled in, then I'll get some over to you. Yes, it should warm up soon with all these bodies.' Dot managed to catch her eye and Peggy smiled over at her. 'Boy, am I glad to see you. We could do with an extra pair of hands this afternoon.'

'Me? No, I—'

'Never mind all that nonsense. I said I need an extra pair of hands. Go and round up some blankets, would you? You can get one for your mother-in-law there, and hand out the rest to the people down this end. Make sure you look after the elderly and the babies first.' Without another thought, Dot did as she was told. She returned with a pile of blankets and found Beryl happily knitting away while chatting to a woman of a similar age. Relieved that she had a reason to leave her to it, she continued on and handed out the blankets in the order that she saw fit. Everybody was thankful for her help, and the youngsters didn't seem upset that she had prioritised others over them. She felt as if she was doing a good job, and it gave her a boost. It also stopped her from thinking about the terrifying sight of all those planes outside, and the way the sky had been lit up by flames.

As the noise and the chaos settled down, Dot could hear the distinct sound of a child sobbing above the rumbles of chatter. Looking around, she couldn't see a youngster in tears anywhere. So, she started picking her way through the crowds of people, stepping over feet and apologising for nudging backs as she went. Finally, she found a little girl curled up next to an elderly woman who was fast asleep and snoring loudly. Dot was impressed that she was able to sleep so soundly on the cold, hard floor. After getting over her admiration for the woman's sleeping skills, she knelt down next to the little girl. She must only have been about four years old, and her face was blotchy from crying.

'Is this your grandmother?' Dot asked her softly. The little girl shook her head sadly. Dot looked all around. 'Is she with you?' she asked the family sitting next to the pair of them.

'No, we thought she was with that lady,' the mother answered.

'Well, she's not. She's all on her own and she's obviously terrified,' Dot replied sternly. She couldn't quite believe that anybody – let alone a mother – would sit by and watch a youngster who was so visibly distressed and not step in to help. Her heart broke for the girl. 'What's your name?' she asked her.

'Ivy,' she whispered through her still-flowing tears.

'Did you come down here with your mummy?'

'I left the house with Mummy and my brothers. We walked with lots of people and when I got down here, I looked around and they were gone.' She sniffed before breaking into a huge sob.

'Don't worry, we'll find them,' Dot promised, although she wasn't sure how. Surely if there was a mother without her child down here, then she would be screaming her name and searching for her. Even through the hundreds of bodies, a mother looking for her child would stand out. 'Come with me,' she said, carefully helping Ivy to her feet. She started trying to guide her through the crowd before giving up and picking her up to carry her. Ivy snuggled her head into Dot's shoulder, and she felt a wave of something rush over her. She could hardly call it love – she didn't even know this little girl – but it felt similar. Suddenly Dot was transported back to when Tommy had proposed, and all the excitement and anticipation she had felt – all the possibilities that had opened up to her in that moment.

'You're the only one for me,' he'd told her as he'd gotten down on one knee in their favourite restaurant. 'There's nobody else I want to spend my life with.' She had been desperate to start a family with Tommy – to have a child – a little part of each of them, who would snuggle into her in this way. But it hadn't happened for them yet – as Beryl so often liked to remind her. Finally, Dot spotted Peggy again and breathed a sigh of relief.

'I know who her mum is,' Peggy replied confidently, after Dot had explained the situation. She retrieved a long list from her jacket pocket and started looking through it. 'She's not down here yet. I don't know how we missed Ivy being down here all alone. She shouldn't have been let in without an adult. Bring her to the entrance in the church and wait there with her. I'm just off out to round up any stragglers, so I'll go to their house first.'

Dot held Ivy in her arms at the entrance to the crypt for what only felt like minutes before she spotted Peggy rushing back towards them, a frantic-looking woman just behind her holding the hands of two young boys. The woman pushed past Peggy and grabbed Ivy from Dot. The look on the little girl's face when she saw her mother brought tears to Dot's eyes. She had never seen love like it. As they continued their emotional reunion, Peggy explained that Ivy had become separated from her mother and brothers as they made their way to the church.

'There was a sudden rush of people and Ivy must have just gone with the crowd, confident that her family were still behind her. Poor love must have been so panicked when she looked around and couldn't find them. I found her mother running up and down their street screaming Ivy's name. She was terrified the Germans had come and taken her or something crazy like that.'

Dot let out a long sigh. 'What's it like out there now?' she asked.

'It's really quietened down. The docks in the east have been attacked heavily and every fire service has been called there. But the Germans seem to have backed off again now. I'm hoping we won't be down here for too much longer.'

Despite herself, Dot felt a twinge of disappointment.

'It was quite a nice feeling to help people while I was down here,' she admitted shyly.

'You did really well,' Peggy replied, smiling. Dot smiled back, but before she had a chance to say anything else, the solid tone of the all-clear started ringing out. Dot took the chance to slip out of the crypt before the crowds rushed forward. There was no way she would be able to fight her way back through all those bodies coming at her to get to Beryl. She couldn't believe what she saw when she left the church and looked up at the sky: it was blood orange now. She shuddered as she thought about all the buildings going up in flames over at the docks. When she spotted Beryl emerging from the church and drawing closer, she held out her hand to take her bag from her. She was grateful she had picked it up for her as she had been worried her mother-in-law might leave it in the crypt out of spite. She wouldn't have put something like that past her.

'I didn't abandon your stuff like you abandoned me.' Beryl tutted at her, continuing to walk after shoving the bag into Dot's hands.

'You were quite happily knitting and talking, and I wanted to help. I reunited a little girl with her family. She'd been terrified.'

'Family! What do you know about family?' Beryl spat. 'You just enjoyed bossing everybody around, is all.'

'Oh, stop being so mean!' Dot yelled angrily. Beryl stopped walking and turned to face her, open-mouthed in shock. Dot stared back at her, just as shocked at her outburst, as the crowds of shelterers dodged past them making their way back home. 'I mean it,' Dot said firmly, looking around her anxiously as people gawped at them. She realised that she sounded more confident than she felt standing up to her mother-in-law. But something inside her had flipped. She had felt good in there, and she wasn't about to let Beryl take that away from her. 'I did well. One of the other wardens even told me so.' Beryl scoffed and Dot felt her cheeks redden. Beryl started laughing and then turned and continued walking. 'I might even join the team,' Dot shouted indignantly after her.

'Yes, Dorothy, dear. Anything you say, dear,' Beryl mocked, waving her hand back at her dismissively. As Dot fell into step with another group of people, she decided it was time to make something of her life at last and prove Beryl wrong at the same time. Surely Tommy would understand that the country needed her – this was different to sitting in an office all day. He didn't want her to work, but he had never actually said anything about her volunteering. Besides, London needed her. Dot was going to track Peggy down the next day and put herself forward as an ARP warden. She had never felt so excited and yet so terrified in her life.

5

Peggy found an empty room and sat on her own to drink her tea. Her colleagues were all in the kitchen talking about how relieved they were that the bombs had fallen far away from Chelsea, but she couldn't bring herself to celebrate the fact. She couldn't stop thinking about the houses and families that would surely have been affected. How many people had lost their homes, or worse – their lives – this afternoon? She had heard that the rest centres in the East End were already overrun with people with no-where to go.

She was also annoyed with Stan for allowing Ivy into the crypt all on her own. He had been standing outside guiding everybody into the church – how had he missed the fact the little girl had been without her family? She had tried to bring it up with him as they had been helping everybody out and back to their homes in the dark, but he had simply sneered at her and walked away. She had gone off on her own, then, to check on the residents on her patch, before making it back to the ARP base an hour or so after the all-clear had sounded. Peggy looked around her at the children's drawings on the walls and smiled sadly. It upset her to think of how alive these rooms used to be. She had been hoping everything would go back to normal soon enough. But, after today, it felt as if everything was just starting to get going. Who knew when the children who used to fill these rooms with life and laughter would be back? And who could tell how drastically different their lives might be? Peggy shuddered at the thoughts filling her head. She had done her best to stay positive throughout everything so far, but the sight of those planes this afternoon, and the still-glowing sky surrounding them, was making it harder and harder.

When Peggy finished her tea she ventured back into the kitchen, hopeful that Stan would have gone out on his rounds. But she braced herself when she spotted his balding head from the doorway. She knew he would make some comment or other about her when she walked in – he could never help himself. And, as always, none of their colleagues would stand up for her.

'That poor girl was all on her own in there, and Peggy hadn't even noticed,' Stan's voice boomed out as she entered the kitchen. She felt her blood boiling. She had pulled him up on being the one to let Ivy into the church without her family, and now here he was turning this around on her?

'Who let her in on her own, Stan?' she asked firmly. He obviously hadn't realised she was there as he jumped and turned at the sound of her voice. As he stuttered and spluttered, she grinned at him. She had caught him in the lie in front of his friends. Peggy felt proud of herself for standing up to him, even if it meant he might give her a harder time from now on. She was a good warden, and she wasn't going to let him tarnish her name. Just as he looked ready to reply, the wail of the air-raid siren cut him off. Peggy raised her eyebrows at him in victory – she had managed to get the last word in before he could make up any more fibs about her.

Everybody flew into action, putting on their jackets and tin hats and rushing out of the kitchen. Peggy thought she was the last one out, but, as she walked through the dining hall, she heard heavy footsteps behind her. Before she could turn around to check who was there, she felt a hand clamp down on her shoulder. She knew immediately that it was Stan. Of course, he wasn't going to take too kindly to her standing up to him – and of course a coward like him would wait until they were alone to do anything about it. Peggy searched desperately for signs of a straggler, but all their colleagues had left the building ahead of them and Victor would be sitting in the headmaster's office at the other end of the building manning the phone.

'Pull something like that again and I will make life *very* hard for you,' Stan whispered in her ear as they walked through the hall together. He was still gripping her shoulder and he squeezed it so tight that she let out a yelp of pain. Suddenly, he stopped walking and turned around to block her path, pushing her back slightly with the hand that had previously been on her shoulder. Fear coursed through Peggy as Stan stepped forwards, leaned down and put his face right into hers. For once, the sound of the siren wailing outside brought her some comfort because she would be missed during an air raid – meaning that Stan couldn't get away with keeping her here for long.

'I need to get going,' Peggy said firmly. His hot, rancid breath was making her feel nauseous. She flinched as he brought his hand up, then she held her breath as he ran his fingers through her hair. She had her warden's hat in her hand, and she wondered quickly if hitting him around the head with it would be enough to fight him off.

'You're too pretty to be so disobedient. Remember, you're in a man's job. Don't go getting ideas above your station, or I might have to knock you down a peg or two.' He tapped her lightly on the cheek twice with his open palm before walking away, shaking his head. Peggy stood frozen to the spot, anger raging through her. She was shaking but she wasn't sure if that was from fear or fury – probably a mixture of the two. How dare he try to intimidate her like that? She couldn't let him get away with it. She'd heard about men like him. They pushed and pushed to see how far they could go. She needed to nip this in the bud before it went too far and he did something to hurt her. But that would have to wait, she decided as she put her hat on and walked out into the night – right now she needed to get back onto the streets of Chelsea again to keep people safe from whatever the enemy was bringing their way this time.

6

Viv jumped when the sirens sounded a second time. They were back for more already? She'd heard the East End was ablaze and she could see that for herself from the colour of the sky. Had they not done enough damage? If the Germans were trying to show London what they were made of, then they had certainly done a good enough job already. Viv had been relieved not to have had any call-outs during the first wave tonight, but she had a feeling she wouldn't be so lucky this time around. She checked the clock on the wall of the canteen at Danvers Street Ambulance Station; it was 8.35 p.m. Only two hours since the all-clear had sounded.

'I think we're about to get busy,' her colleague Dennis muttered as he marched through the room towards the ambulance bay. Viv got quickly to her feet. She hadn't been sent to anything significant since she had started as a driver here – it was mostly people walking into lampposts in the dark of the blackout or stumbling into the path of a car after having a few too many drinks and forgetting that their dipped headlights would make them harder to spot. She had become used to spending her evenings dozing on the camp beds and stretchers set up in the dugout – a concrete-topped shelter built into the corner of the brick shed housing the crew and lined with sandbags. When she had seen the planes flying overhead earlier, she'd thought William had been right and she might finally have to put some of her training to good use. But then it had all calmed down. She followed Dennis out to the cars.

'Do you think they're coming back?' she asked nervously.

'I know they are,' he said confidently as he checked over the first-aid kit in his ambulance. The London Ambulance Auxiliary Service had six divisions and one hundred and twenty stations, each with up to fifty personnel, seven ambulances, and five cars. The site of the Danvers Street station had been requisitioned from its owners and consisted of two double-height, brick-built sheds. One of the sheds housed the vehicles and the other housed the crews. It also had a petrol pump and an office. Other stations were converted warehouses or school buildings.

Dennis was in charge of one of the ambulances at Danvers Street, while Viv was responsible for driving one of the donated saloon cars. She preferred her little car to the big ambulances, even if it didn't feel as though it would offer as much protection once bombs were raining down around her. But she supposed that if a bomb was going to land on or near your vehicle, then it didn't really matter what you were driving – you were in big trouble whatever metal was surrounding you.

'The blackout doesn't mean anything now, Viv,' Dennis continued as he counted the hospital blankets in the back of his vehicle. She furrowed her brow in confusion. 'Look around you!' he cried, waving his arms in the air. 'The Germans have lit up a route into the city for their next load of planes! That's what the raid was for earlier! They have the perfect path to come in by with all the fires they started a few hours ago! And now, instead of blindly dropping bombs

The Blitz Girls

53

and hoping they'll hit houses and businesses, they can see all their targets as clear as day!'

Viv felt a sense of dread sweeping over her. William *had* been right after all. This was it. After all these months of waiting in fear, getting prepared and then becoming complacent because nothing seemed to be happening – now they were really at war.

She took a moment to hope that William stayed safe before she got to work, checking her first-aid box and blankets. She had done all these usual checks at the beginning of her shift. There was no need at all for her to do it all again seeing as she hadn't been anywhere since, but she felt an urgent need to be doing something useful while she waited for the inevitable. She also needed to keep her mind busy so that it couldn't think too much about the enormous danger William would be facing right now. After reassuring herself that her hospital blankets were in the back of her car, all folded lengthways on the stretchers, and that she still had gas suits and fire extinguishers on board, Viv looked around for Paul, her partner for the shift. They found out at the start of every shift who they would be paired with, and Viv liked going out in the car with Paul. Unlike some of her other male colleagues, he never passed any comment about her driving and just focused on the task in hand.

Anticipation and nerves coursed through Viv as a rumbling started in the sky. She didn't want to look up, but she couldn't help herself. She felt sick as she saw a barrage of planes thundering overhead. Her instinct was to run for cover, and she felt her legs jolt just before she stopped herself. Taking long, deep breaths, she did her best to stop her body from shaking. It had certainly felt easier to go out into the blackout while the sirens were blaring when there hadn't been any sign of enemy aircraft in the sky. She had rather enjoyed putting on a brave face in front of William and her friends when they talked about how courageous she was to be doing what she was doing. But the reality was that, now she was faced with real danger for the first time, she was terrified and desperate to flee to a shelter to seek safety along with everybody else. She took another deep breath: this was what she had trained for and she knew that, despite how frightened she was, she was ready to get out there and help.

Suddenly, all the other drivers on shift were filing out of the ambulance station and getting into their cars. Everybody knew something terrible was coming – even worse than what they had seen just a few hours earlier. When the first whistling noise started, Viv took a moment to work out what was happening. The huge boom that reverberated around the ambulance bay shortly afterwards made her realise it had been a bomb being released above them, and it had exploded somewhere nearby. Before she knew it, the sky was throbbing. There were continual whistling, whooshing noises coming from all around her, followed by dull, heavy thuds. In a short break of silence, the sound of the office phone rang out. No sooner had it stopped than it started up again. Viv finally got into her car and jumped as more whistling started up. She looked up to see more and more German planes soaring overhead. Then she spotted a figure emerging from the ambulance station – one of her colleagues, clutching a small piece of paper. He got into the passenger side of Dennis' ambulance and the vehicle immediately started up and left the yard. Suddenly more and more volunteers were filing out and into vehicles until she spotted Paul. Without thinking, she whipped out her lipstick. She felt ready for anything with her favourite shade of red on her lips.

'Oakley Street. One of the bastards hit a boarding house,' Paul said, climbing into the passenger seat next to her and stuffing his piece of paper into his pocket. Viv knew that their boss, Station Officer Spencer, would have written down the location and whatever vague details had come through from the control room before thrusting the report at whoever was standing in front of him waiting to go. She knew from training that they would only ever get a few scant details. The wardens and rescue teams already nearby the wreckage would be assessing the situation and trying to get to casualties while they made their way there.

Viv drove the car carefully out of the yard. Hers was a Hudson. The bodywork behind the front seats had been pulled out and replaced with a van-back kitted out with basic wooden bunks, blankets, and stretchers. To make it easier to get patients in and out, the back doors had been removed and a cloth curtain strung across. She had been disappointed on first joining not to have been trusted with one of the ambulances, but she had grown to love her Hudson, or 'Hudsy', as she had affectionately named it. Hudsy did the job well enough, anyway, and that was the most important thing. She drove slowly through the glowing streets. The speed limit was capped at 20 mph during night-time because it was difficult to navigate in the darkness of the blackout and with the car's headlights being dipped and masked. Although, of course, that wasn't an issue this evening with the city illuminated by fire. It felt surreal being able to clearly see where she was going for the first time in months.

Driving along Old Church Street, Viv's heart sank when she saw a row of houses ablaze, a big chunk taken out of the side of the one in the middle. As they crawled past the fire-fighters tackling the flames and the rescue workers shouting for assistance, she could see half a bedroom on show. The bed was nowhere to be seen and Viv hoped the occupants had made it out and to a shelter in time. She winced when she was forced to crunch Hudsy over debris. She tried not to look at anything littering the streets around them, prefer-ring to ignore the fact that she was further trampling over these poor peoples' possessions. Every time another whistle rang out, her heart lurched. There didn't seem to be any way of identifying where they were coming from or where the bombs would land.

'It's all right to be frightened,' Paul whispered as Viv pulled Hudsy to the right to avoid the remains of a double bed in the middle of the road. They were two roads along from the house with the hole in the bedroom. She couldn't believe the bed had been blasted that far. Turning into Oakley Street, Viv gasped when she saw the remains of what used to be one of the boarding houses for refugees. Most of the top floor was gone, and there was just a huge pile of rubble and broken furniture next to what was left of the rest of the building. Rescue workers were already tackling the blazes with stirrup pumps while firefighters got themselves set up. A warden flagged Viv down before she had a chance to get upset. She was directed to park at the top of the road, well away from the bomb-hit boarding house, and they got out of the car and walked towards the wreckage together.

'Was there anybody still inside?' Paul asked the warden as they walked towards the scene. The warden was young with a pretty face and long, curly hair. Viv recognised her from some first-aid training they had done together a few weeks previously.

'Evening, Peggy,' she said. Peggy gave her a curt nod in return. Viv was briefly taken aback; she wasn't sure what she'd done to deserve such a cold greeting from this woman. But then she turned her focus back to the job – whatever Peggy's problem was, it wasn't something that she was going to let bother her, particularly not when she had such an important job to do.

'It seems as though everybody made it down to the cellar, which was their designated shelter,' Peggy explained. 'The entrance has been blocked by rubble, but the rescue team have managed to clear enough to open up a line of communication. We've cleared the rest of the street, so if anything collapses, then it's only us and the group in the cellar to worry about.' Viv looked over at the group of men slowly and carefully removing brick after brick, taking care each time not to shift the rest of the wreckage for fear of bringing it all down on top of the refugees stuck beneath.

'Are there any casualties?' Viv asked now, just as she took in the sight of a tiny crib amongst the rubble. Peggy answered her question, but Viv couldn't hear her due to all the blood rushing through her ears. The sight of the crib sitting on top of the piles of bricks and stones had shaken her to her core. The thought of a tiny, innocent, defenceless baby being harmed – it was just too much to bear. She closed her eyes as her mind tried to take her back to what she had been through only a few years before. She knew she had to do something quickly before the grief consumed her. She couldn't let it stop her helping these people.

'They need a smaller body to get in closer to the entrance!' one of the rescue workers yelled. Viv looked over and noticed that all eyes were on her and Peggy. She looked to Peggy, who shrugged her shoulders before making her way over to the group of men. Viv followed, glad of the distraction.

'We've cleared as much as we can, but we're too big to get in any closer,' the worker explained, pointing to the path they had cleared in the rubble. 'If we take too much more away on either side, then the whole lot might collapse.' Viv shivered at the thought. Not only would the people sheltering inside be crushed, but it was likely that everybody out here trying to help would be harmed. 'We've been talking to them through the blockage that is left, so we know we're nearly there. We just need one of you to crawl in there and clear enough room to guide them out. It will be a tight squeeze, but there's more chance of one of you doing it than one of us.' Looking at the tall, burly chap, Viv had to agree.

'According to my records, it's a boarding house for refugees, and there should only be women and children down there,' Peggy offered. 'So hopefully we won't be trying to get anybody larger than ourselves out.'

'That just leaves the question of which one of you is going in,' the man added. Viv glanced at Peggy just in time to see the colour drain from her face. She was just as scared as she was, then.

'I think we should do it together,' Viv offered. She was too terrified to do it on her own, but there was no way that she was going to send another woman in alone. Safety in numbers, and all that. 'One of us can lead them out, and the other can come out last – to help anybody who struggles and to make sure nobody is left behind.' Peggy's back straightened and she nodded her head in agreement. Paul grabbed Viv's arm and held her back.

'Take it as slowly as you can and move as little rubble as you need to. Just take your time and you'll be all right,' he whispered in her ear, and Viv smiled gratefully.

As she got onto her hands and knees in front of Peggy and started crawling through the narrow tunnel the men had cleared, she had to take deep breaths to stop herself from shaking. One false move and the whole lot would come down on top of them. Every time she moved a piece of rubble, she winced and held her breath. It felt as though somebody was pulsing electricity through her body. It seemed as if all the rescue workers and everybody in the shelter had stopped breathing, too; in the occasional breaks in noise from the planes, guns, and the bombs in the skies, you could hear a pin drop around them as every-one waited with bated breath.

'We're nearly there!' Viv shouted once she spotted a gap in the pile of bricks up ahead. It seemed to have taken for-ever but now she could just about make out the silhouettes of some of the people waiting for them. Despite how close they were to rescuing the group, she was still petrified – what if she got this close and then brought it all tumbling down? It was certainly possible. Somebody could even stumble on the way out and cause it all to collapse. Suddenly there was another pause in the booming background noise, and through it came the piercing cry of a baby. All Viv's fears disappeared, and she automatically started clearing rubble faster.

'Slow down, take your time,' Peggy hissed from behind her. But all Viv could think about was getting that baby to safety. A long-forgotten maternal instinct had engulfed her, and it was all her mind could focus on. Relief swept over her when the rubble finally opened up and they made it into the cellar.

'Oh, thank goodness!' somebody yelled, and a round of applause started up from the men waiting out on the street. Viv could just about make out a group of women and children huddled together in the darkness. They looked dazed.

'We don't have much time – this could all collapse at any minute,' Peggy explained from behind Viv. 'So, if you are able to crawl out of here with us, then we'll check you over for injuries outside.' Everybody seemed to be nodding. Viv's eyes fell on a woman holding a baby to her chest.

'Is your little one all right?' she asked.

'Yes. Asleep again now. Somehow,' the woman answered.

'They don't call it sleeping like a baby for nothing,' Peggy said with a laugh. But Viv couldn't bring herself to join in with the joke. She was transfixed by the little bundle in the woman's arms. She felt a pang in her chest before a nudge from Peggy startled her back into action.

'I'll lead everyone out, and check people over with Paul as they emerge,' Viv said. Peggy agreed to come out last, to make sure nobody was left behind. As Viv started to carefully pick her way back through the narrow tunnel, she silently prayed that the women behind her were going to be as cautious and as gentle as she was being.

7

The woman in front of Peggy paused. Peggy took the opportunity to breathe deeply and focus on the fact that they must nearly be out of the narrow rubble tunnel. She had never felt so claustrophobic or so desperate to get out of anywhere in her life. Even when her mother had forced her to take those awful sewing lessons when she was younger. Goodness, they had been dull. She had even stabbed herself with a needle one week to try to get away early, but the teacher had simply mopped up the blood and made her carry on. She never had quite got the hang of sewing; a fact that had always upset her mother.

As Peggy's mind jerked back to the present, she was disappointed to find that the woman in front of her had still not moved on. She couldn't see past her to check if there was a hold-up further ahead, but she couldn't hear any voices or commotion, so she suspected the owner of the feet and bottom that she was staring at was responsible for keeping her cooped up and in danger.

It seemed to be taking forever to get back through the tunnel from the cellar and her feelings of anxiety were rising dramatically every time they were forced to stop. She hated being stuck back here with no control over what was happening. She was beginning to wish she had led the way back out instead of Vivian. It really felt as if she had drawn the short straw here. But, then again, she had been surprised that the older woman had volunteered for the job with her at all. When the male rescue worker had asked the two of them who would go in, she had expected Vivian the glamour puss to make her excuses and leave Peggy to it. Surely anybody who turned up to a bomb site wearing bright red lipstick would baulk at getting down on her hands and knees and being covered in dirt and dust? She already knew from her limited contact with Vivian Howe that she was well-to-do and a regular on the dance circuit despite the ongoing war and threat of air raids. Peggy had been shocked to hear her talking about her night out at The 400 when they had done some first-aid training together a few weeks before. Peggy hadn't even been aware that there was a dance hall in the basement of the Green Park Hotel until she'd heard Vivian harping on about how much fun she'd had there. She couldn't understand how people were still going out and dancing and drinking champagne when the country's men were fighting to protect everybody and when London was at such risk. Peggy also wasn't quite sure why somebody so concerned with looks and style and dining out had signed up for such a hands-on job, but tonight she had seen that she had been quite wrong about Vivian. She had to admit that she still wasn't completely sure about the woman, but she could now accept that she could rely on her in a tricky situation – which was a step up from what her views on her had previously been.

'Is everything all right?' Peggy shouted ahead now.

'I'm sorry,' the woman in front of her called back. She didn't have enough room to turn her head round to face Peggy, but Peggy could hear her well enough. 'My arm. It is hurting very much. I need to rest.' This wasn't good news.

They needed to get out of here as quickly and as gently as they could.

'They will help you with your arm once we're back on the street,' Peggy replied. 'I know it hurts, but please try your best to keep going. Can you crawl out using just your other arm? It might be better to take the pressure off your bad arm?'

'All right. I try,' the woman said. Peggy breathed a sigh of relief as the woman started to slowly edge forward, bit by bit, obviously struggling with her arm. But at least they were moving again. As they got further out, the noise from the skies became louder and less muffled. Peggy wasn't sure where she felt safer. When she could finally see the glow of the amber sky again, two figures came forward and helped the woman out of the tunnel. She yelped when one of them took hold of her arm.

'Careful – her arm might be broken!' Peggy shouted.

'Ah, sorry, love,' a gruff voice replied as Peggy watched the woman being led away. As Peggy finally emerged, a pair of hands appeared to help her out. She looked up gratefully and then her heart lurched when she saw Stan's smirking face looking down at her.

'What a hero you are,' he said sarcastically while she dusted herself off. Peggy ignored his comment. She thought the best thing she could do would be to stay professional when she had to work with him and avoid him as best she could the rest of the time.

'That's everybody out,' she said firmly, looking him in the eye. She wanted him to know that she wasn't intimidated by him.

'Good job we've got some little women helping out, ain't it? I can't see that any of us men would have fit through there to rescue that lot.'

Peggy glanced down at his pot belly but thought better of saying anything about it. 'Well, so long as we're good for something, hey?' she said lightly before quickly walking off. She wanted to get away from him before he had a chance to tell her what else she was good for. Peggy picked up her pace to catch up with the woman who had been in front of her in the tunnel. Two rescue workers were guiding her over to Vivian's ambulance car at the top of the road. Vivian was busy with the young mum and her baby, and her colleague was patching up a nasty-looking gash on another woman's head.

'I'll take a look at her arm,' Peggy offered, and the rescue workers nodded before turning and walking back towards the bomb site. The woman was holding her arm protectively, but Peggy could see from the bone sticking out that it was indeed broken. 'I don't think I could have made it through there with my arm in that state,' she said. The woman grimaced. She was clearly in a lot of pain. Peggy was about to start helping her when Vivian called her over.

'This woman doesn't have anything for her baby,' Vivian said when Peggy approached. 'Is there anything we can do to help?'

'Yes, there's a rest centre nearby – I'll take everyone there once you've checked them all over. Although I think the last lady out will need a lift to the hospital as her arm is broken.'

'Right, we'll see to her. There are first-aid posts set up at the Royal Hospital, we can take her there. Everybody else is just cuts and grazes and they're gathered over there.' As Peggy led the young mother and her child over to the rest of the group, she caught Vivian staring at the baby and she could have sworn she could see tears in her eyes. *Must be the dust from all the rubble*, she reasoned, subconsciously rubbing her own eyes.

8

The ground around her seemed to shake as the dreadful bangs and crashes from outside filled the crypt. Dot drew her knees up to her chest and closed her eyes, taking a deep breath. She had been shocked when the sirens had gone off again. She and Beryl had walked back to the crypt together wordlessly, both still silently fuming from their earlier confrontation. When they had found some space to sit down next to each other, Beryl had immediately started on her knitting. Dot hadn't been able to see Peggy anywhere, and she had held off from offering any help to the wardens who were milling about down here. She was feeling a little sheepish after her altercation with Beryl, and she couldn't bear the thought of her mother-in-law making any more snide remarks about her. She also wasn't sure if Peggy's male colleagues would be as welcoming as she had been and the thought of them rejecting her offer of help in front of Beryl was just too much.

The noises seemed to be so much louder this time around, and Dot was certain she could feel the walls moving after every blast. The Germans were surely attacking closer by this time. She couldn't shake the feeling that they weren't going to get out of here in one piece. And she knew others were feeling the same. There wasn't the same atmosphere there had been when they had gathered here just a few hours previously. Everybody was a little quieter, more sullen. Everybody, that was, apart from Beryl, who continued with her knitting as if she was sitting in her armchair at home – she didn't even seem to react to the noises and movement from outside. The friendly chatting between neighbours, which had been present during the previous raid, had all but dried up. There were a few men trying hard to keep spirits up, but their efforts seemed to be falling on deaf ears.

'We'll be back in our beds again in a few hours, just you wait and see,' one chap, who Dot recognised from living at the end of their street, had said to her when he'd seen her jump at the sound of a bomb falling. She had simply closed her eyes and turned her head to the ceiling in response, too terrified to even pretend to believe him.

As another loud whistle echoed around the dark room, Dot flinched. *Bang, bang, bang* came the bombs. What were they doing out there? She tried putting her coat over her head to muffle the sounds, but it was no good. She couldn't stand it any longer – she had to be *doing* something. Something to distract her from the thoughts in her head. She couldn't just sit here, waiting to be killed, thinking about all the ways it could so easily happen. She got to her feet, ignoring Beryl's hard stare as she did so. She didn't need to explain herself to the other woman and she wouldn't. Her survival instinct had kicked in and it was stronger than her need to avoid confrontation with Beryl. Dot picked her way to the warden at the entrance to the crypt.

'They've got the docks real bad,' he was saying to an older gentleman who was sitting alone. 'We've drafted in firefighters from as far as Bristol and Birmingham to help, but the fires are still going strong. A boarding house has been hit in Oakley Street so far round here, and a row of houses got struck at the end of the road our ARP base is on, but I ain't heard of nothing else yet.'

'Is there anything I can do to help down here?' Dot asked as soon as there was a pause in the conversation. The warden looked her over warily. 'I'm sorry, but I can't just sit here waiting to see if we get hit,' she said quietly, looking around her carefully; she didn't want to upset anybody else with her anxious thoughts. 'I helped Peggy earlier – handing out blankets and making sure people were comfortable. Maybe I could see if anybody needs anything?' she pressed gently.

'I'm not one to turn down help,' the warden said warmly, his face relaxing as a grateful smile filled it. He had seemed confused about what it was that Dot wanted at first, but he appeared to understand now. 'If you want to keep yourself busy, love, then you can always have a wander around and check on people – ask if they need anything, make sure they have everyone with them that should be with them. Sometimes, in the rush and chaos to get down here, people get left behind and they're not missed for quite some time.' He paused and looked past Dot to the back of the crypt. 'You might be good at comforting the nervy ones, actually. There's a woman over near the back, being really jumpy. Red coat and blue hat – you'll know who she is when you spot her. Why don't you go and have a word before she rubs off on too many of the people around her? I've tried but I think it might need more of a woman's touch, and Peggy's off dealing with the Oakley Street bomb.'

Dot wasn't sure that she was the best person for the task – after all, she was offering to help in order to keep herself distracted so she stopped being so jittery. But she wasn't about to admit that to this warden. If she did a good job, then he might be able to put in a good word with his boss about her. 'I'll go and see to her now,' she replied just as another whistle rang out around them. She did her best to keep calm and not launch herself to the ground. 'I'm Dot, by the way,' she said with a smile when the loud noise had subsided and they were left with the constant background sounds of planes and guns.

'I'm Charles. Pleased to meet you.' They shook hands and then Dot made her way back through the crowds to the far end of the crypt. She spotted the woman Charles had mentioned straight away. The poor thing was shaking like a leaf. She had her hat in her hands and she was fiddling with it manically, stopping every now and then to make the sign of the cross over her chest. A large space had opened up around her, and the people closest to her looked as if they were doing their best to keep calm, but their eyes were being warily drawn towards her every time she jumped or muttered something. *This is no good*, Dot thought to herself as she got closer. She eased herself down onto the ground next to the woman.

'Terrifying, isn't it?' she said quietly, leaning her head to the side so that her face was just inches away from her target's. The woman looked at her cautiously, but she continued to shake. Another bomb fell somewhere in the distance and her body leaped in the air as she cried out. Without even thinking, Dot reached her arms out and pulled the woman into an embrace. Thankfully, she melted into her. Dot felt the shaking stop almost immediately.

'It's going to be all right. You're safe down here,' she whispered in the woman's ear. She wasn't a very tactile person normally; not one to hug her friends. But it had just seemed like the right thing to do to comfort this woman – this stranger – in this way. And at least it seemed to be working. She felt the woman's breathing slow down and deepen.

'I'm so scared.'

'I know. We all are,' Dot murmured, running her hand gently over the woman's dark hair. As she put everything she had into easing the other woman's fears, Dot found that her own worries disappeared. Gradually, the people around them started talking more loudly; they had obviously relaxed now that the woman had calmed down. Whenever the noise outside grew louder, Dot whispered reassurances to the woman, and she found they put her own mind at ease, too. 'Just keep taking deep breaths,' she told her. 'We're all here together. There's nothing we can do. We have to ride this out, but we'll be home soon, safe in our beds.' After what must have only been an hour but felt like ten times that, she felt the woman's body go limp in her arms; she had fallen asleep. Dot wasn't surprised – it was late at night, and she must have used up an awful lot of energy with all her panicking. A man opposite them caught Dot's eye, and he gestured to his blanket. She nodded her agreement and smiled gratefully as he came and laid it over the woman. Then he took off his jacket and folded it up. Dot nodded again and shifted herself to the side so that together they could ease her into a lying position, her head resting comfortably on the makeshift pillow.

'I can stay next to her and come and find you when she wakes up,' he offered. 'So that you can get back to your duties.'

'Oh, I'm not a warden,' Dot replied bashfully. She thought the lack of uniform would have made that obvious.

'But they seem to need you,' he replied, pointing to the entrance where Charles was now standing with Peggy. They were both waving to get Dot's attention.

'Well, in that case, duty calls,' Dot said lightly. She was pleased to have something else to focus on now that the woman was asleep.

'That was impressive,' Charles boomed as she drew closer to him and Peggy. Dot could see remnants of brick dust on the other woman's shoulders and in her hair. She wondered what she had seen out there and what she'd had to do. But now wasn't the time to ask.

'You've obviously got the magic touch,' Peggy chimed in. 'I told you that you should apply to volunteer. We're desperate for more wardens.' Dot paused for a moment, trying to muster the courage to admit that she wanted to sign up to help. Was this really what she wanted? It could open up a whole world of problems for her with Beryl and Tommy. A long-buried memory tried to push its way to the surface, from the last time she had spoken to Tommy about the fact she wanted to work. Dot quickly pushed the memory away – she couldn't let the past destroy her future. Tommy was away, and she knew she had to do *something*, especially now London was under attack. She decided she had better get on with it before she had a chance to think about it too much and got cold feet.

'Actually, I wanted to ask for your help with that. I'd really like to get involved.'

'That's great news! Why don't you come to the ARP base over at the school tomorrow afternoon?' Peggy offered. 'I'll be back on duty, and I can introduce you to our senior warden, Victor – he'll be able to sort it all out for you.'

'I'll put in a good word for you. We could do with more calming influences down here,' Charles added.

Dot smiled her thanks, but secretly she hoped she wouldn't have to spend all her shifts down in the crypt. Carrying out warden duties during a raid was certainly a good way to distract her from her own fears, but she felt strongly that she would fare better out on the streets. It seemed like a silly thing to assume – so she kept it to herself. But, in the crypt, she felt like a sitting duck, just waiting for a bomb to hit. It's why she could understand the distress of the woman she had comforted so well. Somehow, she felt like she would be in less danger out there. At least she would have more control, then, and there would be more for her to do to help. And she would be able to see a bomb coming and she might just get a chance to run away from it and get to cover. She put her hands behind her back and crossed her fingers for a role out in the thick of it, hoping that she wouldn't end up regretting it.

9

When Peggy roused herself the next day the sun was shining through the thin curtains in her bedroom, despite the chill in the air. She was shocked to realise she had slept through until lunchtime, but then she remembered the events of the night before and her stomach lurched. When she had signed up for ARP duty, she had never imagined things could be as horrendous as they had been the previous evening, and she had an awful feeling that it was going to get a whole lot worse before it got any better. Looking around her, she felt grateful that she still had a roof over her head. Although who knew how long that would last? The bomb at the boarding house in the next road over had really shaken her. She couldn't stop thinking about Lilli and the possibility of losing her.

Peggy allowed her mind to go back over everything that had happened the previous evening. The planes and the bombs had kept coming and coming. There hadn't been many more incidents on their patch thankfully, but she had been devastated to learn of a row of houses hit on Old Church Street. When Charles had broken the news as she'd caught up with him in the crypt following her crawl through the rubble at the boarding-house site, she had been immediately panic-stricken. She knew everybody on that street. But after learning that all the residents had been accounted for, she had breathed a sigh of relief and set to work letting them all know about the nearest rest centre and the help they could expect there.

The all-clear had finally sounded at 5 a.m. After signing off at the school she had gone straight home to check on Lilli. Creeping into her room, she had been relieved to find her fast asleep in bed. Knowing she wouldn't have managed to get much rest in the cellar during the raid, she hadn't wanted to disturb her and had tiptoed back out again to her own room, where she had collapsed into her bed, exhausted, and fallen straight to sleep. And now she was due back on duty in just a few hours.

Peggy almost tripped over when she left her room to go to the bathroom down the hall. She tutted and then smiled to herself when she realised what the obstacle outside her door had been; a slice of toast and a cold cup of tea. Dear, sweet Lilli must have left them there for her after getting no answer when she had knocked with them earlier that day. Or maybe she hadn't knocked at all, worried about waking her up after such a busy night. Clearing them away and feeling guilty about the waste, she wondered whether she should encourage Lilli to start using the public shelter instead of going down to the cellar with the rest of the boarding-house residents. The women and children at Oakley Street had had an extremely close call last night. Being in the cellar rather than anywhere else in the house had certainly saved them, but one false move from anybody and they could have all perished. Surely the crypt would be safer for her friend?

The perfect solution, in Peggy's eyes, would be for Lilli to join the ARP. If the teenager was patrolling with Peggy, then she would be able to keep a constant eye on her and do her best to keep her safe. But she had already checked with Victor, and he had confirmed Lilli was too young to volunteer. Peggy had only just made it in herself. Anyway, she knew the notion was selfish of her and, besides, Lilli was far too timid to assert authority like air-raid wardens were required to do. She was just desperate to keep her close.

Peggy decided to head over to the school for her shift a little early and ask Victor for his advice again. She needed to tell him about Dot before she turned up to see him, anyway.

The walk to Cook's Ground School was eerie. It was like the city was waking up with an almighty hangover. The contrast between the horrors of the night before and the calm as she made her way through Chelsea was unsettling. The streets were quieter than normal, but the people Peggy did see were wandering around as if in a daze. Nobody could quite believe what had happened. The switch from being blasé about the Germans ever attacking to a full state of emergency was harsh and abrupt. It seemed that everybody was still in shock from the night before, assessing all the damage and trying to take in what had happened and what it meant for the future. Peggy didn't like to think about how their troops would retaliate, and how that would make things escalate even further.

When she arrived at the base, she found Victor in his office. From there he would field calls coming in from the telephone girls at the control room and allocate jobs to wardens and messengers during a raid, and then file the casualty and damage info back to the head office once it had been reported back to him. The other wardens on duty from the previous shift were still out doing rounds, and Peggy was happy to get some time alone with Victor. He was in his sixties – too old to go off and fight, and with his thinning hair and his round belly he reminded her of her grandad, although she would never upset him by telling him that. Victor was kind and caring – a good senior warden, but he acted as if he felt younger than his years. Peggy didn't often catch him on his own, but she enjoyed chatting with him when she did.

Peggy had been so disappointed to learn that Stan was Victor's brother-in-law. The two men were so vastly different. Victor was courteous and respectful – he treated her the same way he treated the male wardens and never looked down on her or expected less of her because she was a woman. Whereas Stan was just a creep and a bully – and it seemed his only problem with her was that she was a woman. Peggy appreciated the two men weren't related by blood, but it still confused her that a pair of sisters could have fallen for such polar opposites.

'Big night last night,' Victor said with a sigh when Peggy walked into his office. He gestured for her to take a seat next to him. She nodded morosely and flopped down into the chair. 'How are you feeling? Some of the lads at the other posts are struggling with what they've seen – we got off pretty lightly in Chelsea.'

'We've just got to get on with it.' Peggy shrugged. 'People are relying on us to help.'

'That's the spirit,' Victor said, pride in his voice. They sat in silence for a few moments before Peggy started telling him about Dot. 'Charles mentioned her when he was here filling out one of his report forms last night. Sounds like just the kind of lass we need – so long as you can also vouch for her?'

'Oh yes. She'd be great at all this, as far as I'm concerned,' Peggy replied, grateful to have her opinion respected. Just then, a voice rang out from down the hall.

'I'm in the office!' Victor yelled. A flushed-looking man poked his head round the door. Peggy recognised him from some of her nights in the crypt, but she couldn't remember seeing him the previous evening.

'Just thought I'd better let you know – the missus had the baby last night. A bouncing baby boy!'

'Congratulations, young man!' Victor cried, clapping his hands together in glee. 'What a night for it! I hope they're both all right?'

'Couldn't be better. I'm afraid I was the nervous wreck through it all. I couldn't stop worrying about the Jerries dropping one on us, but I guess my missus had other things to focus on.' He fiddled with his hat and shrugged his shoulders. He looked like he was getting emotional.

'It sounds like she did you proud,' Victor said solemnly.

The man smiled as a tear escaped his eye and ran down his cheek. 'Anyway, erm, I've written down all the details here – address and names, so you can add him to the records.' He handed a piece of paper to Peggy. There were rows and rows of files in Victor's office, full of details of every person who lived in every property on their patch.

'We'd better chalk him up,' Peggy said cheerfully as she checked the address on the scrap of paper and started looking in the right drawer for the file for that road.

'Have you heard from Bill?' Peggy asked once the new father had left. As a dockworker, Bill had been exempted from signing up to fight in the war, but he spent his days and nights off patrolling as an air-raid warden with them. Peggy didn't know where he got the energy from for his shifts after working at the docks, but a lot of people did their volunteer roles around full-time jobs.

'You just missed him. He spent most of the night helping tackle the fires, but he popped in on his way home. I told him to skip his shift here later, but he wouldn't hear a word of it.'

'But surely he'll only get an hour or so of sleep before he has to come back,' Peggy exclaimed. She was exhausted and she hadn't done anything near as brutal as tackling flames all night – plus she'd had the benefit of a good rest.

Victor shrugged his shoulders. 'I can't force him to sleep it off. Besides, if we get another raid tonight, then he won't get any rest anyway. People like Bill need to be out helping, they can't sit back and watch people suffer without doing anything.' Peggy nodded in agreement. 'We're the same, Peggy. If you'd seen those fires last night, you wouldn't have been able to run to safety. You'd have stayed put and done whatever you could to help.' But Peggy hadn't heard Victor's last sentence. She was too busy focusing on what he'd said about another raid.

'Do you really think they'll come back?' she asked, failing to hide the quiver in her voice.

'Of course they will. They mean business, Peggy, and they're going to make sure we know it. They're going to try to scare us off, beat us down. But it won't work.'

'Was it bad, over at the docks?'

'It still is, from what Bill says. The fires are still blazing although they have them under control now. They lost twenty men fighting them. And the streets surrounding the docks took a pounding, too. Some of them have been completely wiped out. Just gone. Nothing left in the whole road but a load of rubble. They reckon more than eight hundred poor sods lost their life last night across the whole of London.' Peggy's eyes widened in disbelief. She tried to fight off the tears that had suddenly sprung to her eyes. She wanted Victor to think she was strong, but the level of destruction, the loss of life – it all felt so overwhelming. And he was telling her about it so calmly. She wondered how he could talk about it without any emotion, but then he suddenly and loudly cleared his throat before turning his head away from her. 'Bastards,' he muttered under his breath. When Victor turned back around Peggy was certain his eyes looked red, but she purposefully looked away.

'I'm worried about my friend Lilli, the refugee who's staying at my boarding house,' she said, keen to change the subject. 'She's been taking shelter in the cellar at our boarding house – it's where I take shelter when I'm off duty. But after crawling through the wreckage at Oakley Street last night, well, I'm not so sure she's safe there. Do you think the crypt would be better for her?'

Victor sighed. 'You haven't heard about the Columbia Market shelter?' he asked quietly. Peggy shook her head, her stomach suddenly churning. 'A bomb went through the ventilation shaft. They must have lost at least forty people. About the same amount carted off to hospital but goodness knows how many will make it out again. Then there was the one that hit Keeton's Road Rest Centre.' He shook his head sadly.

'But the shelters are meant to protect people,' Peggy said in dismay.

'There's only so much they can do,' Victor replied remorsefully. 'If a bomb finds its way to one, then that's very bad luck. Look, to be honest, nobody is safe while the Jerries are hurling bombs down on us. But if I was your friend, I would be taking my chances in a shelter rather than in a cellar. Don't get me wrong, both have their risks, but that's just where I would feel safer. And, remember, it's our duty as wardens to encourage the public to use the shelters.'

Peggy had to admit that she felt the same. But what if she advised Lilli to go to the crypt and it was blown up? On the other hand, what if she did nothing and the boarding house was hit, collapsing into the cellar with Lilli inside? She really was in a difficult situation. Peggy's thoughts were interrupted by the arrival of Dot.

'I followed the voices along the corridor; I hope you don't mind me intruding,' she said politely from the doorway.

'This is Dot, the new recruit I was telling you about,' Peggy said proudly, getting to her feet to welcome Dot into the office.

'I don't know about that,' Dot said nervously, fiddling with the buttons on her smart jacket. She had obviously made an effort to dress up for the meeting. 'Don't I have to pass some type of interview first? How do you know I'm up to the job?'

'I've heard everything about you, young lady, and two of my finest wardens have vouched for you.' Victor smiled. 'I'll put you forward for training right away. There's a new recruit training day coming up.'

After Peggy had shown Dot around the base, she made her a cup of tea in the kitchen. 'Well, that was easy,' Dot said with a grin.

'I told you, you're a natural. And, besides, I don't think they're going to be turning away volunteers any time soon.

Not after last night.' She winked at Dot, to make sure she knew she was just being cheeky, and thankfully Dot laughed along with her. Then they both stopped suddenly. Peggy wondered if Dot felt as bad as she did for laughing at the situation.

'Sorry. I shouldn't joke about it. Last night was horrific.'

'I think we have to look at the bright side,' Dot replied quietly, staring into her tea. 'You must keep smiling, Peggy. We have to be strong.'

'I think you and I are going to get along just fine,' Peggy said. She was so grateful to be facing whatever was coming next with somebody like Dot.

10

When the sirens started, Viv braced herself. She had made it through the first terrible night of bombing – and she had done a pretty good job of it, if she did say so herself. She was ready to head out into it again. It seemed quiet and still around her in the ambulance bay – she had been carrying out some extra checks on Hudsy after his first full night in the thick of it, and she took a moment to enjoy the calm before the storm. Now the siren was wailing, it wouldn't be long before the Jerries flew over and started attacking again. Soon enough the office phone would be ringing, and Viv's colleagues would start pouring out of the building, ready to get to work. She bent down so she could use Hudsy's wing mirror to apply her lipstick. She was just finishing up when she spotted Paul's smiling face in the mirror coming up behind her. She straightened up and turned around to wave a greeting back at him.

'I'm glad to see you have your warpaint on,' he said jokingly.

'I feel ready to take on anything once this is on my lips. You can give it a go if you like?' she teased. Paul laughed. Viv was happy to have been partnered with him again tonight. They had worked well as a team the previous evening, and she was grateful that Station Officer Spencer had obviously recognised that despite all the chaos he'd had to deal with.

He had mixed up a lot of the other pairings. It seemed he was trying to find the right fits amongst them all.

'How are you feeling after last night? Did you manage to get much sleep?' Paul asked. The lightness had gone from his voice now, and his expression had turned serious.

'I was physically exhausted, but my mind just wouldn't stop whirring,' Viv admitted. She had tossed and turned for hours before finally falling asleep. But it had been so fitful that she had woken up feeling as though she hadn't had any rest at all. 'I couldn't stop thinking about all those people with nowhere to go. It sounds like the East End suffered the worst. There are thousands of people who lived near the docks with nothing left. No food, no clothes, no money, no jobs. What will they do? And I can't even allow myself to think about all the lives lost.'

Paul put a hand on her arm sympathetically. 'Maybe it's best not to think about it. I mean, it's only going to get worse. We got off lightly over here last night, Viv. I've heard of some terrible scenes in other parts of the city. We've got to stay strong so we can cope with it when it's in front of us. We have to stay focused on helping the people who need us.' A rumble started up in the air, and suddenly Viv had snapped out of her sadness.

'We're ready, right?' Paul said firmly and confidently.

'Absolutely,' Viv said back, mirroring his tone. 'I'll wait in the car while you go to the office to find out where we're off to.' As she watched Paul walk away, a stream of drivers left the building to get into their cars. Sitting in the driver's seat of Hudsy, Viv felt anxious. She realised she had felt a lot more confident with Paul by her side. It was easier to believe the act when you were putting it on for somebody else. When the first whining whizz came down, she held her breath, waiting for the explosive to drop. It sounded far enough away not to trouble her or her colleagues and she breathed a sigh of relief before feeling guilty that other people's pain and misery was giving her a reprieve. But it wasn't long before the whizzing grew closer. Viv covered her ears and ducked her head as an extraordinarily loud one came down. She panicked that it was so noisy it just had to be for her. She found herself debating whether she should get out of the car and run or stay put. But before she'd had a chance to decide, a massive boom rang out and the metal of Hudsy shook all around her. Viv cried out in shock. There was an eerie silence following the explosion, and she tentatively lifted her head. She was terrified she would be faced with nothing but destruction, but all the other ambulances and the station buildings were still standing. The boom had been so loud, it must have been nearby. Viv was just about to get out to investigate when the station door swung open and Paul and one of their colleagues came rushing out. Viv hadn't even registered the office phone ringing.

'We haven't got far to go,' Paul said as he leaped into the passenger seat. One of the ambulances pulled out in front of them. 'He's got even less distance to travel,' Paul muttered as Viv eased Hudsy out behind the vehicle. When they pulled out on to Danvers Street, she could see exactly where the ambulance was going. A fountain of flames was flying out of a hole in the middle of Paulton's Square, reaching the height of the houses surrounding it. There was smoke and dust everywhere. A large crowd of onlookers was already watching as quick-thinking locals did what they could with stirrup pumps until fire crews arrived. 'Next road along for us,' Paul instructed as Viv shifted her focus back to the dark road in front of them, only slightly lit up by the fire in their wake.

'Beaufort Street,' she replied, proud of her knowledge. 'They really did come near,' she added under her breath, giving an involuntary shudder. As they turned into the road, Viv let out a gasp. They'd reached the scene so quickly due to their close proximity that the rescue workers hadn't managed to get much in order yet, and people were wandering around the rubble looking bewildered. An air-raid warden waved them in as close as they could get without getting stuck in the wreckage or ripping any of Hudsy's tyres. Ambulance crews were supposed to wait in their vehicle for casualties to be brought to them, but Viv already knew from the night before that Paul, like herself, was unable to sit and do nothing while everybody else got their hands dirty. Just like the previous evening, they both got out of the car without even discussing the fact they were going against the rules.

The relief effort at bomb scenes was coordinated from an incident post set up as soon as possible. Viv spotted the female warden from the night before placing two blue lamps on top of one another to mark out the area. She signalled to Paul and they both made their way over. Viv tried not to look at the ghastly sights surrounding them, instead focusing her gaze on Peggy.

'They hit one of the apartment buildings,' Peggy explained. 'And there was a direct hit on Cadogan Shelter. It looks like it's blown in the sides of it.'

Viv tried to stay calm as she took in the enormity of what had happened. She hated the brick-built street-level shelters that had been put up across the city, like this one. They had been constructed with the view that raids would take place during the day – they were not suitable for people to spend all night in, and they certainly weren't as safe as being underground.

Taking in the remains of the shelter, she wondered if there would even be any survivors left to help. She took a tentative look around. People seemed to be filing out of a block of flats. 'We're evacuating the building – it's uninhabitable now and there's no gas or water.' As Peggy spoke, a group of men who Viv assumed were from the heavy rescue squad assembled near the shelter – or what was left of it. Viv couldn't take her eyes off the huge slabs of concrete trapping twisted bodies, blackened from the blast and dust. 'They'll work on stabilising the collapsing walls and shut off the water and electricity so we can extract the living, and later the dead, from the ruins,' Peggy added. Her voice dropped with the last few words, and she looked down at the ground.

'We'll stay here so we can get patients straight to the ambulance as they're brought out,' Paul said. Viv was glad he'd spoken, as she seemed to have lost the ability herself. She just couldn't seem to digest everything that was happening around her. She felt as though she was in the middle of a bad dream. 'Focus,' Paul whispered in her ear. His prompt helped her shake off the thoughts that were clouding her mind. As planes roared over them and more whistling rained down, Viv straightened herself up.

'It looks like the stretcher parties are dealing with the minor injuries,' she observed as they waited for the rescue teams to do their work. The stretcher bearers were there to assess if casualties should be taken to a first-aid post or to hospital, and to prepare them for transportation. They tied parcel labels to the patients: 'X' for internal, 'T' for tourniquet and 'M' for morphine. Then they would guide them to Viv and Paul to drive to hospital. But there were so many walking wounded tonight that they seemed to be content with Viv and Paul loading up the badly injured casualties themselves, while they got people with less serious wounds and scrapes to a first-aid post. Everybody was just mucking in where they could while survivors wandered around with faces blackened with soot and dirt, pieces of brick and shards of glass embedded in their skin, their clothes torn and bloody, either screaming or eerily quiet and unable to answer simple questions.

'They're coming!' a voice shouted over all the noise. It fell eerily silent around them, apart from the sounds of planes and bombs, as people started stumbling out from an opening the rescue workers had made into the shelter. Every single one of them was covered in dirt and dust and they all looked completely disorientated. None of them spoke.

'I can't believe people have managed to walk out of that,' Paul muttered. Then he pointed to a man sitting on the floor. His legs were stretched out in front of him, and he was staring silently at the big bone sticking out of the left one. 'He may have walked out, but he won't be getting much further. I'll splint it and then get him in the car,' Paul added, heading for the casualty.

Viv nodded and kept watching the shelterers emerge, waiting for somebody in need of her help. The flow seemed to stop, and then she spotted a rescue worker helping some-body out, his arm firmly around her waist. Viv rushed forward and supported the woman from the other side. Together, they walked her over to Hudsy. It was only when they got there that Viv realised she was soaking wet. They sat the woman down on the edge of the pavement and at that point Viv realised with horror that it wasn't water making her feel wet – it was blood. The thick, red liquid was pouring out of a gaping wound in the woman's side. Viv grabbed a pile of bandages from Hudsy but when she turned back to the woman, she had passed out in the rescue worker's arms. Viv got to her knees and desperately felt for a pulse. Relief ran through her when she found one. It was only very faint, but it gave her hope. She loosely covered the wound with the bandages and together she and the rescue worker lifted the woman onto one of the bunks in the back of Hudsy.

'I need to get her to hospital quickly or we might lose her,' Viv said. They were the first words she had spoken to the man, who nodded his head solemnly and then made his way back to the shelter. Viv looked across to the other bunk in the back of the car and saw that it was crammed with five casualties all sitting close together. Paul had climbed in and was perched on the edge of the bunk the woman was lying on. 'You've been busy,' Viv said with a smile, before running around to the driver's side. She quickly wiped the windscreen clear of dust from the pulverised buildings before getting in. An ARP warden guided her through the rubble and she somehow managed to make it out without ripping a tyre. She winced with every bump in the road, thinking of the poor people in pain in the back. But she knew Paul would be looking after them. His task was to watch over them for signs of deterioration or shock, and also to stop anybody from trying to climb out through the curtains in confusion.

The drive to St Stephen's Hospital only took a few minutes, but it felt like a lifetime as Viv was forced to stick to the lower speed limit. As Hudsy crawled along the streets, all she could think about was the bleeding woman with the fading pulse in the back. When she pulled in, Paul was out of the back before she had even made it out of the driver's seat. He helped the nurses get the woman off the bunk and onto a stretcher as Viv guided his casualties out and into the arms of other waiting nurses. Once Hudsy was empty, she exhaled a long breath.

'We've only just started,' Paul chirped, hopping into the passenger seat. Viv wasn't sure how he could be feeling so exhilarated after what they had just seen. But she supposed you did what you had to do to get through it.

They made the journey back to Beaufort Street in silence. Paul's bravado seemed to fade as they got nearer to the scene. There was a crowd of patients waiting for them next to the shelter. Walking towards them, Viv suddenly noticed bits of bodies lying in puddles of water, blood and filth. She quickly put her hand over her mouth to try to hide the retching she could feel starting as bile rose in her throat. She must have been so focused on getting the bleeding woman to the ambulance that she had missed all of it before. Thinking of the woman reminded her of the blood covering the right side of her uniform. She wasn't sure she would ever get that out. When they reached the bodies, Peggy was waiting for them.

'Don't worry about the ones covered in blankets – there's nothing we can do for them,' she said matter-of-factly. 'I put a splint on that chap's leg,' she continued, pointing to a man who was sprawled on the floor groaning in agony. 'It looks pretty badly broken, and he has a head wound, too.' Another groan rang out from amongst the survivors and Viv and Paul leaped into action. The stretcher party helped them get the people unable to walk to the car, while around them the bombers continued droning heavily, AA guns fired, and high explosives shrieked down. They also had to compete with the noise of the rescue workers sawing and drilling and shouting instructions to each other.

Over the rest of the night, Viv lost count of the number of trips they made to St Stephen's and back. Every time they returned, there were more patients waiting for them. But even more shocking was the volume of dead bodies. The pile just kept growing. Viv stopped herself from looking at them, in the end, but eventually she had to because in the early hours of the next day, she and Paul and some of their colleagues were tasked with transporting them all to the mortuary.

Paul had been doing his best to keep their spirits up as they helped and transported the casualties to hospital, but he couldn't keep them up now. They worked together silently, treating the corpses with respect. They refused to just haul them into the back of Hudsy, instead taking their time and being gentle, making sure to wrap them in blankets. A lot of the poor souls had limbs missing, and Viv found herself hoping that they had died quickly, without suffering too much. Every now and then, they had to pause what they were doing when a rescue worker called for silence. Everybody would stand still so the diggers could listen for a faint cry from within the rubble to help them focus on the best place to burrow. Viv couldn't believe that they were still excavating people alive after all this time.

When they eventually made it back to Danvers Street, both Viv and Paul were caked in dust and rubble and blood. The trips to the mortuary had outweighed the trips to St Stephen's; a fact that brought tears to Viv's eyes.

'You did well tonight, Viv,' Paul told her reassuringly, as if he could feel her despondence. 'We did everything we could, and a great many people are waking up to see today because of us and all the other rescue workers. Yes, a lot of people died – but think of how many more would have perished if we hadn't been there.'

Viv nodded. She knew he was right. She found herself longing for William more than she had ever done before. When she returned home that evening, she allowed herself to think briefly about what he might have been doing while she was out helping casualties. He was at so much more risk than her, flying his plane around the coastline and trying to ward off the enemy planes. She suddenly hated herself for the way she had turned him down when she had last seen him – brushing him off so lightly when her true feelings ran deep. She hoped against all hope that she would get to see him again to make it up to him.

11

When Dot's first training day finally came around, she woke feeling excited but apprehensive. The Germans had returned every night since that first awful round of bombing – four nights so far – and she wasn't sure if she could cope with another evening in the crypt. She kept herself as busy as she could down there – the other wardens were happy for her to pitch in and help – but it was hard to escape the whistles of the missiles drawing closer when you were trapped in a space like that. She longed to be out in the open and *really* helping, not just handing out blankets and water and telling people they were safe when she wasn't entirely sure that they were.

There was a growing feeling that the public shelters weren't all that safe, after all. But then the Anderson shelters were just as risky. She could understand why a lot of people were simply taking their chances by staying at home – if a bomb was for you, it was for you, and it didn't make too much difference whether you were surrounded by metal or your own home's walls – once that explosive landed it was going to take out everything in its wake so you might just as well wait for the end in comfort.

Dot had heard of people trooping down into underground Tube stations to wait out the raids, despite the fact the government had banned the areas from being used for shelter. She'd overheard somebody in Woolton's saying that the London Underground staff were so outnumbered that they had no choice but to let people in with their bedding, radios, snacks and magazines. The woman had commented on the fact the noise of the bombs, planes and the guns were just a distant rumble from down in the stations. Dot liked the sound of that, and she supposed that the shelterers were probably safer down there than at home or in their Anderson shelters – or indeed somewhere like the crypt. But she found it hard to believe that anywhere was immune to danger at the moment.

When Dot had finished her morning cup of tea and breakfast, she crept from the kitchen back through the living room, past Beryl who was asleep in her chair. Her mother-in-law had mostly been giving her the silent treatment since their cross words in the street on their way back from the crypt following the first night of bombing. She relented occasionally to moan about something or other, or to mock Dot for mucking in down in the public shelter, but apart from that the silent treatment suited Dot just fine, if she was honest. But she was feeling anxious about what Beryl would say and do on Tommy's next visit home. She didn't want his mother to cause any trouble between the two of them. And she certainly didn't want her mouthing off about how she had been helping the wardens down in the shelter before she had a chance to explain everything to her husband herself.

Of course, once Dot had passed her training and officially become a member of the ARP, then there would be no hiding the fact from Tommy and Beryl. Dot paused for a moment to think about the potential fallout. She was so determined to go through with this that she had been in denial about the possibility Tommy could react badly to the news. Because the last time they had discussed Dot going out to work, Tommy had grown so angry he had lashed out and hit her.

A tear sprang from Dot's eye as she finally allowed herself to relive that moment. She hadn't thought about it in so long – she'd pushed it out of her mind so well that she could almost have believed it had never even taken place. It had only happened the once, and Tommy had been full of remorse afterwards. He'd promised her he would never raise a hand to her again, and she had believed him with all her heart. Tommy had stayed true to his word and Dot had buried the incident deep down inside.

Tears streamed down Dot's face now as the hurt and confusion she had felt after Tommy had hit her flooded back. But it *had* been a one-off, she was certain of that. She had to be – otherwise how could she justify staying with him?

Dot had always thought that if a man was violent towards her, then she would have no problem walking out of the door. But with both her parents gone and the family business in Tommy's name, she had felt trapped after he'd lashed out. If Dot had left Tommy, what would she have done? Where would she have gone? She didn't have any other family. She had also worried that, having taken so long to find a husband in the first place, it would be too late for her to find happiness with anybody else. Anyway, regardless of all of that and despite what he had done, Dot still loved Tommy. She felt foolish, but she couldn't deny it.

So, she had stayed. And she had been so scared of upsetting Tommy that she hadn't disagreed with him over anything since. Thinking about it all now, Dot realised the whole situation had made her feel resentful. She hated the fact that she felt too weak to stand up to Tommy and his mother. Maybe that was why she was feeling such a pull towards the ARP work; this could be her way to show them that she was strong enough to live her life the way she wanted – with or without their support.

If she went ahead and joined the ARP, it could make or break her and Tommy. She found herself hoping her new-found independence and skillset would impress him and make their marriage stronger. She refused to listen to the voice that tried to tell her it would all end in disaster. Dot wiped the tears from her eyes with her sleeve. Of course, she had to accept there was a chance Tommy would get angry when he found out about her new role. But she had weighed it all up and decided it was worth the risk – the satisfaction of helping her country would outweigh the devastation she would feel if Tommy was violent towards her again. And, besides, this wasn't work – she was volunteering at a time when London needed her and lots of other women to pitch in and help where they could. Maybe, just maybe, she could make her husband proud. Dot smiled at the thought.

Dot had thought about writing to Tommy to let him know she was joining the ARP, but when she'd sat down to put pen to paper, she'd found herself unsure of where to start or what to say. She was so worried about writing the wrong thing and upsetting him that she had screwed up the piece of paper and decided not to say anything at all, instead opting to wait until he was home to reveal her news. That would also give her time to settle in to the role and she hoped she would have tales of rescuing people from ruins and helping poor homeless victims of the raids find alternative accommodation to astound him with.

*

Despite all her background worries, Dot made her way to Cook's Ground School for her training day with a spring in her step. She knew that she had hours and hours of lectures ahead of her – she had to rack up ten hours in the classroom before she could don the ARP uniform. Nonetheless, she was looking forward to learning everything she needed to know in order to carry out her new role. When she arrived, she was led to one of the old classrooms, where ten other new recruits were sitting patiently waiting to learn the ropes. She was pleased to see two other women in the room, and she sat herself down next to one of them.

Dot nodded a silent hello to the woman and then proudly produced her notepad and fancy pen – a set she still had from back when she had worked as a receptionist at her father's garage. One of the things that upset her most about Tommy's refusal to allow her to work was that she had been working when they'd met, even if it had just been for a few hours a week for her father. But Tommy had told her father that he wanted to look after her himself, so she didn't need the job any longer. And, just like that, her independence had been snatched away in an act of chivalry that she felt was more a show of control. Then, of course, her father had died before Dot had had a chance to ask for his help in talking Tommy round. While Dot was waiting for the first lecture to begin, she was handed a leaflet. Reading through it, she felt slightly overwhelmed.

Air-raid wardens must possess the following knowledge:

1. *Understanding of poisonous gases, including how to detect them and protect against them*
2. *The methods of tackling incendiary bombs*

3. *How to protect against HE explosions, including the construction of private shelters and the provision of public shelters*
4. *The techniques for fitting gas respirators*
5. *How to use and maintain the equipment supplied at the ARP Post*
6. *A deep understanding of the local ARP and Civil Defence organisations and systems, including:*
   - *The sequence of local air-raid warnings*
   - *Address and telephone number of the Report Centre*
   - *Contact details for police and fire services*
7. *An intimate awareness of the physical and practical layout of his locale*

Dot looked across at her neighbour and widened her eyes as if in shock. 'This is an awful lot to learn in a day,' she whispered, being careful that none of the men sitting near them could hear what she was saying. She didn't want them to think she wasn't up to the job, even if she was beginning to doubt it herself.

'Don't worry.' The woman smiled reassuringly. She had long grey hair scraped back into a bun, and a kindness behind her eyes. She looked older than Dot; she was in her fifties, at a guess. 'My friend joined up a few weeks back and she says she could have done it with her eyes closed. A lot of it is common sense and knowing the area. I guess you've lived round here for a long time?'

'I've been here most of my life,' Dot replied, suddenly feeling a burst of confidence.

'Well, then, you'll already know a lot of the vital information – like where the water hydrants are, the hospitals and ambulance stations, police boxes and telephones, addresses of doctors, nurses, chemists and veterinary surgeons.' Dot furrowed her brow in confusion. 'My pal, she's based in Westminster by the way, well, she had to get a vet out of bed a few nights ago. A dog had gone back into a house to try to help his trapped owner. Poor thing singed his paws something rotten, but the rescue crews would never have found the old boy who owned him if he hadn't done it.'

Dot suddenly understood. *Of course* people like vets and doctors weren't always on hand at bomb sites. She knew there would be first-aid posts, but she had never heard of a vet being on duty at any of them. And she supposed they might run out of doctors and nurses at the first-aid posts when things got hectic, as well as needing more senior health workers at other times. 'Well, I know where our local vet, Mr Pritchard, lives,' she said almost smugly. 'He lives just round the corner from me with his wife and two children. And his assistant, Miss Page, lives in the next street over.'

'You see? You'll be fine.' Her new friend beamed. Dot was just about to ask her name when a stern-looking man with a moustache walked in, and the room fell silent as he began to speak.

'In time of war, an air-raid warden should regard himself first and foremost as a member of the public chosen and trained to be a leader of his fellow citizens and, with them and for them, to do the right thing in any emergency. The keynotes of his conduct should be courage and presence of mind.'

Dot sat up a little straighter, feeling proud of herself for taking on this challenge. Suddenly, all her fears about Tommy reacting badly to the news disappeared. This was such a vital task – how could he be anything but impressed by her taking it on of her own accord?

She took reams and reams of notes throughout the morning; she learned about anti-gas precautions, first aid, casualty rescue, incendiary bomb control and dealing with unexploded bombs. There was a short break for lunch when the other recruits sat and talked together while they ate their homemade sandwiches. Dot didn't join in with the group – she was too busy going back over her first-aid notes. They were taking part in a training exercise that afternoon and she was desperate to get everything right.

When the group was split into two and sent off to different streets for the training exercise, Dot's heart raced as the locations were revealed. It then sank right to the pit of her stomach when it was revealed she and her fellow trainees would be practising their new-found skills on Lawrence Street. It was just her luck she would get sent to her own road when she was trying to keep a low profile from Beryl. She breathed a sigh of relief when they got to Lawrence Street and she saw that her house wasn't along the section cordoned off for the training exercise. However, she would be visible if Beryl decided to look out through the window at what was going on. She took a deep breath and told herself not to panic. Beryl was going to find out about her new job soon and at least, on the bright side, she wasn't going to have to carry out any mock first aid on her and put up with her cutting jibes in front of her new colleagues. She found herself laughing when she thought of the short shrift the organisers would have been given by Beryl when they'd knocked to ask if she would take part in the drill.

As it was, Dot's friend Sally was one of the volunteers. Dot smiled and waved at her, grateful for the friendly face, as the trainer explained to the group that they would be tasked with rescuing Sally from various locations, as well as administering 'first aid' on a number of her pretend ailments. When it was Dot's turn to treat her 'broken leg', she remembered what she had learned in one of the morning's lectures about using a newspaper as a makeshift splint until she was able to secure the services of a doctor or ambulance driver. After doing what she thought was a pretty good job of the newspaper splint, she helped Sally over to an ambulance worker who was waiting further down the road next to her car. They had to walk past Dot's house to get to the car, and she was certain she saw the curtain at the window next to the front door twitching slightly. She could just imagine Beryl working herself into a frenzy over Dot 'disobeying' her beloved son's wishes. But she took a deep breath and reminded herself that this wasn't any old job, and Tommy would understand.

'That's very good for a first attempt,' the ambulance worker said as she checked Sally over. Dot couldn't help but grin in response. 'On a normal night, I would replace this with a normal splint, and then get your patient into the back of my car and take her to a hospital or a first-aid post.'

'You would drive?' Dot asked, failing to hide the shock in her voice. She knew women were driving the ambulances now, but she hadn't come across a female driver yet and she had assumed this woman was playing a role, like Sally was. Even in her overalls, which on closer inspection looked to be stained with blood and goodness knew what else, this woman just oozed glamour with her pretty face, long, shiny hair and perfect red lips.

'How is this one getting on, Vivian?' Peggy's voice sang out from behind Dot, and she spun round to see her walking towards them with her senior warden, who Dot was sure from memory was called Victor – but not confident enough about that to address him by name.

'She's doing brilliantly,' the ambulance driver replied, smiling at Dot before showing Peggy and her boss Dot's handiwork.

'They told us to use what's around us to help patients, and to focus on getting them comfortable until the ambulance gets there,' Dot said, feeling her confidence rise.

'What do you think, Victor? Can we keep her?' Peggy joked to the senior warden, and Dot silently congratulated herself on remembering his name correctly. It was amazing how well her brain could work when she put it to some good use for once. She felt invigorated by what she had learned so far, and by meeting so many new people.

'All recruits back to me!' the trainer bellowed, and Dot said a rushed goodbye before dashing back to him. As much as she was enjoying showing off her new skills to them, she didn't want to get into trouble for slacking during her training. Even if it was likely that Victor would be her senior warden, he wasn't in charge of her at this moment, so it was more important for her to impress the trainer.

The group went through a number of other drills, including 'rescuing' someone from a fire in their bedroom, and treating a severe head wound. Dot even got the chance to practise using a tourniquet when Sally pretended her leg was hanging off. She found herself praying that she would never have to put that new expertise to use. When the drill was over, the group walked back to the ARP base together, where Dot was pleased to find Peggy getting ready for her shift.

'Are you back again in the morning?' Peggy asked her.

'I am indeed,' Dot replied. She was anxious about what Beryl was going to say when she got home, but she was comforted by the fact she would be out again all of the next day, so she wouldn't have to deal with her for very long. Plus, as much as she didn't want there to be another raid this evening, it was very likely that there would be one – meaning she would be able to avoid Beryl in the crypt and keep herself busy helping the wardens down there.

'How did you get on with the training?' an older man asked her. Dot looked up at him, surprised. Despite his height and his broad shoulders, she hadn't seen him standing next to Peggy when she had walked in.

'It was a lot to take in, but I think I'll be all right,' she replied confidently.

'My apologies, I should introduce myself. I'm Bill – one of Peggy's colleagues,' he said, holding out his hand to Dot.

She offered her own hand forward and as they shook hands, she found herself wondering if he worked outside in a physical job, because his hands felt so rough and calloused. Inspecting his face more closely, she saw that his skin looked weather-beaten. His dark hair, streaked with grey, looked dry and unkempt. Dot guessed that he was probably in his forties.

'Dot here did a brilliant job today. We'll be lucky to have her on our patch,' Peggy said brightly.

Dot smiled gratefully. She felt lucky to have befriended somebody so welcoming and encouraging. This whole thing would have been a lot more daunting without Peggy's support. In fact, she wasn't even sure if she would have gone through with it if she hadn't bumped into her that day in Woolton's.

'It sounds like you'll be joining the team in no time,' Bill said warmly.

'I do hope so,' Dot said nervously. 'They said today that we could get posted anywhere in London, but I live around here, and I know the area so well. I would find it hard to learn everything you need to know about somewhere new.' She stopped abruptly, aware suddenly that she had started babbling. She wasn't sure why she had said all of that to Peggy and Bill – both of whom barely knew her. But the worry had been eating her up since the trainer had explained the post allocations earlier that day. And it wasn't as if she could go home and offload her fears on Beryl.

'Victor will make sure we hang on to you – he'll have me to answer to if he doesn't,' Peggy said firmly.

'It's funny, but before the war I didn't know a soul in this neighbourhood, despite having lived here for most of my adult life,' Bill was saying now. 'I moved here when I got my first job, and I suppose I spent so much time working that I never got around to getting to know everybody. I would leave for the docks before light and come home after dark.' That explained the weather-beaten look and calloused hands, Dot thought to herself.

'Now everybody knows your name.' Peggy chuckled, and Bill's face broke into a warm smile. 'Honestly, all I ever get asked about is Bill. Every time I knock on a door or offer to help somebody to a shelter, they want to know if Bill is on duty. Everybody wants to be your friend.'

'Well, not everybody – but I certainly feel like I know every household now, and I finally feel like I belong.'

Dot felt a rush of tenderness sweep over her. It clearly meant a lot to Bill to have been accepted the way he had been by the people he had lived alongside anonymously for so many years. She hadn't been speaking to him for long, but she could feel warmth and kindness radiating out of him, and she imagined that was what people were drawn to – especially during such worrying times.

On her walk home, Dot thought about what Bill had said and smiled hopefully to herself. She hadn't realised it before, but she had never felt like she fitted in around here. Now she thought about it, it was something she longed for – she longed to belong. And maybe, just maybe, this would be the start of that.

12

Creeping back into her boarding house after a long night of ARP duties, Peggy was intent on getting straight into bed. She needed to visit her refugees later that day and she was in desperate need of some rest beforehand. Helping with the training session the previous day had been fun, and she was hopeful her presence at the drill had put Dot at ease – but she really had missed those extra hours of sleep.

Peggy was always very careful not to make any noise when she came home after a shift. She knew the other residents didn't get much sleep down in the cellar during the raids, and she would hate to disturb anybody once they'd finally managed to drop off to sleep in bed following the all-clear – those who had to get to work would only manage to snatch a few hours of rest before doing so. She remembered just in time that she had broken her drinking glass the previous day, and in her rush to get to the training day she hadn't had a chance to clear up the mess or get a replacement from the communal kitchen. With a groan, she fumbled her way along the darkness of the hallway – the sun had not yet come up. She had to walk through the dining room to get to the kitchen, but she took one step and then stumbled straight over something soft.

'What on earth,' she muttered after landing on the hard floor. The object she had tripped on started groaning and stirring. Looking slowly around her as her eyes adjusted to the dark, Peggy realised she was sitting in a room full of bodies. Angrily, she got to her feet and picked her way over the forms to the light switch. Cries ran out and hands shot up in front of eyes as all her neighbours were woken by the light and commotion. 'Please tell me that you didn't all spend the raid in here?' she boomed over their protests.

'Oh, Peggy.' Mrs Martin sighed, pushing herself up to a sitting position. 'It's just so hot and stuffy down there. And there are no facilities, so to speak.' Peggy was disappointed. Mrs Martin, a widow following the Great War, was one of the oldest residents at the boarding house and Peggy really had thought she was old enough to know better. 'Don't look at me like that.' Mrs Martin tutted, flattening her grey hair down. She at least had the decency to look ashamed of herself despite the tone of her voice.

'You all know I'm a warden. I've told you how important it is to be as safe as you possibly can be during the raids. Have you not seen the destruction out there?' Peggy waved her arms around as she spoke, getting angrier and angrier. Then she noticed something. She was in a room full of women. 'Where are all the men? Were they sensible enough to spend the night in the cellar?'

'The men are in the living room. I thought it decent to keep them separate from the women,' Mrs Martin replied haughtily.

'Oh well, at least when they drag your broken bodies and limbs out, they'll know there was no funny business going on before you were blown to bits,' Peggy retorted sarcastically.

'Come on, Peggy, don't be like that,' one of the girls near the back said with a groan. 'Mrs Martin is right. There's not enough room for us all down there, and it's so uncomfortable. It was all right when it was every now and then, but it's been every night – sometimes for fourteen hours. And they're even coming during the day now.' She had a point – it was cramped down there. And there had been more and more raids during the day lately. But it was safer in the cellar than it was up here. And Peggy couldn't bear the thought of them all being at risk like this. Especially not Lilli – who she expected Mrs Martin to look out for in her absence. She wished again that she was able to keep the teenager with her all the time.

'Do you not think I know all that? I'm out there dragging bodies out of crumpled buildings and trying my best to help people while you shelter from the danger. I don't want to have to pile your bodies up to be taken to the mortuary.'

A stillness fell across the room. Peggy felt bad for losing her rag, but this just seemed senseless. It was true that she knew that her neighbours weren't completely safe down in the cellar, but they would be more protected than right here in the dining room, or in the living room. At least in the cellar they would stand a chance if a bomb hit the building.

She sighed. 'There doesn't seem to be much point in arguing with you about this. But all I ask is that you think very carefully about where you take shelter when the sirens next go off. And if you must insist on bedding down in here, then please do not go talking about it to anybody outside of this house. I would be in a lot of trouble if my senior warden discovered this was going on and I knew about it.' Nobody spoke as she made her way through to the kitchen and then returned with a glass and a broom.

★

Later that day, Peggy walked to the refugee house with Lilli. She was glad that Lilli was her unofficial translator for these trips. She had been so busy since the raids had started that the two of them had hardly spent any time together. It was nice to have an excuse to catch up with her, even if they did have important business to tend to. However, Lilli was unusually quiet, and Peggy suspected her friend was upset with her about the morning's confrontation. She wondered if it might be a good time to try to encourage Lilli to start using a public shelter. She had still been uncertain about the best place for Lilli to sit out the raids, but if it was now a choice between the dining room and the crypt rather than the cellar and the crypt – well, then that changed things significantly. She wasn't sure if she could rely on Mrs Martin to look after her any longer.

'It's not safe to spend the raids in the dining room, Lilli.'

'I know. But they all go there. No-one goes to cellar. I don't want to go alone.'

'Maybe you could try a public shelter?'

Lilli's eyes widened. She looked terrified.

'They're not as bad as everybody says.' Peggy laughed. 'The crypt doesn't get too crowded because there are a lot of houses with gardens around here, and those people have Anderson shelters to go to. There are also a lot of cellars.'

'But Claude says people were rude when he went to the public shelter with his family. They said he was German and should leave.'

Peggy's brow furrowed. Claude was one of the refugees she was looking after – meant to be looking after, anyway. If he had been treated badly in the crypt, then why hadn't he told her about it? Why hadn't she picked up on it? She was exhausted from all the air raids, but it was no excuse for neglecting the people she was supposed to be looking out for. 'I'm sorry to hear that. I didn't know. If I had been there, then I would have stepped in to help.'

'But you are so busy with the bombs,' Lilli said sadly.

'If you shelter at the crypt, then I promise I will look after you.' An urge to protect Lilli had taken over before she'd spoken, but now she had said the words she felt anxious. It was an unrealistic promise, and she knew it. She hardly spent any time in the crypt anymore – there was always so much to do above ground. But there were regulars down there who she could ask to keep an eye on her friend. People like Dot who were always happy to pitch in while the wardens were off doing other things. She would do her best to protect her. Besides, a few ignorant Londoners assuming from her accent that Lilli was German and giving her the cold shoulder was nothing compared to her being asleep in the dining room when a bomb hit. This was surely the best course of action, she assured herself. 'You could even take a pack of cards with you and show off some of your new skills,' Peggy added with false enthusiasm.

'Okay, I go to crypt from now on,' Lilli said confidently.

Peggy breathed a sigh of relief, hopeful she had given her friend the right advice.

At the refugee boarding house, they practised some English and Peggy promised to search out some more clothes for the children. They had already outgrown the items donated to them when they had arrived. Peggy sensed a growing feeling of resentment amongst the group. It was the first occasion she had been able to spend some proper time with them since the raids had begun, and they seemed to be feeling bitter at being put up in London after their experiences of escaping to England. Peggy could tell that they were all terrified. She felt the same way, but she couldn't very well admit that to them. She tried to reassure them that they were safer here than they had been where they were before, but she wasn't sure if anybody believed her. She wasn't sure if she believed it herself anymore.

Peggy normally came away from the afternoons with the refugees feeling a little lighter and good about the fact she was helping people who had been in a dire situation in some small way. But on this occasion, she left feeling disappointed in herself. She had been at a loss as to how to make them feel better about anything. How could she possibly do that when there wasn't really anything positive to be taken out of what was going on at the moment? She made her way to Cook's Ground School with her head hung low and her mood even lower.

13

Swaying on the dance floor at Café de Paris, Viv smiled at her friends who were dancing happily around her. The four of them had decided to get together on one of Viv's rare nights off. The raids so far had been relentless – London was coming under siege day and night now, and she was needed at Danvers Street more than ever. But even Station Officer Spencer had been forced to admit that the drivers and assistants needed a break from it all now and then. Mistakes were more likely to be made if workers were tired and didn't get time to process everything they were having to deal with, he had said when Viv had offered to come in anyway. She hadn't been grateful for the respite – time off was simply more time to think about the horrors she had witnessed, the people she had been unable to save despite her best efforts. And she couldn't think of anything worse than sitting out a raid doing nothing. So, when her friend and flatmate Jilly had suggested a night at their favourite haunt, she had jumped at the chance.

Viv knew that certain people would judge her for doing something so lavish and carefree at a time like this, particularly when it was almost certain that there would be yet another air raid tonight. But, for her, trying to relax at home would have been futile. All she ever saw when she closed her eyes was death and destruction. She needed to keep herself busy with going out in Hudsy and helping people, and seeing as that wasn't an option, then the next best thing was to let loose with her friends and pretend, for just one evening, that she wasn't witnessing such horrific things every day. And, looking around her at the bustling club, she could see that she wasn't the only one to feel like that. Some people just needed a sense of normality to be able to get through something like this.

Viv reckoned they were as safe down here on the dance floor as they were in a public shelter, anyway – it was two floors beneath the pavement, after all. And at least they were having fun instead of cowering in a cramped and smelly space, surrounded by people she would normally cross the street to avoid. She would happily defend her decision to anybody who challenged her on it. That young air-raid warden – what was her name? Oh yes, that was it: Peggy. Viv knew that she would certainly have something to say about it. Peggy had looked at her with such disdain when she'd mentioned her nights out the first time they'd met. And that had been back before the Germans had even invaded. If she had thought it in bad taste to go dancing back then, Viv could well imagine what she would have to say about it now! She didn't understand what Peggy had to be so stuffy about. She looked like she could do with a good night out herself.

When Jilly signalled that it was time to get another drink, Viv followed her friends to the bar. She called them her friends, but strictly speaking they were Jilly's friends. Viv had simply inherited them from her flatmate. But Ruth and Emily were good-time girls and that was what Viv needed at the moment more than anything, so they had been getting along fine so far. Jilly's parents, Mr and Mrs West, were long-time friends of Viv's mother and father. Viv's father and Jilly's father had attended boarding school together, in fact, so the friendship went back an awfully long way. Viv and her family had been to stay with the Wests in their London residence countless times while the girls had been growing up.

But as soon as war had been declared, Jilly's two brothers had signed up to fight and their parents had left London for their house in the country. When Viv had heard her friend was still in town alone, she had jumped at the chance to stay with her. Jilly's family had given up their main residence to house refugees, but Viv moved into their small city flat with her. She'd been finding the flat she was renting on her own quite lonely and she relished the chance to spend some time with her old childhood friend. Viv had only moved to London a few months before war was declared but she and Jilly hadn't spent much time together despite their proximity.

Jilly had befriended Ruth and Emily when they'd attended secretarial school together. Viv had enjoyed getting to know them since moving in with Jilly. The three of them were all volunteering at one of the rest centres now that their offices had closed.

Waiting for their drinks at the bar, Viv's thoughts wandered to William. The last time she'd been to Café de Paris was the night he had driven down from Sussex to see her. She couldn't help but think about him now. She was having fun with her friends, but she found herself longing to be near him. She hadn't told any of them about his proposal as she knew they would chastise her for turning him down, and she wasn't ready to admit the real reason for her refusal to accept his offer.

'How is William getting on?' Jilly asked her now, as if she had read her mind.

'I don't know,' Viv admitted honestly. 'I wrote to him after his last visit, but I haven't heard anything back yet.'

'Oh, I wouldn't worry about that. I haven't heard from my brothers for weeks, but there is no point in panicking until you get that telegram. You must keep the faith.'

Viv's stomach flipped. That wasn't even something she had considered. She didn't actually know William all that well, with all things considered, so, if something terrible happened to him, then how would she ever find out? She certainly wouldn't be getting a telegram with the news – that would go to his parents. She didn't even know their names, much less how to contact them. And she didn't know any of his friends that well. Would she have to wait and read his name on a casualty list in the newspaper? Panic gripped her. Far from reassuring her, Jilly's words had made her feel ten times worse. But she didn't say anything. She felt silly for being so worried about William, and she didn't want to spoil the evening with her fears.

'We'll have to go to the Savoy or Grosvenor House next time,' Ruth was saying now.

'Oh yes! I heard they've installed camp beds in the basement,' Emily chipped in excitedly. 'Customers are turning up in evening attire, carrying their nightwear and toothbrush as well as a gas mask. It sounds like a hoot!'

'They're doing it at The May Fair and the Lansdowne, too,' Jilly added.

As they continued the conversation, Viv tried to join in, but her mind was elsewhere. She couldn't help but feel a little distant from her friends. She respected them for working at the rest centre and she couldn't deny that they, too, were bearing witness to the horror of the war. But they were seeing the aftermath and she wasn't sure they understood everything she was going through. Sure, they would lend an ear if she asked to talk it through with them – but that was the last thing she wanted to do. She felt a sudden wrench towards the women she had been working alongside recently. Peggy clearly didn't like her much, but they had pulled together when it mattered, and she was somebody who would understand what Viv was going through without her having to explain. That new ARP warden, Dot, seemed as though she would be a good companion, too. She just felt as if being in the company of people who were experiencing the same horrors as her would bring her some comfort.

Viv tried to join in with her friends again, but now she couldn't stop thinking about William. She tried to assure herself that not hearing back from him wasn't unusual; he was busy with his RAF duties at the best of times and his role defending the British coastline would surely be a lot more demanding right now. But that was what kept niggling at her. He was in direct danger now, and she couldn't help but feel anxious about that. There was also the possibility, of course, that he was more upset than he had let on about her turning down his proposal. Maybe he had decided to give up on her altogether. The thought made her sadder than she would have expected, and she wondered briefly if all these concerns meant she was sweeter on William than she would like to admit. But she just as quickly dismissed the thought and forced herself to tune back in to her friends' conversation.

When the sirens went off an hour later, Viv grabbed Jilly and they walked back to the dance floor. A rush of people left the venue. Viv laughed to herself at their panicking. She supposed that once you had been out in a raid and seen what she had seen, you might well feel safer on an underground dance floor, too. She wondered if she would be one of the panickers if she hadn't had the ambulance work to keep her busy so far. It must be hard, when all you could do was sit and listen to the bombs and guns and planes, waiting for one to hit you. Well, that wasn't for her tonight. The band ramped up the volume and she cheered along with her friends and the other revellers who had stayed on to enjoy the rest of the evening, despite the threat flying over the London skies above them.

14

Dot felt a mixture of excitement and dread as she made her way home following her second and final training day. She was proud of herself for what she had achieved but at the same time anxious about Beryl's reaction to her new role. After yet more lectures and another training exercise, she had been presented with her Card of Appointment by the Chief Constable. She took it out of her pocket now to admire it.

This is to certify that Dorothy Simmonds, of 27 Lawrence Street, London, has been duly appointed as an air-raid warden.

She had also been given protective overalls, a civilian duty respirator, a steel helmet, an eye shield, badge and armlet, a whistle, an electric torch and a gas rattle. She'd had no idea Peggy and her fellow wardens had been carrying around so much equipment in their shoulder bags when she had come across them on duty before now. They all seemed to make the bags look so light to carry, yet she was straining under the weight already. She had been wandering the streets near her home for an hour or so since leaving the school, putting off facing Beryl for as long as she could manage. She knew her mother-in-law must be aware of what she was up to by now – she had certainly spotted her during the training drill the day before. Beryl had kept up her silent treatment that evening – even going so far as to keep her comments to herself when Dot presented her a dinner that she knew very well wouldn't be to her liking. If she couldn't even bring herself to criticise Dot's cooking, then that meant she was furious with her. They had walked to the crypt in silence that night when the sirens had sounded, and then Beryl had spent the entirety of the raid glaring at her daughter-in-law as Dot, in turn, tried to keep herself busy and distracted by comforting other shelterers.

The whole evening had been excruciating. Dot knew Beryl was bursting to confront her about her training; she could *feel* it. But she was keeping it in – which was what she did when she was extremely angry about something. Instead of sniping and pushing as she normally would, she stewed on it until she erupted, and it all came flying out. Dot could feel her brewing and she felt like she was walking on eggshells waiting for the onslaught. She was pretty sure that walking into the house carrying her overalls and her ARP kit would be enough to push Beryl over the edge, which was why she kept walking up to Lawrence Street and then losing her nerve and circling back towards the Thames.

Staring out into the water, Dot wondered if Beryl had written to Tommy to let the cat out of the bag. She started to regret giving up on the letter she had thought about writing herself. He probably wasn't going to be happy about it to begin with, but surely she had more hope of talking him round if the news came from her, along with a list of all the reasons why it was a good idea? Maybe she still had time, though. Beryl's fingers weren't as supple as they used to be.

Though she could still knit like there was no tomorrow, she often called on Dot to finish writing letters for her as the finer movement made her fingers ache. If she had started a letter yesterday, then there was a good chance she hadn't managed to finish it just yet. Maybe Dot could get her on side before it was too late.

Feeling a little more hopeful, she decided to take the plunge and go home to face the music. The sooner she got this out of the way, the better. She took a deep breath and readied herself to grovel to Beryl. She might even have to beg. But it would be worth it to make sure the news of her air-raid warden role reached her husband via herself instead of via his mother, delivered with venom.

Dot was enjoying her stroll back along the river when the sirens started sounding. That was just typical. Normally she would be grateful for the reason to avoid spending time alone with Beryl. But on the one night she actually wanted – no, *needed* – to have some one-to-one time with her mother-in-law, the Germans had to go and scupper her plans. She groaned and changed direction, heading towards Upper Cheyne Row. She was hopeful that the warden on the door would allow her to leave her overalls and equipment somewhere safe near the entrance, as the last thing she wanted to do was to walk in with them and push Beryl to boiling point with the sight in front of everybody. They needed to make it through this raid, and then they could have a civilised conversation about it all tomorrow, in private.

When Dot got to the crypt it was full of the chaos that normally ensued shortly after the sirens went off. Hordes of people were packing into the space under the church, calling out to find friends and family, and clambering for the best spot to settle into. After leaving her ARP kit with Charles at the entrance, Dot made her way through the crowds, looking for Beryl. Dot had come a long way from where she had been on the river to get here – a lot more distance than Beryl would have had to cover from the house – but she couldn't see her anywhere.

She tried to keep calm, but all she could think about were the terrible things that could have happened to the older woman to stop her from getting to safety. The bombs hadn't started falling yet, but Beryl could have tripped coming down the stairs to leave the house or taken a funny turn as she got pulled along in the throng of people rushing through the streets. Some people were so concerned with getting themselves to safety that they didn't even seem to notice they had pushed others out of their way to get there quicker. This was the first time they had ever had to come to the shelter separately, and Dot suddenly felt guilty for having left Beryl to make the journey on her own. If she had gone straight home, then she would have been there to escort her.

Dot looked around her. The bedlam had started to calm now, and people were settling down together, tucking up under their blankets ready for another long night of turmoil. She watched the latest group of stragglers arrive. Beryl wasn't with them. It never took them this long to make it here, even when Beryl was purposefully dragging her heels in order to annoy Dot. As the sound of planes roared above them, and the guns started firing from the ground, Dot knew what she had to do. Beryl might make her life a living hell a lot of the time, but she was family. She loved her despite their differences, and she couldn't stand the thought of her being in pain at home or out on the streets somewhere, desperate for help. This was Tommy's mother, and he would never forgive her if anything happened to her. She would never forgive herself.

'I need to find Beryl,' she said to Charles as she dashed past him and grabbed her belongings. She had considered leaving them where they were but reasoned that they might come in handy seeing as she was going out onto the streets in the middle of a raid. She put her hat on as soon as she was outside. After walking for a few yards, she heard a whistling sound and ducked behind the nearest garden wall to wait for the missile to land. She took a deep breath and braced herself, then breathed a sigh of relief when it landed some distance away. *This is what I trained for*, she told herself as she went back to join the remaining few groups of people heading to the shelter. Another whistle whizzed through the sky. The previous one had landed so far away, and Dot was desperate to get to Beryl as soon as possible. She was so near to Lawrence Street now. She decided to forge ahead.

Suddenly she was flying through the air, a heavy force on her back, before landing on the pavement with a thud. Lying on the ground, Dot felt a rush of debris whooshing past her. She wondered why none of it had hit her before opening her eyes and realising she couldn't see anything. Fear gripped her as she tried to work out what had happened. Too scared to move, she ran over the possibilities in her mind. Had shrapnel struck her eyes and blinded her? Maybe she was in too much shock to feel the pain yet? Had a building fallen on her? Tentatively, she tried to move, but there was something holding her down. Her heart was racing. Was she going to be one of those people who was trapped for days before eventually being dragged out of the rubble, minutes from death? Or would she simply die here? She was the one who was meant to be doing the rescue work – not making rescue work for others. Abruptly, fresh air swamped her and the mass weighing her down slowly eased off until it was gone completely. But even with the weight gone, it felt warm. Too warm. Like she was standing too close to an oven.

'Phew. That was close,' a voice whispered. 'You can get up now,' it added, laughing now. Dot had been too terrified to move. She slowly and carefully got to her knees, checking herself over for damage as she went. Up ahead she could see a house in flames. That explained the warmth. People were rushing towards the flames with buckets of water and stirrup pumps. She could hear voices shouting, trying to establish whether anybody was in the building where the bomb had struck, and if the walls were likely to collapse. In the distance she could make out Peggy approaching the scene, blowing her whistle.

Dot looked behind her. The voice had been coming from the ambulance driver from the training exercise the day before. She was on her feet now, busy shaking dust and dirt from her hair, which somehow seemed to shine in the glow of the flames. She still looked glamorous, but her jacket was ripped and shredded. It had looked expensive, too.

'This old thing? I've got a hundred at home,' she joked, catching Dot's eyes taking in the state of it. 'Are you all right? I think my coat took the brunt of it. Sorry if I startled you. You didn't seem to be bracing for cover and I just wanted to get us both under something. I didn't realise my own strength.'

So, this woman had shoved her to the ground and sheltered them both from the debris and shrapnel from the bomb with her coat? Dot had acted recklessly and nearly got herself killed. And this woman had put herself in danger in order to help her instead of leaving her to it and looking out for herself. 'But, your coat – it's completely ruined.'

'Rather the coat than you, dear.' The ambulance driver smiled, taking a stick of lipstick out of her pocket. 'If I was worried about my fancy clothes, then I'd have gone back to the country to be with my family when these wretched raids started. But enough about that – what on earth were you thinking back there? I'm pretty sure I just saved your life. I thought air-raid wardens had more common sense than to ignore a bomb falling at their feet.'

The comment sounded harsh, but it was no more than Dot deserved. And, somehow, this woman's tone and the friendliness behind her eyes as she spoke had managed to make it sound like a light-hearted dig rather than a reprimand. 'I know. And I'm sorry.' Dot flushed with shame. No sooner had she qualified as an air-raid warden than she had let herself down. 'I'm worried about my mother-in-law, and I just wasn't thinking straight.' There was another boom, this time further away, and the guns started up again.

'You've got to keep your wits about you. You can't let anything personal get in the way of what you're doing out here. It could make the difference between life and death. You'd be no use to your mother-in-law blown to pieces, now, would you?' The woman was gathering up Dot's bag and overalls from the floor. Dot hadn't realised they had left her grip when she had been thrown to the floor. The woman handed them back to her and helped her to her feet. 'My name's Vivian, by the way. Viv to my friends.'

'I'm Dot.' She smiled back. She suddenly felt terrible for having assumed this obviously very capable woman was anything but that simply because she presented herself so well when they were surrounded by such horror. Her first impression at the training exercise had been that she was too glamorous to carry out such a role. Her posh accent had further convinced Dot that she wasn't cut out for war work. But Viv had undeniably proven her wrong tonight.

'I take it you passed the training?' Viv asked, looking pointedly at Dot's kit. Dot nodded. 'Well, I'm sure we'll be bumping into each other a lot more from now on. Now, what's the problem with your mother-in-law?'

Dot's stomach suddenly flipped. She had been so distracted by the commotion she had wandered off track spectacularly. 'I've got to find her,' she said, panicked. 'She's not at the shelter. She's angry with me. For joining the ARP.'

'Try to stay calm,' Viv said soothingly. 'You'll be no use to anybody in this state. And you'll only get yourself hurt.'

Dot took a deep breath. She was right, of course. Everything she had learned seemed to be going out of the window now she was out in the thick of it. Thank goodness Viv had come to her rescue.

'Do you need me to come and help?' Viv asked, checking her watch. 'I'm late for my shift but they're used to it. It's quite common to get sidetracked by someone in need of help on the way in.'

'I'm almost home, I'm sure I'll find her there. But thank you. And thank you again for saving me. I really do owe you.'

'Don't mention it,' Viv said kindly. 'Here,' she added, holding up her stick of lipstick. She swept a slick of it over Dot's lips. 'That's better. I always find a bit of warpaint puts me back together. Good luck out there.'

'Good luck to you, too,' Dot said before turning on her heel and running off down the street at speed. She felt ashamed of herself for making such a foolish mistake, but she wasn't going to dwell on it. If what had just happened had taught her anything, it was that she needed to keep her mind on what she was doing. She couldn't afford to get distracted during times like this.

When she reached the house, she turned her key in the lock and braced herself, convinced she was going to find Beryl in some awful state. There couldn't be any other reason for her not to have made it to the crypt. And she knew that she hadn't become stuck between here and there as Dot had just covered that journey and there hadn't been any sign of her. Dot fumbled her way through the house in the darkness. When she reached the living room, she was able to make out the silhouette of Beryl in her chair. Her heart raced as all the possibilities ran through her head. Had she suffered a stroke or heart attack? Maybe she had choked on her dinner.

'Beryl!' she cried, lunging towards the body, desperate for a sign of life. Just as Dot placed her hand on the older woman's arm, Beryl let out an almighty roar.

'What on earth are you playing at?' Beryl yelled. Any doubt that her mother-in-law had met a grisly end disappeared. Dot felt shame and rage race through her as she thought about the risks she had taken to get back here to help her, and how worried she had been. She'd almost got herself blown up! 'Well, what are you staring at me like that for? You silly girl, you could have seen me off, giving me a fright like that!'

Dot would have laughed at the irony of the statement had she not been so furious. 'I was worried about you. I thought something terrible must have happened when you didn't turn up at the crypt.'

Beryl tutted. She reached over to turn on a lamp and in the light, Dot could see that she was shaking her head at her. 'You weren't worried about me. You were only concerned about how it would look to everyone else – you down there doing your Good Samaritan bit and your mother-in-law nowhere to be seen. You don't care about me, you only care about looking good in front of everyone else.'

'That's not true,' Dot replied. She was used to Beryl saying hurtful things to her, but this had hit a nerve. She was doing this to help others; she had never given a second thought to what anybody made of her. She was even risking rocking the boat with Tommy, which wasn't something she looked upon lightly given the history between them. But she bit her tongue. There was no point in arguing with Beryl about this. Besides, they didn't have time to have this out here – they needed to get to safety.

'I'm not going to that bloody shelter,' Beryl snapped, folding her arms across her chest. 'I've had enough of watching you parading around down there.'

'Well, you had better get used to it, because I've joined the ARP,' Dot retorted. She instantly regretted it. She had wanted to break the news to Beryl gently, to try to help her understand her reasons so they didn't have a big argument about it.

'Of course you ruddy well have. I saw you out there yesterday, you know. You must think I'm stupid! That's why I didn't go down there tonight. I couldn't stand the thought of you waltzing in with your uniform, looking all pleased with yourself. And it looks like I was right.' She stared pointedly at Dot's lips. Suddenly, Dot remembered she was wearing lipstick. Tommy hated make-up and his mother knew it. This would just back up Beryl's assumption that Dot had joined the ARP for the wrong reasons. Why hadn't she wiped it off before she entered the house? She had been too worried about her mother-in-law to think about anything else, she thought to herself, feeling foolish.

Beryl tutted. 'Goodness knows what Tommy will make of all this,' she said.

'He'll be proud of me.'

'I wouldn't bank on it! He knows as well as I do that a woman's place is at home, taking care of everything. Looking after her family. You've only just joined and already you've abandoned me and started tarting yourself up.'

Dot was growing angrier now. She had felt awful thinking about what might have happened because she hadn't been here to help Beryl to the shelter. But she had been sitting here like a petulant child – and she had put them both at risk. She took a deep breath and reminded herself not to bite back, though. She needed Beryl onside, and this was starting to get out of hand. 'Please. Will you just come to the Anderson shelter with me, so I know you're safe? And let me explain why I've volunteered. I want to help people. It's as simple as that. I can't stand to sit around and watch while everyone suffers. I think Tommy will be pleased I'm doing my bit.'

'So, you haven't told him? I *knew* it! I *knew* you were keeping secrets from my son as well as from me.'

Dot felt a rush of relief. At least Beryl hadn't told Tommy before she'd had the chance to. But there was still a risk she would if she couldn't talk her round tonight. 'It wasn't like that. It all happened so quickly. I was going to write to him to tell him, but I realised it was better done face to face. I wanted to be able to tell him about all the good work I've been doing next time he comes back.' Beryl tutted. '*Please*, let me be the one to tell him. I don't want this to upset him, and I think I can make him understand if I can talk it through with him. But he'll surely get upset if he hears it from anybody else.'

'Oh, don't you worry, dear. I'm not getting involved in this. This is *your* mess, and *you* can clean it up. I won't be the one to tell him his wife has been cavorting around with all sorts of different men while he's been off defending the country.'

Dot's blood boiled at the accusation, but she stopped herself from getting defensive. Beryl wasn't going to tell Tommy about the ARP. She could think what she liked about what Dot was doing; so long as Tommy understood the truth of it, then that was all that mattered. She knew that he thought more of her than that. At least, she hoped he did.

'Thank you,' she whispered. Beryl didn't respond. 'Now, please, will you come to the Anderson shelter with me if you still won't come to the crypt?' There was silence until an explosion rang out around them. It didn't sound dangerously near to Dot, but it was close enough to shake the walls of the house. One of the pictures on the wall fell to the floor with a crash. Beryl let out a small yelp and was getting to her feet before Dot had a chance to say anything.

'I'll sit in the shelter with you, but I've not forgiven you for lying to my boy,' she said shakily as she made her way to the back door. It was a start, Dot thought to herself, as she followed behind.

15

Peggy smiled when she walked into the canteen and spotted Dot kitted out in her uniform and ready for her first shift.

'I was worried when I didn't see you at the crypt during the raid last night,' she said after admiring the little flourish Dot had given her drab overalls – a small daisy in one of the top buttonholes. There had been another raid earlier today, but Peggy had managed to convince Lilli and a few of her other neighbours to go down into the cellar with her to sit it out.

Dot sighed. 'Oh, I had a bit of a night of it with my mother-in-law.'

She looked tired. Peggy remembered how drained she had felt after doing all her training. And she hadn't even had nightly air raids to contend with at the same time. But she had faith that her new friend would find the strength and energy to pull through. It's what they all had to do – there was no choice, really, when it came down to it.

'I'll fetch us a cup of tea and then you can tell me all about it. Victor will be in soon, along with the rest of the men on shift. We normally have a quick catch-up and then I go and do my rounds. Hopefully I'll get a chance to complete them before the sirens go off tonight. Victor said I can take you with me and show you the ropes.'

'That sounds great,' Dot said with a smile.

Peggy felt the most positive she had done since the raids had begun as she boiled the water. It felt good to have some female company on her shift at last. She had managed to avoid Stan over the last week. The raids had kept everybody so busy that even when she had come across him at a bomb site, he hadn't had a chance to make any of his usual remarks. She had caught him sneering at her a few times, but mostly he seemed to be too preoccupied with what was going on around him to give her a second thought. She had noticed he tended to take a lot of time and care with the bodies of the dead, showing them a respect she would never have expected from somebody like him. Maybe he did have a heart and was affected by all the suffering he was witnessing as much as she was. Peggy would never have thought that the Germans attacking London so regularly would have an upside to it, but it seemed that it did. As much as she hated the man, though, she had to admit that she would happily put up with his full attention if it meant the Germans left London alone. While she was on her own in the kitchen, she was reminded of the little mantra she used to recite at the start of every shift.

'Please keep the bombs away for another night,' she whispered now, rolling her eyes and tutting to herself. How foolish she felt today for thinking that would have done any good. She thought back to those long nights on shift, before the Germans had started attacking the city. What she would give to go back to that. She wondered with a heavy heart if the Germans would ever stop attacking them. Hitler didn't seem like the kind of man to back down, and she knew that her country would never dream of surrendering. Where would it all end? Peggy was dragged back to the present when she heard Stan's loud laugh travelling through from the canteen. She quickly finished the teas and hurried back in, keen to save Dot from his clutches.

'Ahhh, Peggy. I was just offering to take the new recruit out and show her what's what,' Stan said. He gave Peggy an over-exaggerated wink that made her feel sick to her stomach.

'Don't worry, Victor has asked me to show her the ropes,' Peggy replied, trying to keep her voice calm and even. She didn't want him to know how much he rattled her, or how desperate she was to protect Dot from him.

'Oh, I see. Girls together, is it?' Stan scoffed bitterly, look-ing slowly between the two of them. He rubbed his grubby hand over his big belly and laughed quietly. 'Well, I suppose you're probably better off in pairs. Two of you will be about as effective as one man, anyway.'

Dot flushed red and nervously played with her fingers. Peggy was furious that this bully was belittling her before she had even started and had been given a chance to prove herself. She went to say something cutting back to him, and then she remembered his threat from before. As much as she hated bowing down to someone like Stan, his behav-iour that night had really shaken her. She knew how easy it would be for him to catch her on her own again. Her shoul-der flinched as the muscles remembered how tightly he had squeezed them. She didn't even want to think about what he would do if she put him down in front of somebody else again. As much as she hated this man and did not want to let him get away with what he was saying, she was going to have to unless she wanted to be constantly looking over her shoulder waiting for him to punish her for it.

When Bill and Charles walked in together, Peggy took the opportunity to get Dot talking to some of her kinder colleagues. She didn't want to scare her away before she had even started her first shift. She knew Dot had met them both previously, and she was pleased when they both had a positive reaction to her joining the team. When Charles produced his pocket watch, she knew that Dot had his seal of approval. Charles was picky about who he shared the history of his watch with, but once you were in his confidence then you could be sure to hear the story repeatedly. Peggy thought she must have heard it at least a dozen times already.

'I was young and sprightly enough to fight for our country during the Great War,' he was telling Dot now. Bill looked over at Peggy and playfully rolled his eyes. He had probably heard the story more times than she had. 'Now, you see this dent here?' he said, pointing to the back of the pocket watch. Dot nodded, looking intrigued. 'This watch saved my life,' he declared proudly. 'That dent right there is where a bullet hit it. If it wasn't for the watch, then I'd have been a goner. It was in my breast pocket when it got hit.'

'My goodness,' Dot exclaimed.

'I won't go anywhere without it now,' he added.

'I don't blame you. It must be your lucky charm.'

After a brief catch-up with Victor, everybody headed out to their patches to check on the blackout and compile a list of who was home that evening. Victor had told Dot to learn Peggy's patch like the back of her hand. They were to team up when they were on shift together, and once Dot was confident enough then she would be able to cover Peggy for time off and vice versa. Peggy was delighted at the prospect of having safe hands to leave her residents in. She was extremely protective of them.

'I'm really sorry about Stan,' Peggy said quietly as they walked along in the dark together. 'Turn that light out!' she yelled as a quick aside. There had been a slither of light escaping from one of the houses. No sooner had she made the statement than the light had vanished.

'Sorry, Peggy!' a voice called back from the other side of the window.

'That's Mrs Wicks,' Peggy explained. 'She never quite pulls the blinds down far enough and then she insists on reading her paper by the lamp right next to the window. I've been trying to convince her to move her reading chair to the other end of the room, so she's away from the window at least. But you know what these old dears are like. They're so set in their ways. Maybe a little bit like your mother-in-law.' The sentence had escaped her mouth before she'd had a chance to censor it. 'Whoops, sorry. I don't know her; I'm sure she's a bit more accommodating than Mrs Wicks.'

'No, no, she's just as stubborn.' Dot laughed. 'Probably a little more so. And she would never apologise for being in the wrong.' The two of them giggled conspiratorially, but Dot's face quickly turned serious again. There was clearly something bothering her, but Peggy got the sense that she might not be ready to talk about it.

'I'm sorry again about Stan back there,' Peggy said, deftly changing the subject. 'He seems to have a real problem with women joining the ARP. I want you to know that I normally would have stuck up for you – but he got quite nasty with me last week, so I'm doing my best to avoid riling him up. It's probably best if you do all you can to avoid him. I'd thought he was only picking on me because I was the only female warden at our base, and that he might not be so brave once you were here. But it looks like I was wrong about that.' She suddenly realised what it sounded like she was saying. 'Not that I only encouraged you to join in the hopes of getting that ogre off my back, of course,' she added hurriedly.

'I wasn't thinking that. But I wish I had been more help. He made me feel uncomfortable, but I was so thrown by it that I'm afraid I just stood and stared at him while he talked down at me. I feel a bit ridiculous now.'

'Please don't feel like that. As much as you probably wish you had stood up to him, believe me when I say it was for the best that you didn't. I've learned that it's better not to antagonise a bully like Stan. I know it's incredibly unfair, but we have enough to be worrying about and dealing with without fearing repercussions from somebody like him. Bullies like him always get their comeuppance in the end.'

'I hope you're right.'

Peggy hoped she was right, too. They continued in silence for a little longer. Peggy could sense that Dot was mulling something over in her head. She was keen to talk some more and get to know her better, but she decided to stay quiet a little longer, hoping it might encourage Dot to get whatever was bothering her out in the open.

'What you've said has made me feel a little better about how I dealt with my mother-in-law last night, actually,' Dot finally said.

'Beryl, isn't it?' Peggy asked encouragingly.

Dot nodded. 'She's really angry about me doing this. She can't stand to see me doing my bit. That's why she didn't go to the shelter last night. I was so worried about her that

I ended up rushing back to the house – I was so distracted that I nearly got myself blown to bits in the process, and then we had a bit of a row about it all. I really wanted to stand up to her, but I'm worried she'll tell my husband about the ARP before I get a chance to, so I backed down to keep her onside. I was feeling a little pathetic this morning but now . . .'

'It's so frustrating,' Peggy blurted. 'But, like I said, bullies always get their comeuppance.' In the silence that followed, she panicked. 'I've done it again, haven't I? I'm so sorry – I'm sure Beryl isn't a bully. Family situations are so difficult, especially mothers-in-law. Well, from what I hear, anyway. I don't have one of my own.' She was rambling now, and she knew it, but she didn't seem to be able to stop. She really wanted to be friends with Dot, but she kept saying the wrong thing. She suddenly realised that Dot was laughing.

'You are funny,' she whimpered through giggles. 'Please, stop worrying about offending me. When it comes to my mother-in-law, there really is nothing you can say that is worse than what I think of her. Don't get me wrong – she's family and I love her – but my goodness can she be a nasty piece of work!'

As Dot told her about the way Beryl treated her and all the little snipes that she made at her all the time, Peggy couldn't help but feel sympathy for her new colleague. What an awful way to live. Her family had always been so loving that she couldn't imagine existing in such a horrible atmosphere.

'What's your husband like?' Peggy asked cautiously. She wasn't sure if she was probing too far, but she couldn't help but wonder. If Beryl was as bad as Dot was making out, then what else was she having to deal with at home? The man surely took after his mother. How much of a bully was he? She had heard of women stuck in marriages with wretched men. One of her aunties had even stayed with her husband despite the fact he beat her regularly. For reasons that Peggy still couldn't fathom, she insisted that she loved him and was convinced that he loved her too. But he went too far one day and almost killed her. Peggy's father had whipped her out of that situation before she'd had a chance to recover and protest. But Dot jumped to Tommy's defence without missing a breath.

'Tommy is nothing like his mother. He's protective of me, of course. That's why he didn't want me working once we got married. That's the reason Beryl thinks he won't like me doing my bit now, but I think she's wrong. This is different, isn't it? He's going to be proud of me. I'm going to do him proud.'

Peggy wasn't sure if Dot was trying to convince her or herself, but she was the one rambling now and she couldn't help but think that it was very telling. She had listened to her auntie defend her husband in the same sort of way many times.

'He'd be silly to be anything but incredibly proud of what you're doing. Especially as he knows how much you have to put up with from his witch of a mother.' She hoped the last part would be taken with the humour she had intended and she was relieved when Dot started laughing again. But behind her laugh she was certain she could see sadness in her eyes. She hoped Dot wasn't going to have to stop volunteering when Tommy found out what she was doing. She thought the fact that she had kept it from him was very telling as well, but who was she to judge? 'Anyway, we got sidetracked. I was going to ask if you managed to convince Beryl to go back to the shelter in the end?'

'I think the Germans convinced her more than I did.' Dot smirked. 'I managed to get her into the Anderson shelter after backing down to her during the row. We've never spent an actual raid in there – just the false alarms. Well, the raids are quite a different experience in those flimsy underground burrows, I can tell you.' Dot shook her head dramatically and let out a long breath. 'It's just as noisy and just as scary as being out on the street while the bombs are dropping. I don't think she was prepared for that. She spent the whole night whimpering and shaking.'

'Oh well, at least you got some peace from her sharp tongue,' Peggy joked.

'Well, yes, that was certainly a bonus.' Dot giggled. 'As soon as the all-clear sounded she whispered that she would go back to the crypt from now on – but only if I stay away from her in my uniform, and don't tell anybody that we're related.' Peggy could just about make out Dot rolling her eyes in the darkness.

'Everybody knows she's your mother-in-law.'

'Exactly. But I just nodded and agreed. Whatever makes her happy, I suppose. At least she regretted putting her foot down with me and refusing to go there in the end.'

'Yes, but she could have regretted it a lot more.'

Dot nodded thoughtfully. 'When the sirens went off this afternoon, she shot out of the door and down to the church faster than I've ever seen her move. I think last night really shook her up.'

'Serves her right.' Peggy grinned playfully.

'Anyway, enough about Beryl. I'd love to know about your family, Peggy. Do you have any brothers or sisters?'

Peggy's heart filled with warmth and longing simply with the thought of her family. 'Both my older brothers are serving in the Navy,' she said with pride. 'And my father is off fighting too. My sister, Joan, is working as a land girl, and my three youngest sisters are at home in Sussex with our mother. They've taken in two evacuees so far.'

'You must miss them all terribly,' Dot said quietly.

Peggy nodded. 'I've struggled being away from Joan the most. She's only a few years younger than me and we've always been incredibly close. Lee and Jamie were always off on some adventure in the woods together when we were growing up, and Joan and I stayed home to play with our dolls and play mummies and babies.' She laughed to herself. 'Our mother always used to laugh about how desperately maternal we both were – we'd argue constantly over who was going to be the mummy. I always used to throw in that I was the oldest and that meant she had to play the baby.' Peggy paused to enjoy the memories. She hadn't thought about those games in such a long time. It always made her feel so nostalgic and homesick, but she was beginning to find that sometimes it was good to embrace those feelings.

'You said you had even younger sisters, too? I bet you both loved it when they were babies?'

'Oh, of course!' Peggy exclaimed, thinking back to the days when she and Joan would rush home from school for cuddles with their sisters. 'Mother would go for a rest and leave us in charge until dinnertime. We loved to dress them up and push them around the village in their prams. It was like we were proudly showing off our own offspring.' She chuckled. 'Silly, really, when I think about it now. We treated the poor little things like dolls.'

'I'm sure they enjoyed all the love and attention from their older sisters.'

'They certainly did. I worry about how they're getting on without me and Joan – but they have each other and they have our mother.' She sniffed and hoped that it was too dark for Dot to see how wet her eyes had become. She would give anything to be back at home with them all now.

'Have you heard from Joan since you came to London?'

'She writes to me as often as she can, but she's busy and I understand that. I've grown close to one of the refugees at my boarding house – Lilli. I think I was drawn to her because her soft, caring nature reminded me of Joan. She's become a bit of a surrogate sister, now I think about it. I seem to have this need to look after people wherever I go.'

'That's a great quality. I'm sure you'll make a wonderful mother one day.'

Peggy bristled with pride at the kind words before turning her focus back on their patrol. She stopped to knock on another door. She loved talking about her family, but she needed to concentrate on keeping other families safe right now. They knocked on a few more doors over the next hour or so. Peggy introduced Dot to more of the residents and she was pleased to see her making notes about them all in her pocketbook.

When they were on the way back to the ARP base, Peggy started to wonder when the sirens would sound. The thought brought with it the usual fear, but it was stronger tonight. Lilli might have assured her she would shelter in the crypt from now on, but Peggy knew how anxious she was about going there, and she knew she couldn't stay with her the whole time to look after her. Lilli would be tempted to stay with her friends in the dining room at the boarding house and Peggy couldn't stand the thought of her being so exposed and vulnerable while bombs dropped on the city.

'I wonder if Beryl will be one of the first to the crypt this evening, after her awful experience in the Anderson,' Dot joked as they made their way back to the school. It was like her new friend had read her mind.

'That's it!' Peggy cried jubilantly.

'What's what?' Dot asked in confusion.

'Lilli and Beryl!'

'What about them?'

'They're going to be crypt companions. It's perfect!' Dot still looked none the wiser – and it was no surprise – so Peggy explained her idea. 'The residents at my boarding house have started sleeping in the dining room during raids.' Dot raised her eyebrows in shock. 'I know, I know. I was furious when I found out. But they're saying the cellar is too cramped and some of them won't budge on it. I'm terrified I'm going to end up having to dig them all out of there one day soon. Anyway, I've convinced Lilli to shelter at the crypt, but she doesn't know anybody. She went last night but she really struggled to mix with the other shelterers. Maybe I could send her Beryl's way?'

Dot laughed so hard that it came out as more of a snort. 'Sorry,' she blustered. 'It's just that Beryl is hardly the maternal type. I can't see her looking after a young Belgian down there.'

'Yes, but Lilli is such a kind and gentle soul. I've seen her melt the hearts of even the hardest, toughest men. It's one of the reasons she reminds me of Joan so much. It's got to be worth a try. If anything, it might keep Beryl distracted from her vendetta against you for a little while?'

'When it comes to that, I'll give anything a go.'

'That's that decided, then.' Peggy smiled. When the siren started wailing shortly after, she felt ready to get to work and to put their new plan into action. They helped guide residents from their patch to the crypt and checked in on the people who Peggy knew would insist on staying at home. They were on their way to the crypt to introduce Beryl to Lilli when an incendiary dropped just yards in front of them. Peggy was impressed at Dot's speed in getting hold of the nearest stirrup pump and putting out the flames. After the brief delay, they were on their way to the church again when the rumbling of a plane roared overhead.

'Get down!' Dot yelled as they both threw themselves to the pavement at the same time. A succession of bombs rained down, followed by the sickening sound of one of them hitting a building. They stayed in position until the planes had continued on past them.

'It sounded as if it was a few roads along,' Peggy said shakily. She got to her feet and went over to Dot to hold out her hand and help her up. They ran together towards the heat of fire. As they got closer, Peggy felt her knees go weak when she realised the flames were worryingly close to the church spire. But she dismissed her worst fears. Suddenly one of the ARP messengers rushed around the top of Upper Cheyne Row, obviously on his way to the school to log the incident with Victor.

'Tell the boss we'll take this one!' Peggy shouted over to him as they drew closer together. She was near enough to see his face now. It was a shocking shade of white despite all the heat surrounding them.

'They've hit the crypt,' he shouted.

16

Almost as soon as Viv pulled Hudsy out of the ambulance station, she was deafened by the noise of planes flying overhead. Shortly after there followed explosions and a mass of activity in the sky. She knew she wasn't supposed to take her eyes off the road, especially with the risk of so many obstacles and the added difficulty of the reduced lighting. She kept focused for as long as she could manage. When she turned the corner, there was a huge thudding noise. Wardens immediately started running up the street, blowing their whistles and shouting for hordes of confused and panicked people to take shelter. Suddenly, there was an almighty explosion.

'Keep going,' Paul muttered, keeping his eyes on the sky. Viv's knuckles had turned white from gripping the steering wheel so hard as Hudsy had been violently shaken. She could see clouds and dust floating up into the air in the corners of her vision, but she kept driving on, keen to get to their destination as quickly and as safely as they could. She knew Paul would divert her or tell her to stop if it was too dangerous to continue. She'd been shocked when he'd got into the car and told her they were going to Upper Cheyne Row. That was where the church was – where people sheltered. She was praying now that it hadn't been hit. Bombs hitting houses with people inside were bad enough, but the carnage of the Cadogan Shelter had been almost unbearable. She wasn't sure if she could cope with another. Paul suddenly gasped. Viv couldn't help it – she had to look up to see what he had seen. She slowed a little and followed his line of sight. She gasped too when she saw the raider, flying worryingly low, being chased by a Spitfire.

'It's unloading as it goes,' she just about managed to hear Paul saying as both planes roared over them, filling her head with unbearable noise. 'We're probably going to have to get through a few bomb sites to get to Upper Cheyne Row. It's sure to have taken out some houses on our route.'

Viv hated driving past people who needed help, but she knew it was important to get to their destination as soon as they possibly could. There were people waiting for them there. People who had been in pain longer than those they would have to pass on the way. The bombs that had only just landed would be being called into Control right now, and fresh crews would soon be dispatched to the casualties there. Viv closed her eyes briefly and took a deep breath as she spotted some poor soul's severed leg at the side of the road. She kept her eyes fixed forward, then, not keen on discovering the rest of the body. As they drove on, the streets became brighter – lit up by the burning caused by incendiary bombs and explosions. There were wardens and residents working together to put out fires with buckets of water and stirrup pumps, desperately trying to calm the flames until the fire service arrived. Viv wished it was pitch black again, and that her route wasn't being illuminated by the carnage from people's homes and businesses – and lives – being destroyed. But as everyone around her scrambled for safety and shelter, she kept driving towards the danger.

Turning into Upper Cheyne Row, Viv felt bile rising in her throat. Her prayers that the shelter hadn't been hit had fallen on deaf ears. *Like most prayers these days*, she thought bitterly to herself. She felt sick thinking about how many innocent people would have been sheltering in the crypt when the bomb had ripped through it. The one place they would have felt safe.

Searching around for ARP wardens, she spotted Dot and Peggy waving her over. She parked up a few houses down from the church – as close as she could get without shredding the tyres to pieces – and she took a moment to digest the rubble and flames before leaping into action.

'What a night to work your first shift,' she said to Dot as lightly as she could manage as they stood staring at the smouldering wreckage. She tried to block out the groaning and wailing that she could already hear coming from trapped survivors.

'I don't think there was ever going to be a good night to start,' Dot replied, fixing her hat and smiling weakly. Suddenly, a worrying thought popped into Viv's head. They hadn't been far from here when she had saved Dot from the shrapnel the previous evening. And Dot had been on her way home. She didn't want to ask the question – too afraid of the answer. But she had to.

'You live around here, don't you? Do you know anybody who was in there tonight?'

Tears filled Dot's eyes despite her obvious attempts to stop them. Peggy took hold of Dot's hand as they both continued to stare at the horror in front of them.

'We both do,' Peggy croaked, her voice shaking.

'My mother-in-law is in there,' Dot whispered. 'Beryl.'

'My friend Lilli was down there, too. I *made* her go down there,' Peggy said next. Before Viv could respond, the pair of them started running towards the burning church.

'Wait! You need to wait for the rescue teams!' Viv shouted, chasing after them.

'They're taking too long. We need to get that fire under control before it's too late,' Peggy called back. A group of locals had appeared carrying buckets of water and stirrup pumps. Peggy and Dot each took a stirrup pump and disappeared into the church, followed by the rest of them.

'There's only one way in and the fire is blocking it,' Viv heard somebody else saying. She went to lift a bucket of water, but somebody grabbed her arm and pulled her back. She turned around to see Paul staring at her.

'I want to help too, but we're better off out here,' he explained calmly.

'I can't just leave them to it,' Viv protested.

'The fire service will be here soon enough, along with the rescue teams. We need to be ready and waiting to help the people who make it out of there alive. What will they do if we get injured trying to free them?'

Viv reluctantly relented. She had to admit that he made a good point. She just found it so difficult to stand by and do nothing while she could hear people shouting for help. Just then, a fire engine pulled up and Viv breathed a sigh of relief. As the team set straight to work, she waited anxiously, praying there would be some survivors for them to assist. She couldn't face a night of only driving to and from to the morgue. When Dot and Peggy finally emerged, covered in soot and dust and coughing while they helped a woman stagger out, Viv rushed over to them. The woman's leg was dragging behind her and as Viv got closer, she could see it was covered in burns – the flesh black and red and melting.

'Can you get her to my car?' Both wardens nodded and Viv went on ahead to get some bandages ready. As she worked on doing the best she could for the woman until she could get her to the hospital, she waited for Peggy or Dot to update her on the situation in the crypt. Paul brought over a little boy with a broken arm, and they worked together to splint it. The boy didn't make a noise throughout.

'You're very brave,' Viv told him. He must have been in so much agony, she wondered if the shock and the confusion had kicked in and blocked out the pain.

'Where's Mummy?' he whispered, his bright eyes watering as they looked up into hers expectantly.

'She'll be here soon,' Viv replied confidently. She immediately felt guilty for the lie. But what else could she say? She glanced over at Dot and Peggy, realising neither had spoken a word since emerging. They were both as white as sheets. Stepping a little way away from the boy so he couldn't hear them, she asked, 'What's it like in there?'

'They've got access now,' Dot whispered. She was silent again for a long time before adding, 'It's like something from a horror film down there.' Suddenly, there was an influx of survivors being helped outside. Yells of pain and anguish drowned out the noise of the guns and planes. Viv tried to zone out all the background noise, instead focusing on each patient as she got to them. The car was full very quickly. She looked around for Dot and Peggy but couldn't see them anywhere. She guessed they must have gone back inside to help the rescue teams.

'It will be Cheyne Hospital from here,' she said to Paul as he climbed in the back with the casualties. 'Keep a close eye on that one for shock,' she added, pointing to the woman with the burns on her legs. She was relieved to see another woman had taken the young boy under her wing, as well as a little girl who had suffered burns and a head wound and was also missing her mother.

The hospital wasn't far away, and they were soon on their way back to the church. Viv found herself worrying about what to say to Peggy and Dot about their loved ones missing in the crypt. What were you supposed to say in that situation? She knew what she should say – what she had been trained to tell distraught survivors waiting outside a collapsed building, desperate for some miracle to help their loved ones make it out alive. She was expected to soothe them, assure them it would all be fine even though it was obvious that it would not be, and then gently coax them away. But she couldn't do that with Dot and Peggy. They would see straight through it – they would have been taught the same thing, after all. And they certainly weren't going to be leaving the bomb site any time soon – they were constantly going in and out of the crypt, trawling through the wreckage. They might even discover the bodies of the people they were searching for. Viv shuddered at the thought. It didn't bear thinking about.

Viv looked over at Paul briefly and then turned her eyes back to the road. He looked drained – emotionally and physically exhausted. His eyes were puffy, and his face was drawn.

'It was crowded in there tonight,' he whispered. The noise from the planes and bombs had died down – for now – and the streets were eerily quiet. 'A lot of people were wiped out when the bomb hit. From what they can tell, it struck the church at an angle through a window and penetrated the floor before bursting amongst everybody taking shelter down there.' Viv recoiled as she thought about what everybody down there would have suffered. 'It sounds as though the bomber we saw being chased was trying to get Lots Road Power Station. He seems to have hit everything around here but his bloody target.' They turned into Upper Cheyne Row again, and Viv could see an ambulance being loaded up with more casualties.

'I really hope Beryl and Lilli are in there,' she said to herself.

'Who?' Paul asked.

'You know those two female wardens I was speaking to earlier? Well, one of them had a mother-in-law in there this evening. The other had a friend inside.' Paul shook his head.

'There's a doctor doing the rounds of the survivors,' a warden informed Viv as she made her way across to the churchyard where the injured were gathered. He was tall and balding, and she was pretty sure from memory that his name was Stan. She'd caught him staring at her for just a little longer than was necessary a few times, but there was no hint of any letching tonight. 'He's been telling the other ambulance crew who needs to get to hospital first and who can wait, so you might want to liaise with him.'

'Thank you.' Viv smiled faintly.

After a few more runs to the hospital the church grounds were thinning out and Paul and Viv found themselves able to stop for a few minutes to catch their breath. Viv looked around for Peggy and Dot. She had caught glimpses of them as they had been going backwards and forwards but there hadn't been an opportunity to speak to them. She spotted

Dot comforting three young children at the side of the road and went over to her. Dot smiled as she approached, but from the weakness of the smile Viv could tell that she hadn't found Beryl yet.

'There's no sign of Beryl or Lilli,' Dot whispered as the children cuddled into her.

'They could still make it out alive. I've heard of people being rescued after days buried in the rubble.' Dot winced and Viv realised her words hadn't been as reassuring as she had hoped.

'Charles didn't make it.' Dot's voice was hoarse. 'He was one of our colleagues. He was always so nice to me. He's one of the reasons I signed up. I guess his lucky charm wasn't so lucky after all.' Dot was staring into the distance now. She looked numb. 'Peggy found him in there,' she added quietly.

Viv didn't know what to say, so she didn't say anything. She was beginning to realise that sometimes that was for the best. She heard her name being called and turned around to see Paul near the entrance to the church.

'We need a stretcher!' he yelled over to her. Viv nodded and quickly turned back to Dot.

'If I find Beryl, I'll take good care of her,' she said firmly before running off to Hudsy.

17

As the sun started rising the following morning, Dot's hopes of Beryl making it out of the crypt alive were fading fast. She couldn't quite believe this was happening – and so soon after she had pushed Beryl to start sheltering down there. She had even made her promise to return when Beryl had refused to go. If she had left her to it and let her have her tantrum about not wanting to see her in the shelter on duty, allowed her to sit out the raids in the Anderson shelter in the garden, then she would still be alive now. She scolded herself silently; she needed to stop thinking about that. There was still a chance Beryl was alive down there – Viv had spoken about people being rescued after days trapped in the rubble. Yes, Dot had shuddered at the thought of it, but that outcome was certainly better than the alternative. Viv and her partner had swapped their trips to the hospital for trips to the morgue now, but that didn't mean there wouldn't be any more survivors getting pulled out of the wreckage.

There had been no sign yet of Peggy's friend, Lilli, either. The two of them had kept themselves busy helping home survivors who had miraculously emerged with hardly a scratch. They had also been wandering along the streets running parallel to the church to help at other bomb sites and direct people who were now homeless to rest centres. Dot had even escorted three young children to a rest centre herself. She'd been unable to locate their mother and the poor siblings were terrified. Dot knew their mother was most likely dead, but she had told the children she would probably be along to pick them up soon enough. She hated herself for the lie, but she felt like they'd been through enough that night and they deserved to feel a little bit of hope for just a short while longer before they were forced to accept that their lives had been torn apart.

'I can't stop thinking about Charles.' Peggy's voice cut into Dot's thoughts. She sat down heavily on the kerb next to her and put her head in her hands. Dot put a comforting arm around her shoulder. The raid had finished, the all-clear siren having sounded a few hours before, but neither of them had been able to tear themselves away from Upper Cheyne Row. Victor had turned up not long ago, after a messenger had passed on the news about Charles. He had tried to convince them both to go home – or to at least take a break back at the school. But neither of them felt able to leave the site until they knew for certain what had happened to Beryl and Lilli. 'I wish I hadn't turned him over. I knew it was Charles. It was obvious he was dead. I should have left him there for the rescue team to get him out when it was time. But something in me just needed to be certain he was gone. That I couldn't have helped him.'

Dot was relieved she hadn't seen lovely, caring Charles in that state. The few times she had ventured into the crypt that night to help search for survivors had left her feeling traumatised. She'd picked her way through flesh and limbs, mixed in with books and hats and shoes and teddy bears. Tears stung her eyes now as she thought about the children who had perished in that shelter. When the rescuers had started bringing out all the body parts, Dot had found herself checking over all the hands wearing rings, desperately searching for Beryl's wedding ring but at the same time dreading finding it. What on earth was she going to tell Tommy? She was meant to be looking after his mother and instead she had sent her to her death. Would he ever be able to forgive her? Dot realised she hadn't responded to what Peggy had said about Charles. She was thinking about what to say when one of the rescue team came and crouched down in front of them.

'We've got the body of a young woman, Peggy. She's got blonde hair and she's wearing a light blue dress. Do you want to come and check?'

Peggy let out a small cry. Then, forcing herself to look the man in the eye, she nodded slowly. She had given a description of Lilli to as many of the rescue team as she had been able to early in the evening, telling them what she had been wearing when Peggy had left for her shift that afternoon. They had all promised to let her know if they found anyone that fit the description. Dot helped Peggy to her feet and together they followed the man to a stretcher laid out on the ground away from the rest of the blanket-covered bodies. There was a sheet covering the body on the stretcher. Dot felt Peggy take a deep breath as the man reached down to reveal the corpse's face. Peggy's hands shot to her mouth, barely supressing another wail, this one more animal-like in sound. Dot tried to support her friend's weight, but Peggy threw herself to the ground, landing on her knees and resting her head on the young woman's chest. Dot found it difficult to draw her eyes away from the woman's face. She looked so peaceful and beautiful – it was as if she had slipped away in her sleep, instead of being taken in such a brutal way. When Dot looked up, the man nodded silently at her and backed away. Peggy didn't need to say anything. It was obvious they had found Lilli.

'I'm so sorry,' Dot whispered. She looked over at the rescue workers heading back into the church and wondered if the next person they recovered would be Beryl. Or would she be one of the bodies pieced together later? Surely there was no way she would make it out alive now. Dot was going to have to start facing the facts. Peggy was stroking Lilli's hair now and talking to her. Dot felt intrusive listening in, so she took a few steps back to leave Peggy to grieve in private – or in as much privacy as was possible given the circumstances, anyway. She saw the man who had found Lilli start walking back towards her. Dot's insides tightened as she braced herself for news of another body – this one fitting Beryl's description.

'I don't want to disturb her, but could you maybe pass on some information when the time is right?' he asked. Dot nodded and waited, relief washing over her. 'It looks as if a piece of shrapnel struck her. It appears to have hit her heart. She's lucky, in a way – she wouldn't have known anything about it, and she wouldn't have suffered.' Dot looked over at Peggy again, sobbing over Lilli's body. 'I hope that brings your friend some comfort,' the rescue worker added before walking back towards the church again. But Dot knew that Peggy would be feeling just as guilty as she was feeling, having persuaded Lilli to shelter in the crypt. She wasn't sure there was anything that could make her feel better about that.

She was about to go back over to Peggy when she felt a large presence looming behind her. She turned around to see Stan. He was staring at Peggy, contempt written all over his face.

'See, this is why women shouldn't be allowed to sign up for this,' he sneered, shaking his head. 'No offence to you, of course, but this here just shows that you lot can't keep your emotions in check.' He was pointing at Peggy as he spoke. Peggy's words about treading carefully around Stan rang in Dot's ears, but she couldn't just stand by while he spouted such cruel nonsense, regardless of whatever consequences she might face.

'How dare you,' she said slowly, trying to control the shake in her voice due to the rage she was feeling. Stan looked confused. '*Us lot* are more than capable of doing just as good of a job as the men.' Stan tutted but Dot continued before he had a chance to say anything. 'You have no idea what's going on here. Peggy has just lost one of her best friends.'

'It's not professional, weeping all over a corpse in the street. She needs to pull herself together.'

'None of this is professional!' Dot shouted, waving her arms around at the devastation that surrounded them. 'There are no rules, Stan! Besides, she isn't even on duty anymore, so you have no right to say any of this. But if there was still a bomb raid going on, then I can assure you that Peggy would be out there doing what she needed to be doing, and she would take the time to grieve afterwards.' Stan was glaring at Dot now. It was obvious that he wasn't used to being spoken to in this way, and Dot was already beginning to regret her outburst. But she hadn't been able to stop herself. She had risked so much to get here, and she hadn't done that to put up with comments like his. He'd sounded like . . . when the realisation hit, it struck her like a brick to the face. When Peggy had been telling her about Stan and his bullying, manipulative ways, it had all sounded vaguely familiar, but Dot hadn't been able to work out why. Now she knew. Stan had the same attitude towards women working that Tommy did. Tommy had always dressed it up as a desire to look after her and protect her, but he gave away hints of disdain over the years that she had chosen to ignore. And, of course, his lashing out at her when she had pushed to be allowed out to work should have been the final straw for her – it should have made everything clear – but she had been blinded by her love for him and she had chosen instead to erase the memory from her mind and pretend it had never happened.

It had felt natural to Dot to defend Tommy when she had been talking to Peggy about him, but she was suddenly beginning to understand that he was a bit of a bully himself. Just like Peggy was fearful of the repercussions from standing up to Stan, Dot had grown to be fearful of how Tommy would react to certain things that she did. So she had just behaved in the way that he wanted. But her determination to join the ARP had forced her to confront what was really going on in their relationship. She had spent years telling herself it was her problem when, really, Tommy was the one with the problem.

Her husband was a bully. Pure and simple. He just wasn't as obvious about it as people like his mother and Stan were. Dot suddenly felt stupid; how had it taken her all this time to realise what was going on? She had married a tyrant and she'd been in denial about it all this time.

She'd just put up with his behaviour, never questioning anything. Maybe Beryl's behaviour had distracted Dot from what the real issue was. When Dot looked up again, Stan had wandered away and Peggy was getting to her feet.

'Was he hassling you? I heard raised voices.'

Dot was relieved Peggy hadn't heard the exchange. 'Nothing I can't handle. Although I might need to look over my shoulder for the next few days. I gave him a bit of a mouthful.'

Peggy sighed. 'I think there's a bit too much going on now for him to get away with any funny business. But just make sure that you're always with someone, just in case.'

'How are you feeling?' Dot didn't want to think or talk about Stan anymore and she was certain that Peggy probably felt the same. Tears filled Peggy's eyes and she tried to talk but sobs came out instead. 'You should get home.'

'But what about you?' Peggy managed to ask through her tears. 'I take it there has been no sign of Beryl? Maybe you should pop home on the off chance she slipped away without you noticing, or decided against going to the shelter again?'

Dot shook her head. 'No, she wouldn't have gone to our Anderson. She was terrified that night we ended up in there. As much as she didn't want to watch me on duty, she wanted to be in there on her own much less. And as awful as Beryl is, she wouldn't leave me to worry and search for her if she had made it out. She would have tracked me down or got a message to me once the all-clear sounded.' Dot was confident in what she was saying. No matter what had gone on between the two of them and how much Beryl disliked her, she just couldn't imagine her leaving her to worry like this.

It was cruel beyond comprehension. 'I'll wait here until they've finished. But you should get home.'

'I'll need to tell everyone,' Peggy whispered, fresh tears filling her eyes.

'Go. I'll be fine,' Dot urged. There was nothing else for them to do here, and Dot was only staying put because she didn't know what else to do until Beryl was found.

As Peggy walked away, Dot searched around for a glimpse of Stan. She wanted to be certain her friend wasn't going to pass him on her way home. She didn't want him lashing out at her on the quiet streets, in anger over what Dot had said to him. And if she walked past him near the bomb site, then she didn't trust him not to make any further snide remarks within her hearing. She caught sight of his balding head in the graveyard, where all the dead bodies were laid out waiting to be transported to the morgue. Dot didn't like to think about how many trips backwards and forwards Viv and her partner had made by now.

She breathed a sigh of relief that Peggy was heading off in the opposite direction. But she wondered what Stan was doing over there. His shift was over, too, and there was nothing else for the wardens to do at the crypt, much less in the graveyard.

As Dot kept watch intently, Stan ducked down suddenly, out of sight. Intrigued, Dot walked towards the graveyard and peered over the wall. Stan was creeping from body to body, peering underneath the blankets. She felt a wave of sympathy for the man. Maybe he had known people in the shelter, and he was searching for somebody. But what she saw next made her blood boil. Her heart raced as she watched in disbelief as Stan lifted one of the blankets and quickly slipped a watch off the wrist of one of the bodies and into his pocket. The movement was so slick and fast that if Dot hadn't been staring closely at him and instead just glanced in his direction at the moment that he was doing it, then she would have missed it altogether. That made her think that it was a well-practised move.

Dot couldn't believe what she was seeing. The shock of it was rooting her to the spot. He lifted another blanket and rummaged about, before grabbing something and shoving it into his pocket. Dot wanted to scream at him. She couldn't let him get away with it. She had to confront him.

Movement just behind her distracted her, and she looked over her shoulder when she heard voices coming from the entrance to the church. All her rage about Stan's stealing dissipated and was replaced with relief when she saw Beryl talking to two of the rescue workers. Dot took off immediately. Beryl was alive! And she looked fresh as a daisy! She had never been so happy to see her – she might even give her a hug! How had she managed to walk out of there after the rescue team had spent all night digging out survivors and bodies? As she drew nearer, the obvious truth started setting in. But she didn't want to believe it. Dot slowed to a walk as she took in Beryl's appearance. Yes, it would be possible that by some miracle she had been found safe and well in the crypt after all this time – stranger things had happened. But what wouldn't be possible was for her to walk out of there looking so immaculate. Even the survivors who hadn't suffered a scratch had been covered in dust and debris. It was always the same after a blast. It was impossible to walk away without looking a complete mess.

'Beryl?' she said cautiously as she reached the group, who were still talking. Rage was coursing through her now but, just as she hadn't wanted to come to blows in public with Beryl about her joining the ARP, she didn't want to confront her about this in front of the rescue workers who she was going to be working alongside daily.

'Oh, there you are! I might have known you'd still be here, throwing your weight around and helping everybody else but your family! I'm on my way to the shops to get some supplies for breakfast seeing as you're too busy showing off here to do your run to Woolton's.'

Dot was frozen to the spot in disbelief. Not only was Beryl going to launch into an argument with her in the middle of the street, but she was somehow going to turn all of this around on her.

'I thought you were *dead*,' she said through gritted teeth. She was desperately trying to keep her calm in front of the rescue team, but she could feel that she wasn't going to take long to blow.

'You would have loved that, wouldn't you!' Beryl yelled. 'One less thing for you to worry about, and you would be free to galivant around and pretend you're so important to your heart's content!' The rescue workers ducked their heads and shuffled off awkwardly, leaving the two women standing in the street alone. With their audience gone, Dot couldn't help but strike back.

'You need to get this ridiculous notion out of your head, Beryl! All I want is to do my bit to help during this wretched war, instead of sitting around moaning and complaining and doing nothing.' She looked pointedly at her mother-in-law, hoping the slight she meant for her would sink in. 'Where on earth were you, anyway? You do realise that I've spent the whole night worried out of my mind, terrified you had perished in that shelter?'

'Well, thank goodness I didn't listen to you and go down there. You told me it was safer in there, but I think you were waiting for this. You wanted me to be down there when the bomb hit.'

'Don't be so ridiculous,' Dot cried. She paused, surprised at herself for once again standing up to Beryl. The independence this new role had given her had also boosted her confidence, it seemed. Or maybe the old bat had finally pushed her too far. Dot had always been a relatively docile woman who would put up with a lot rather than face a confrontation, but maybe she had reached her limit at last. 'We're told to recommend the shelters, and you've experienced yourself how much more terrifying it is to spend a raid in an Anderson. If a bomb came down on our Anderson during a raid, then there would be nothing left of you. At least in the crypt you would stand half a chance – there were a lot of survivors last night, you know.' She paused again for breath. Her mouth had really run away with her then. But she was glad. Beryl needed to understand her accusations were outlandish. 'You still haven't told me where you were while I was racing into a burning building to try to rescue you,' she said firmly.

Beryl's face softened ever so slightly. 'What? You . . . what did you say?' She sounded shocked and almost sheepish. Dot was happy with that. She wanted her to feel bad for what she had put her through.

'I ran into the crypt just after the bomb hit it, Beryl. While it was still burning. I thought you were inside. I fought the flames until the firemen got here. That's how desperate I was to get to you.'

'I – I don't know what . . .'

'You thought I would just spend the night prancing up and down the street, trying to look good, is that it? Goodness,

Beryl, you really have an awful lot to learn about the ARP and what we do. The uniform and equipment aren't just for show. We do important – and dangerous – work. And I put myself at even more risk than was necessary last night because I was so desperate to save you.' Dot didn't even care where Beryl had spent the raid now. She was too angry to argue with her anymore. She just wanted to get home and get some rest. All she could think about was poor Lilli and what Peggy must be going through having lost her – somebody who was as close to her as her own sister. Dot turned on her heel and stormed off, leaving Beryl standing gawping open-mouthed at her.

18

By the time Peggy reached her boarding house, every-body had cleared the dining room and gone back to their bedrooms or set off for work. She was relieved – she wasn't sure how she would have coped walking in to find them all camped out again. But she also didn't know what to advise them all to do for the best anymore. She had made Lilli go to the public shelter and look how that had turned out. Fresh tears welled in her eyes as her friend's beautiful face, once so vibrant and full of life, flashed into her mind. She wasn't sure if she would ever get over what she had done. But what could she have done differently? Nowhere felt safe anymore. It felt as though it was just a matter of finding the most comfortable place to take your chances in. She wandered through the house in a daze, every corner of it throwing up a fresh memory of Lilli and bringing with it a fresh sense of grief, until she found Mrs Martin in the communal lounge, reading a newspaper.

'Have you heard about Buckingham Palace?' the elderly woman asked, putting the newspaper to one side. 'Day before last, it was. It isn't in the papers yet, but Mrs Skilling from down the road knows one of the wardens who was on duty round there at the time. They did it in broad daylight! Can you believe it? He reckons it was deliberate, an' all.

Third time, too,' she added, shaking her head. 'Nearly got 'em, too.'

She finally looked up at Peggy, who was standing staring at her, tears flowing freely down her cheeks now, unable to stop them from falling. Peggy also found herself unable to respond to Mrs Martin. She didn't know how to talk about anything else after what had just happened.

'Whatever's the matter, dear?' Mrs Martin gasped, slowly getting to her feet. 'Oh, my love. Did you see something dreadful last night? It sounded like we got a good battering.' She put her arm around her and guided her to one of the armchairs, where Peggy slumped down and put her head in her hands. Mrs Martin stood next to her, rubbing Peggy's back as she spoke. 'I keep saying you young 'uns shouldn't be having to go through all of this. It's just too much. You're no age to be witnessing all this death and loss. Someone needs to stop that blasted man and his murdering followers. Otherwise, where will it all end? There'll be no England left for him to take over!'

'She's gone,' Peggy whispered, looking up and into Mrs Martin's eyes. Mrs Martin searched Peggy's face as if she was looking for more information, but she didn't say anything. 'Lilli,' Peggy croaked before bursting into tears again and throwing her arms around her neighbour's waist. As she wept, she could feel Mrs Martin's body shuddering with shock and grief at the same time.

They stayed that way for quite some time although Peggy had no idea how long. She got a vague sense of somebody else entering the room on a few occasions, but each time the visitor paused before thinking better of interrupting and then promptly leaving. When both women managed to stop crying and compose themselves, Mrs Martin went off to make two strong cups of tea, using the sugar rations to make it extra sweet and assuring Peggy that nobody would begrudge them that. Peggy sipped her tea and recounted the night's events in full, wishing now that she could go back to the start of it and warn Lilli away from the crypt instead of encouraging her to go there.

'I only told her to go down there because it was safer than sleeping in the dining room,' she rasped, wiping her tears with the sleeve of her overalls. 'I wish I'd just kept out of it. If I hadn't interfered, then she would still be here. I killed her, Mrs Martin. This is all my fault.'

'You weren't to know,' Mrs Martin soothed. 'The boarding house could have just as easily been hit, and if you hadn't sent her to the crypt, then she could have perished here – and you would have felt responsible because you hadn't stepped in. None of this is your doing, my love. You were in an impossible situation.'

Peggy nodded and sniffed loudly. 'Speaking of which, I need you to make sure everybody starts going back down to the cellar during raids.' Mrs Martin looked uncertain. '*Please*,' Peggy added firmly. 'Like you said, we could be next. And I don't think I could live with myself if you lot were all wiped out in the dining room when I could have done something to stop that happening. I accept that a bomb hitting the house is going to be bad news, and it's likely to happen at some point with the way things are going. But at least if you're down in the cellar, then you'll stand half a chance. Or some of you will, at least.' Mrs Martin was staring into her hands, which she had clasped on her lap. 'Don't make me identify more bodies of people I love. Not when it can be avoided. If you won't do it for me, then at least do it for Lilli.'

'I'll do my best,' Mrs Martin replied quietly. 'Do you want me to spread the news about Lilli around the house? I imagine the last thing you want to be doing is going over it all again and again with everybody.'

Peggy nodded gratefully before excusing herself to her room.

Some hours later, Peggy was startled by a soft knock on her door. With deep sleep still clouding her mind, her initial thought was that it was Lilli with her morning cup of tea and toast. But reality quickly set in, and her heart broke all over again when she remembered that her lovely friend would never be knocking on her door again. More tears threatened to fall, but she fought them back when another knock sounded out and she realised that she had no idea who was seeking her out. After shuffling to the door, she was surprised to find Dot standing outside her room, still in her overalls and with a sympathetic look on her face. She invited her in, and they sat on Peggy's bed in silence at first. Peggy didn't know how to ask her about Beryl so she thought she would let her friend break the news when she was ready. After a few minutes, Dot spoke.

'I wanted to come and make sure you were being looked after. I can't imagine what you're going through.'

'Thank you,' Peggy whispered. 'But what about you? Is there any news on Beryl?' She was devastated to have had her worst fears about Lilli confirmed, but at least she knew what had happened to her. She couldn't imagine the pain of not knowing for certain, and of not having a body to say goodbye to.

'I don't know where she spent last night's raid, but it certainly wasn't in the crypt,' Dot replied bitterly. 'I'm *so* angry with her. I haven't been home yet because I'm too upset with her to even look at her, let alone talk to her.' She let out a soft chuckle. 'How the tables have turned,' she added quietly.

After Dot had explained how Beryl had brazenly walked up to the bomb site and the subsequent confrontation, the two women sat in silence again.

'I wish I could say something to make things better for you, but I feel useless.' Dot sighed. 'And I feel guilty that Beryl is still walking around without a care in the world while Lilli is lying in the morgue with all those other poor souls.'

'Don't feel bad. I'm glad Beryl is safe. Really, I am. I know you probably don't feel ready to admit it just yet, but I know you are, too. Or, at least, you will be once you've calmed down. Thank goodness she's a cantankerous old bat, eh?' Peggy waited nervously for a reaction from Dot. She was pretty sure that she could get away with little digs like that about Beryl, given how Dot had laughed with her about them in the past after her initial shock. But maybe this was a little too soon after everything that had happened. She was relieved when Dot started giggling.

'Her stubborn nature and hatred for me and my new role saved her life last night,' her friend admitted. 'I'll have to talk to her soon as I'm absolutely dying to know what she got up to. There is no way she spent the raid in our Anderson shelter on her own. She was shaking like a leaf the whole time when we spent that night in there together.'

'Maybe she has a fancy man she's started staying with!' Peggy exclaimed lightly. Dot scoffed and they both burst into laughter, until Peggy abruptly stopped giggling, struck with guilt for enjoying a few seconds of joviality.

She supposed that's what friends were for – cheering you up when you were down. But she wasn't sure she felt ready for that yet. She took a deep breath. 'Well, you must go and find out and then you can tell me all about it this afternoon at the teashop.'

Dot looked confused for a minute before understanding filled her face. Viv – as she had instructed Peggy to call her last night – had invited them all for an afternoon tea – her treat, that day, to celebrate Dot joining the ARP. Peggy had smiled to herself when Viv had insisted on it being a Lyon's Corner House – even her afternoon teas were the fanciest of the fanciest. Peggy would have been happy with a sandwich and a mug of tea at a greasy spoon. It was typical of Viv but, instead of making her roll her eyes as things like that had done when they had first met, Peggy now realised it was a part of who Viv was – she just liked nice things and that was fine. It didn't make her stuck up or shy of putting in the effort and hard work that was needed during a raid. Peggy winced whenever she thought about those early judgements she had made about Viv. She really couldn't have been more wrong. After Peggy had mentioned how close she'd been to Lilli, Viv had even been kind enough to invite Lilli along to the afternoon tea, too, despite having never met her. She really was a completely different person to the woman Peggy had assumed all those weeks ago.

'You're still going?'

'Yes. Lilli was really looking forward to meeting you all and making some new friends. I want to go for her. Besides, she wouldn't want me to dwell on losing her. I need some time to myself first, to come to terms with everything. But then I must get back to doing what she was so proud of me for doing.' Peggy swallowed hard and tried to stop the tears that were brimming in her eyes from falling. She wasn't sure how she had any left. 'I'll be turning up for my shift tonight, too. We have got to keep going, no matter what. We can't give up. If I don't turn up for duty tonight, then more people could lose their lives. I won't have that on my conscience.'

'Well, at least that won't give Stan any more ammunition.' Dot tutted. Peggy looked at her questioningly, and Dot suddenly looked as if she had said something she hadn't meant to. 'Sorry, I . . . just ignore that last comment.'

'He said something after I left earlier, didn't he? Let me guess: women are too emotional for this kind of job, and we can't cope with it all. Did he realise I'd just seen the dead body of the girl I was as close to as my own sister?' Peggy could feel rage replacing her grief and coursing through her body now. She wanted to track Stan down right away and give him a piece of her mind and to hell with the consequences.

'I'm so sorry. I wasn't going to say anything yet. I don't think I was going to tell you at all to be honest, but it just came out. He's so pathetic, and you have enough to deal with without worrying about that ogre. But rest assured – I set him straight. I don't think he'll be speaking out of turn about you again any time soon.' Dot took a deep breath before adding, 'I've probably put myself on his radar.' She fiddled with her hands nervously. 'But I can handle myself just fine.'

Peggy's rage was now replaced by fear for her friend. She really was going through all the emotions this morning. As if she wasn't exhausted enough already. 'I really appreciate you sticking up for me. But I don't like the fact that Stan will probably have it in for you now. We must make sure we stick together over the next few shifts.'

Dot nodded gratefully. 'There's something else,' she said, her face lifting slightly, a smile creeping across it. 'I think I know a way to get that bully the punishment he deserves.'

Peggy listened intently as Dot explained what she had seen Stan doing in the churchyard. 'And you're certain? I don't mean to doubt you – it's just, it was the end of a long, highly stressful night. Is it possible you were mistaken?' As she was speaking, her mind cast back to memories of watching Stan seemingly taking care over the bodies of the dead following previous raids. She had been so naïve; of course he hadn't been showing compassion – he'd been looting the corpses.

'Definitely not,' Dot said with confidence. 'I didn't take my eyes off him, and I saw him slip the watch into his pocket. Then he moved on to another body and lifted something from it before I was distracted by Beryl turning up. I'd put my life on it. Should we tell Victor tonight?'

'It's not as simple as that. I wish it was. I can't remember if I told you before, but Victor is his brother-in-law. It's sensitive. And even without that connection, we still need some hard evidence before making an accusation like that.'

'But how can we get that? We can't exactly get Victor down to a bomb site and have him staking out his brother-in-law until he witnesses him looting a dead body for himself.'

Peggy nodded in understanding. 'We need a plan,' she said, suddenly invigorated by the thought of having something else to focus on, something to draw her every thought away from how upset she was about Lilli and how desperately she already missed her. 'Now, we both need some rest. I don't know about you but there's no way I can think straight without some decent sleep. And you need some answers from Beryl. So, let's both get our heads down and we can put a plan together at the teashop this afternoon.'

'That sounds like a good idea to me,' Dot said, jumping to her feet.

When she'd left, Peggy took a moment to try to process everything she'd just learned. It was a lot to take in after losing Lilli. But she was grateful for the distraction and determined to bring Stan to justice.

19

Making her way to the Lyon's Corner House in Coventry Street, Dot let out a huge yawn. The sirens had gone off almost as soon as she'd made it back home from Peggy's earlier that morning, so she hadn't managed to get any rest before leaving to meet her friends. She was feeling tired beyond comprehension, but there was no way she was going to miss out on this get-together. When Tommy was at home, she rarely had the chance to meet up with friends. He was happy for certain companions to come over for a drink and a natter while he was out at work, but he always seemed to get upset if she talked about meeting them elsewhere.

He had never said that she couldn't, but she didn't like seeing him sad and so she had slowly started turning down social invitations until they had stopped being extended altogether. She thought back now to one Saturday afternoon, early on in their marriage, when she had been due to meet Sally for afternoon tea. She had just finished getting ready when Tommy had bounded into the bedroom waving cinema tickets.

'I got us the best seats in the house!' He beamed, picking her up and swinging her round, making her squeal with surprise and joy. When he put her down and she finished giggling and straightening out her dress, she took the tickets from him and frowned.

'But, these are for this afternoon,' she whispered, her heart dropping.

'I know it's last minute, but I had some extra work come in and I thought why not treat my beautiful wife – to say thank you for everything that you do for me and Mother.' He leaned down and kissed the top of her head, which still made her tummy flip the same way it had when they had first started courting.

'But, Tommy, you know I'm meeting up with Sally this afternoon.'

His face fell. 'I completely forgot,' he said, bringing his hand up to his head. 'Oh, I feel rather foolish now. I was just excited to spend some time with you after how hard I've been working lately, I just . . . I didn't stop to think.'

Dot sighed and took his hand in hers. He looked so forlorn.

'I guess I could always take Mother,' he said with a distinct lack of enthusiasm.

'You'll do no such thing,' Dot replied firmly, squeezing his hand. 'I'm all dressed up and ready to go, and there is nothing I'd like more than to spend the afternoon with my husband.' His face lit up and she instantly felt like she was making the right decision. She could see Sally any time she wanted – she wasn't working so she had all the time in the world during the week. And part of her hated the idea of Beryl getting to enjoy Tommy's company in her place. 'I'll just go and explain to Sally,' she said before dashing out of the bedroom.

Sally seemed to understand, and they agreed to rearrange for another time. But the double-booking whenever she had other plans ended up becoming a regular thing. Dot was never that bothered – she saw Tommy as her best friend and it never felt as if she was missing out on anything, as they were always doing something together instead. They joked about how she needed to buy him a diary.

Of course, the invitations from her friends soon started drying up, until it seemed that the only time she ever went out was with Tommy. But it always felt like enough – with Tommy by her side she didn't need anybody else.

Since Viv had invited her along for this afternoon's tea, Dot found she was as excited as a small child at Christmas. She had liked her brief interactions with Viv so far, and she was really enjoying spending time with Peggy on shifts and getting to know her. But they were always so busy and focused on what they were doing. She couldn't wait to sit down and have some proper time with them, to really talk. It would be good to spend time with people who understood how difficult their volunteer roles were – it was something she didn't think you could really appreciate unless you had been through it yourself. Dot also wanted to make sure she was there to support Peggy, who would surely struggle knowing that Lilli was supposed to be there with them.

Dot's excitement about the meet-up made her wonder if she had indeed been missing out by not going out with her friends after marrying Tommy. She had never queried why he hadn't been happy about her socialising without him, but now she found herself questioning it. Her realisation that he was a bit of a bully following her talk with Peggy played over in her mind again. She had always been happy to believe that he'd been keeping her safe at home with him, but perhaps it had simply been about him controlling her. Was he really just so forgetful he continually planned things for them to do when she had told him she was meant to be seeing friends, or had he made all those double plans on purpose, to chip away at her friendships until she only had him left? She wondered how she hadn't seen it at the time – why she had been so quick to go along with it and just cast her friends and social life aside for him. Was it out of love for him, or fear of what he would do if she disobeyed him? It was certainly out of love in the beginning, but, since his lashing out at her, she wondered if she had simply fallen into line with everything that he wanted to avoid any more confrontation. It wasn't something she had realised she had been doing, but maybe subconsciously she had.

She wasn't sure about any of it anymore. This time away from him and her new independence and confidence were casting everything about her life into doubt.

Picking her way through the remnants of London's streets – buildings were being left blown wide open now as it seemed that as soon as anything was fixed, another bomb fell to destroy it – Dot decided that things were going to have to change once the war was over and Tommy was back at home. She had finally started standing up to his mother, and it felt good. She felt liberated. It had made her feel confident enough to consider the possibility of making changes within her marriage. Now she had come to the realisation that she was married to a bully, part of her wished she could just leave him and start anew. But it wasn't that simple. She still loved Tommy. She could still remember those early days full of fun and laughter and she was desperate to get back to that. If Tommy loved her – which she was certain he did – then he would be happy that she had grown more confident and independent. Maybe it would be good for them – the new Dot might remind Tommy of the Dot he had fallen for all those years ago. She certainly felt as if the old Dot was starting to shine through again. This could be their chance to make things work. She didn't want to think about the alternative.

Looking around her at the battered streets and buildings, she hoped London would be able to come out of it all stronger, too. She waved at a man pulling items out of some rubble. He was whistling away to himself, and he smiled and returned her wave. She was proud of this city for the way it was dealing with everything that was being thrown at it. Everywhere she looked, people were carrying on, they were smiling, and they were being kind to each other. She understood why Peggy was insisting on carrying on as normal, despite the pain that she must be feeling. In truth, nobody really had a choice, did they? The Germans would continue coming for them all, so they had to carry on protecting themselves and fighting back until all of this was over, no matter what they were feeling or who they lost along the way. There would be a time to grieve properly, but it wasn't now.

Dot was the first at the teashop, and she took a seat at their table and settled in to enjoy the band that was playing on the floor below. It was loud enough to hear, but not so loud that it would disrupt any of their conversation. She was glad that Viv had picked a Lyon's Corner House to meet in. She felt like she needed the bustling and vibrant atmosphere today. She hoped another daylight raid wouldn't disturb their afternoon tea. She wasn't sure if the customers here would be bothered by the air-raid sirens going off while they were dining, though. She could remember when the sirens had first started sounding during the day – people had dropped the items they were queuing in shops for and fled; meals had been left half eaten while their consumers had cowered in shelters. But people were starting to take their chances a little more now. The planes flying over and the bombs dropping were becoming a way of life. And people wanted to live as normal a life as they could manage. The people of London were starting to refuse to let the Germans send them running scared. After all, people had to be fed, the housewives had to shop – people had to get to their jobs. Life had to go on, bombs or no bombs. It was different at night, of course – it was all very well going about your day while the planes were overhead and trying to avoid getting struck down, but a lot of people still felt safer in the shelters at night.

The raid this morning had sounded particularly brutal, but she hadn't heard any bombs landing nearby. She had returned home just before the sirens sounded to find Beryl in her favourite chair in the living room. But instead of greeting Dot with her usual scowl, her mother-in-law had seemed quite sheepish. When the siren had started wailing, she had agreed to go to the Anderson shelter with Dot without any argument. It had unnerved Dot, but she was relieved because the crypt needed repairs doing before it could be used as a shelter again, and they were too far from the underground stations people had started sheltering in to make it to one in a safe amount of time.

Once they had settled into the Anderson shelter, Beryl had pulled out her knitting. But she didn't ignore Dot to concentrate on it, as she would usually do. She spoke as she knitted away, staring intently at her work and never looking up at Dot. She hadn't gone so far as to apologise for scaring Dot the previous evening, but she had explained where she'd been. It certainly hadn't been what Dot had been expecting, and now she couldn't wait to tell Peggy.

Viv walked into the teashop, and Dot breathed a sigh of relief. Viv and her ambulance partner had clocked off and been replaced by another shift before Lilli had been found, so she didn't know they would be one person down for their afternoon tea today, although she must have had an inkling. Dot was grateful for the chance to explain before Peggy's arrival.

'Is she still coming?' Viv asked, looking shocked after Dot had filled her in. Dot nodded. 'Good for her. We've got to keep on keeping on,' she replied firmly. 'We can't let them break us down.' Just then, Peggy joined them at the table. 'Dot was just telling me about your terrible night,' Viv said sympathetically. She reached over and put her hand on Peggy's arm. 'I'm so sorry about your friend.'

Peggy smiled weakly, her eyes glistening. 'She would have loved it here. She was desperate to get out and see more of London. She really wanted to go to some dances, too, but she never got the chance.' She paused and looked around the room again. 'I wish I hadn't been such a goody two shoes about it all. I should have taken her dancing. I looked down on you for going out and having fun despite everything that's been happening, Viv. But I realise how important it is now. I wish I'd taken Lilli. I wish she'd had more fun in her final weeks.'

'Well, we will have to go to a dance together, in her honour,' Viv declared cheerily. 'And we will have a proper toast to her. While we're there.' She didn't look hurt by Peggy's revelation that she had thought badly of her for going out and having fun during the raids, but Dot didn't think Viv was one to be easily offended.

'That sounds good,' Peggy replied quietly, looking around her again and smiling sadly. 'Anyway, I think we should talk about something more positive. Lilli wouldn't want me to spoil this occasion being sad.'

'I have something that will cheer you up,' Dot blurted out excitedly. She suddenly realised that Viv didn't know the backstory on Beryl, so she filled her in on her mother-in-law from hell as quickly as she could, before delivering her update.

'It turns out she was stepping out with a man last night!' she declared animatedly, excited to see Peggy's reaction. Peggy didn't disappoint; she spat out the drink she had just sipped before coughing loudly.

'I'm off-duty, dear, please don't make me administer first aid,' Viv joked as Peggy tried to compose herself and Dot revelled in the effect her revelation had had on her friend.

'What the? Who on earth? *How?*' Peggy spluttered between coughs.

'A chap called Jim from round the corner. Apparently, he's a lovely man with good morals. So, I'm struggling to understand why he's interested in Beryl, but I suppose living through a war can do strange things to people.' Dot shrugged as she spoke. It felt nice to be talking about Beryl without complaining about her being mean to her, for once. She explained that Jim had called on Beryl yesterday afternoon and asked her out for a friendly drink, to 'settle the nerves' after the last few weeks. Beryl had been flattered and accepted. They had gone to the Savoy, and he had managed to convince her to shelter in the hotel bunker when the raid had started.

'She says she just went down there without thinking, but I know it was to spite me. She knew I would have been worried about her because I'd seen how terrified she was when we spent a raid in our Anderson shelter together. She knew full well that I was aware of the fact she wouldn't go in there on her own.' Dot paused to let out the giggle she had been stifling. 'Anyway, none of that matters. The positive to come out of all of this is that she was so embarrassed at having to tell me about Jim that all my anger at her dissipated. She was acting like a naughty schoolgirl, but I really couldn't give a hoot about her romantic interests.' It had made her laugh that her mother-in-law had spent all this time convinced Dot had joined the ARP in order to indulge in illicit trysts with men when it was herself who was doing all the cavorting.

'Why was she so nervous about telling you? Do you think she feels ashamed of stepping out with a man?' Viv asked.

'I don't understand why she would be. Tommy's father died years ago – long before I met him. But she did beg me not to tell Tommy anything about Jim. I don't think she would have told me had it not been for the crypt getting bombed and all the worry I went through over her. I think she felt as if she owed it to me to be truthful about it after seeing how upset I was.'

Peggy frowned. 'It's strange that she wouldn't want Tommy to know. You'd think her son would be happy to see her having some fun. It sounds as if she's miserable most of the time, especially with the way she treats you. That just screams to me that she is unhappy and taking it out on you.'

Peggy's words struck Dot to the core. She had never thought about it like that, but she had to admit that her friend made a very good point. And Beryl had been so desperate for Dot to keep the news of Jim from Tommy – it was almost as if she was frightened of him finding out. Beryl had always been so fiercely protective of Tommy and convinced he could do no wrong – was that really the case or was there more to their relationship that she wasn't aware of? She had certainly never seen a vulnerable side to Beryl, and it had shocked her. It had also backed up her fears about Tommy's true self. She didn't mention any of this to Viv and Peggy, though. She wanted to keep things light-hearted, and she already felt like enough of a fool when it came to Tommy. What would they think of her if she admitted that she had married a bully but been too blind to see it all this time? Besides, she was determined to turn things around with him and start a new chapter in their relationship. Nobody needed to know how weak she had been in the past.

'So, will you be using the Anderson shelter from now on?' Viv asked. 'I suppose the crypt will be out of action for a little while after last night?'

'It actually didn't need very extensive repairs,' Peggy offered. 'I stopped by on my way here,' she added quietly, staring at her plate. 'I wanted to make sure Lilli's body had made it to the morgue safely.' Viv and Dot smiled sympathetically and waited until she was ready to continue. 'It's ready to be used again already. The organ in the church was destroyed, but the west window and the floor have been fixed. I think they wanted to get it back in action before the King and Queen get here.' There had been rumours of the royal pair visiting Chelsea the next day to try to keep spirits up. It was meant to be kept quiet, but most residents knew about it by now and there were plans to line the King's Road and wave to them as they were driven through. 'I imagine they will take them there to look around.'

'Will people want to shelter there anymore?' Viv asked.

'I'm not sure, to be honest. But so many other shelters have been hit, and people are still using them. I think it depends what alternative you have, really. The King and Queen visiting is sure to encourage people back there. I can't bring myself to advise the others at my boarding house to go there, but I think they can be convinced to use the cellar again.' Peggy paused again, looking deep in thought as she stirred a spoon around in her cup. 'I know it sounds silly, but I just always assumed that the one place that would be safe would be a church.'

'I felt the same,' Dot replied. 'I think I'll go back there during raids when I'm off-duty. And I know Beryl will, even though she's still harping on about not wanting to see me in my uniform. She was shaking throughout our chat during the raid this morning, so there's no way on this earth that she will go in the Anderson on her own. She said she enjoyed being in the Savoy bunker because she could hardly hear what was happening outside, but she can't afford to go down there every night.'

'Unless Jim asks her along again, of course,' Peggy said teasingly, and Dot had to laugh along with her. But she decided to change the subject away from Beryl now. She was here to get to know her new friends better.

'Let's get to know Viv,' she said playfully. 'All we know so far is that you manage to stay glam in the face of destruction, and you love a good dance.'

'That reminds me,' Viv said, fishing around in her handbag and pulling out two items. 'A little present, for my new friends.' She smiled, extending one out to each of them.

'Lipstick?' Peggy asked, taking hers and pulling the lid off.

'My favourite colour. You must promise to slap some on whenever you're feeling in need of a bit of a boost. We all need a bit of warpaint now and again.'

They both grinned at each other and nodded in unison before pulling the lids off. Viv handed Peggy her mirror and she slicked the lipstick on with ease. When it came to Dot's turn, she found herself feeling nervous. She wasn't really a make-up wearer. Tommy preferred the natural look on her. Beryl's face flashed into her mind; the way she had looked at Dot the last time she had worn lipstick. But she was stronger now, she thought defiantly. Beryl had no right to judge her for anything after what she had done.

'Here, let me,' Viv offered. She took the lipstick from Dot and leaned over to apply it. 'Perfect,' Viv declared, clapping her hands in glee before taking out her own and topping up her lips. She didn't even need to use the mirror. She went on to tell them a little about her background, and then talk turned to an RAF pilot she had been courting. When she pulled out a photo of William, both Peggy and Dot gasped.

'He's beautiful.' Peggy sighed, before catching herself and apologising.

'Don't worry, you're allowed to find him attractive. Besides, he's not strictly mine, and I think I've messed things up with him – so you might even have a chance with him yourself.' Viv was trying to sound light-hearted but the expression on her face gave away the regret she was obviously feeling about the situation.

'How do you mean?' Peggy asked cautiously.

'Well, the last time I saw him, he asked me to marry him, and I turned him down. I haven't heard from him since.' She was still speaking in a light and breezy voice, but it was evident that she was upset about it.

'What is wrong with you?' Peggy demanded. Viv and Dot looked at her in shock. 'Why would you turn down a proposal from somebody so handsome? He sounds as if he would be perfect for you, too. Look how dashing he is in his uniform – and you, so glam all the time even in your overalls. You need to track him down before he finds somebody who will snap him up when he proposes.'

Dot stepped in. 'I'm sure she has her reasons.' She was used to Peggy's brash honesty now, but she could see that Viv was worried about the fact she hadn't heard from William, and she didn't think this was helping. 'Maybe you haven't heard from him because he's been hurt in action,' she offered, before realising that would make Viv feel even worse. She wondered whether Viv would ever invite the pair of them out again after this.

'He's either dead or moved on with somebody else because I turned him down? You two really know how to cheer a girl up!' Dot laughed nervously but relief swept over her when she saw Viv smile. 'It's all right. I know I'm a mess when it comes to love. He's probably better off out of it, anyway. I wouldn't be the perfect wife he would be expecting.' Her comment hung in the air, neither Dot nor Peggy sure what she meant or how to respond.

'We need some advice,' Peggy chirped. She was obviously as keen as Dot to steer the subject on to something different after that awkward conversation and cryptic remark. Peggy quickly explained what Dot had seen Stan doing earlier that morning.

'He's got to be selling the items he pinches on somewhere,' Viv mused. 'But the question is, where?' They all sat deep in thought before Viv sat up straight and launched her finger in the air. 'There's a pawn shop round the corner from the ambulance station.' She suddenly hunched back in her chair and sighed. 'But that would be too obvious. Only somebody truly stupid would try selling stolen items on so near to where they were thieving them.' Dot and Peggy looked at each other knowingly.

'That sounds like a great place to start,' Peggy said.

They said their goodbyes shortly after and, as Dot got closer to home, all she could think about was getting into bed for a couple of glorious hours of sleep before she clocked on for duty again. She was so tired she felt as if she could curl up on the pavement and quite easily doze off regardless of the cold and the people rushing about around her. She silently prayed for no more air raids to disrupt her rest. She was walking along the King's Road and visualising getting under her bed covers when she saw a familiar face heading towards her.

'Hello, ARP Warden Simmonds,' Bill said playfully.

Dot smiled and happily stopped to talk, even though it would cut into her precious sleeping time. She had seen Bill around the ARP base a few times, but they had never had a chance to talk properly, which she found a shame as he always seemed so warm and friendly. After she explained where she had been, he offered to walk her home.

'I've not got far to go now; I'm only on Lawrence Street,' she replied.

'I don't like the thought of a young lady walking these streets alone, especially not at the moment,' he said kindly but firmly.

She agreed, suddenly remembering she was wearing lipstick and feeling self-conscious. She hoped he hadn't noticed.

'How are you finding the warden shifts? It's hard going, isn't it?'

'I'm exhausted, but I'd rather be out helping than sitting in a shelter.' A silence fell between them, and she wondered if he was thinking about what had happened at the crypt, like she was. 'Especially after last night,' she added quietly.

'I heard you were there when they found Charles. I'm sorry you went through that. He was a brilliant chap.'

Dot nodded sadly. 'Peggy lost somebody else last night, too. It all seems so unfair.'

'It is unfair. But we must stay strong. I think it's brilliant that you and Peggy are out there doing your bit. I hope your families are proud of you.'

Dot had to stop herself from scoffing out loud. She didn't know Bill well enough to tell him the truth about that. Besides, she was nearly home, and that conversation would take far too long when she just wanted to get to bed.

'I'm just here, so I'll head off now,' she said when they reached the top of her road. She didn't want Bill walking her right to the door. No matter how sheepish Beryl was feeling about her evening with Jim, there was no question that she would make a big deal out of a handsome man walking Dot home. She would accuse her of getting up to no good behind Tommy's back, and that was the last thing Dot needed right now.

'I'm glad to have got you home safely. I'm sure I'll see you again soon,' Bill said, dipping his head.

Dot gave him a wave as she made her way along Lawrence Street, feeling a little lighter for the compliment he had given her and Peggy. She would have to remember to tell her friend later. But when she pushed the front door open, she immediately sensed that something was different. Then she caught sight of a pair of men's boots by the hallstand, and her good mood was replaced by an overwhelming sense of dread. Tommy was home.

20

Viv went home to freshen up after leaving the teashop, hoping to get to a dance floor before the sirens started wailing that evening. Station Officer Spencer had insisted on her and Paul taking the night off after they had reported back on how many trips to the morgue they'd had to make when they'd finally arrived back at Danvers Street to drop off Hudsy and clean up in the early hours of that morning. Viv had no desire to spend tonight's inevitable raid in a public shelter, and so she had planned to do what she did best – dance her troubles away. Dot's mother-in-law sounded like a right old battleaxe, but at least she knew the best way to get through an air-raid was to dance her way through it, she laughed to herself.

There was no sign of Jilly at the flat, but Viv knew she was likely to be busy at the rest centre, with so many people left homeless after last night's raids and the bombing this morning, too. Once she was in her favourite blue dress and had slicked on her lipstick, she started to write her friend a quick note to let her know where she was going to be, just in case she made it back in time to head over and join her. She paused to consider where she was going to go.

So many of her favourite haunts were offering shelter now and she was keen to see what they had to offer. But she couldn't get Café de Paris out of her mind. She knew it was because that was the one place she would bump into William if he was back in town. She sighed and wrote the name at the end of the note. She hated herself for being so desperate to see William that she couldn't bring herself to go anywhere else, just in case.

Nervous anticipation consumed Viv as she wound her way down the staircase to the dance floor to the sounds of the West Indian Orchestra. Their music always brought William to her mind. She wasn't sure what she would say to him if she saw him here tonight – the very fact he hadn't been in touch to tell her he was coming and invite her to meet him would be evidence enough of his changed feelings for her.

She thought back to Peggy's reaction when she had shown her and Dot the photograph of William and explained what had happened the last time she'd seen him. She wasn't even sure why she had confided in the two of them when she hadn't even shared the news with her closest friends. And Peggy had been quite harsh about it. But maybe that was what Viv had needed. She wasn't sure if William would even talk to her if she came across him tonight. He had seemed to take her saying no to his proposal quite well, and they had certainly left things on good terms, but now he had gone quiet. Viv pushed all negative thoughts to the back of her mind. If he was here, then it meant he was alive and well, and that meant more to her than him still being sweet on her. She just wanted to be sure that he was safe, and then she could work the rest of it out.

Viv sighed. She might not be the woman William thought she was, but living through this war was teaching her that everyone was equal, no matter what they might have done in the past. When you were facing down bombs and destruction together, none of that mattered. Maybe, just maybe, she deserved happiness with him.

Looking intently around the room, she felt deflated when she finally had to accept that William wasn't there. She took a deep breath and walked with purpose to the dance floor. She was going to do what she always came here to do – dance to forget the world around her. Swaying her hips and moving her arms around, she closed her eyes until she was lost in the music. All thoughts of William, air raids, injured casualties, severed limbs, homeless people and dead bodies left her mind for the duration of the set, and it felt blissful. When Snakehips announced the band was taking a break, Viv took a moment to get her bearings again.

Background music started playing and some revellers continued to dance, but she was gasping for a drink now, so she made her way to the bar. As she waited to be served, she felt a light tap on her shoulder. Excitement and anticipation rushed through her again as she spun around, expecting to find William staring back at her. But, instead, she was met with another man in uniform who she vaguely recognised. He had blonde hair like William, only it was cut shorter, and he had similar blue eyes. Searching his face for a little longer than felt comfortable, she desperately tried to place him.

'Don't worry, we've only met once – I wasn't expecting you to recognise me,' he said gently. As he spoke, it hit her. This was Johnny – one of the men that William had trained with. She had met him here a few months back when he'd come on a night out with William. She had been convinced at first that the two men must have been brothers because of their similar looks.

'Johnny! I remember!' she exclaimed, looking behind him excitedly now, certain that William must be with him. Otherwise, why would he have come over to see her? Johnny's face fell when he caught her searching the crowds behind him.

'Viv, I'm sorry. He's not here,' he said sadly. He took her hand gently in his and suggested they go somewhere quieter.

'No, just tell me,' she replied firmly, looking straight into his blue eyes and wishing she was looking into William's beautiful blue eyes instead. 'Is he dead?' Somebody jostled Viv from the side. The bar was getting busy. She knew this wasn't the best place to have the conversation, but she was rooted to the spot, and she didn't feel like she could move until she knew what had happened to William.

Why had she shut down his marriage proposal? Why had she been so stupid? If he loved her, then he would have seen past anything she'd done before she met him. And she suddenly knew that he had loved her. He had loved her, and she had broken his heart just before he'd gone to his grave. She wasn't sure if she would ever get over this. Suddenly, she was moving. Johnny had gently taken hold of her elbow and guided her to a nearby chair. She had been so lost in her panicked thoughts about William that she hadn't even realised she had moved, but now she found herself sitting across from him. He held both her hands in his as he spoke. It was an intimate gesture from a man she had only met once, but she knew he had been close to William and, somehow, she felt comfortable – like it was making her close to him again to be in personal contact with somebody who had known him so well.

'Listen to me. He's not dead.'

Viv felt relief rush through her entire body, and she let out a small laugh. She couldn't believe she had got herself in such a state before hearing what Johnny had to say. Of course he wasn't dead! This was William. He was always going to be there for her – he had told her as much. She looked up and found Johnny still staring at her, a sombre look on his face.

'If he's not dead, then . . . ?' Now her mind was really racing. Why had Johnny sought her out like this? What news was he trying to break? Surely William hadn't sent one of his friends to break up with her? She had heard about cowardly men doing much worse, but William wasn't like that . . . was he?

'He's not dead – but he is missing in action,' Johnny said softly, and Viv's heart dropped to the pit of her stomach. 'His plane was badly shot and we think he might have had time to bail out, but we haven't been able to find him. I'm so sorry, Viv. I knew he would have wanted you to know. He never stopped talking about you and even last week he was telling me about how he was going to settle down in the country with you and start a family after all of this is over.'

So, he hadn't been upset with her after their last meeting! She was overjoyed to hear he still wanted a future with her. She smiled in response to Johnny's revelation before remembering what he had told her before that. Would William be alive when the war was over to enjoy that sunny future with her?

'Do you think there's hope?' she asked, staring down at their intertwined hands. He squeezed hers firmly before letting go to nudge her chin gently up with his fingers. Once she was looking him in the eyes again, he replied.

'There is *always* hope,' he said firmly.

★

Later that night, Viv lay in bed as the sirens sounded around her. Johnny had left Café de Paris shortly after breaking the news about William. He had only come to London for a matter of hours on a quest to find her and the club had been his first stop seeing as that was where he had met her previously, and he knew she and William always met up there. Viv had briefly felt as if fate had been at play and that was what had pulled her to Café de Paris that evening, before laughing at herself for thinking in such a way.

She hadn't fancied staying on any longer once Johnny had left. It was a surprise to her that there was something in her life that she couldn't dance away, but she found she just couldn't bring herself to get back on that dance floor once her fresh fears for William were hanging heavy on her mind. Lying there and listening to the sirens, she found she couldn't face going to a public shelter, either. So, she decided to stay in bed. She knew it was risky, not to mention stupid. But she was so consumed with worry for William that she didn't have any left to put into being concerned about the air raid and what might happen to her. As the planes rumbled past overhead and she heard the first whistling of bombing, she turned to face the wall and she pulled the covers over her head, waiting for fate to play its part in her life once more.

21

Dot closed the door behind her and rushed to take her shoes off. Tommy was home, and she couldn't wait to fall into his arms and enjoy at least one day safe in the knowledge that he was off the battlefield and at home with her. But as she placed her shoes next to her husband's boots in the hallway, the sense of dread that had consumed her when she had first spotted them returned.

She wanted to be excited to see Tommy, but she found herself panicking that he would be upset that she hadn't been there to greet him when he had arrived home. He didn't like not knowing where she was. And she also had the sensitive subject of her ARP role to broach with him. Dot took a deep breath and reminded herself of her plans to turn things around with Tommy. This was their chance at a fresh start – he was going to be impressed with the fact she was doing her bit, and it was going to change the dynamics of their relationship.

Dot heard knitting needles clinking together in the living room, and her hopes for a happy reunion with her husband vanished as she realised there was a very real possibility that Beryl had already told Tommy about the ARP. If his mother had told him, along with all her venomous thoughts on the role and what it entailed, then Tommy would not be in the mood for the loving embrace that Dot was craving.

She closed her eyes briefly and prepared herself to walk into the living room. But when she entered, Tommy's chair was sitting empty. Looking slowly to the left, Dot took in the sight of Beryl in her chair. Her mother-in-law kept her eyes trained straight ahead, refusing to look at her.

'You've told him,' Dot whispered. She was surprised at the fact her voice was shaking. She had convinced herself that she would get the chance to explain everything to Tommy herself, and that he would be happy with her volunteer work if it was revealed to him in the right way. She had hoped that after Beryl's confession to her, and her pleas for Dot to keep her news about Jim to herself, that she might have done the same for her. But she should have known that Beryl couldn't be trusted.

Heavy footsteps boomed across the landing above Dot and reached the stairs. Tommy had been in the front bedroom while Dot had been approaching the house. If he had been anywhere near the window, then he would have seen her saying goodbye to Bill. Her mind raced as she tried to work it all out: she hadn't been here when he had arrived home, so she knew it was likely that he would have been looking out of the window, watching out for her and awaiting her arrival – getting frustrated about the fact she wasn't at home where he expected her to be. Dot's heart pumped harder with every step that thundered down the stairs, and she realised with a start that all of her new-found confidence was evaporating the closer Tommy got to her.

'Was that your fancy man, then?' Tommy's voice demanded from the bottom of the stairs. Dot slowly turned around to face him. He had definitely seen her with Bill, then. This was not a great start.

'Of course not,' she replied as lightly as she could manage. She made a failed attempt at a smile as she made her way back into the hallway towards him with open arms, hoping that she could bring him round with a warm welcome despite the coldness emanating from him. 'I've been out for tea with some friends, but that was just one of my ARP colleagues who I bumped into on the way home. I'm sure your mother has told you all about my volunteer work,' she added cautiously. 'I'm doing really well helping to keep everybody safe. I'm so glad you're home so I can finally tell you all about it. You're going to be so proud of me, Tommy.'

Tommy stood frozen still. When Dot reached him, he made no move to welcome her hug, so she dropped her hands down to her side awkwardly and got up on her tiptoes to plant a kiss on his cheek instead. He flinched away and she jumped back, scared he was going to lash out at her. Tommy laughed menacingly as he stared intently at her face.

'And you tart yourself up for all these men you're going about with while I'm away, do you?' he asked in a near-growl. Dot was confused for a moment, but then her heart sank when she remembered the lipstick Viv had given her. She had so willingly and so happily allowed her to slick it on back at the teashop – it had seemed such innocent fun. She felt sick when she thought about how happy she'd been only an hour earlier. Who did she think she was? She wasn't care-free and glamorous like Viv. She should have known trying to be like her new friend was only going to get her into bother. She reached into her pocket for the lipstick.

'My new friend gave me it today. The one I met for tea. Her name is Viv,' she stuttered as she held up the offending piece of make-up. Tommy was glaring at her now and she could feel herself shaking. He had only looked at her this way once before.

The two of them stood, looking at each other, for what felt to Dot like an eternity. Then suddenly Tommy snatched the lipstick out of her hand and tossed it through the doorway and into the living room. Dot jumped, and she heard Beryl gasp in shock at the same time. She quickly looked over at her mother-in-law, and found she was still staring straight ahead, refusing to be drawn into what was happening between them.

'You won't be needing that anymore. You know what I think about women who cover themselves in that slap. It's a good job I came back when I did,' he said. He sounded calm now and, instead of making Dot feel better, the sudden switch in tone made her nervous. Why couldn't he act like the Tommy she had fallen in love with? Where had all his tenderness gone? 'Who's going to look after my mother if you're off at all hours with goodness knows who?'

Dot knew it was a rhetorical question. She wanted to tell him that his mother was more than capable of looking after herself, but Peggy's words about how it was best not to antagonise a bully started playing in her head. Dot dipped her head as her husband continued.

'I thought you were aware that I was only comfortable going off to fight because I knew you would be here looking after the house while I was away. This is where you belong, Dot. A woman's place is at home. I can't get over the fact you weren't here to greet me when I got back.'

Dot wanted to tell him that she wanted more from life than running a household, especially when that involved doing everything for his rude and ungrateful mother. She also wanted to shout at him about the fact he never gave her warning of his visits home, and he couldn't very well keep her on house-arrest waiting for his arrival. But, again, she stayed quiet. She had certainly grown in confidence over the last few weeks, and she may have been brave enough to finally stand up to Beryl, but with Tommy looming over her she felt weak and pathetic and too scared to tell him what she wanted. Maybe she had been naïve in thinking she could change him. She so desperately wanted to make things work between them – but how was that possible when she was too frightened to be herself around him? She had been living a lie, and now she was stuck with a bully for a husband.

'Not to worry,' Tommy said lightly, placing his arm around Dot's shoulder and guiding her into the living room. 'I'm home now. I have a few days' leave from the unit, so we can get everything back to normal before I go back. You wouldn't want me out there worrying about you when I should be focusing on staying alive, would you?' They sat down on the sofa together, opposite Beryl, and he took both Dot's hands in his own, turning his body so that he was facing her.

'But, really, there's nothing to worry about,' Dot said as confidently as she could manage. She wasn't ready to stand up to this man and insist that he let her stay on with the ARP, but she had to at least try to make him understand that the organisation wasn't a bad thing for her to be a part of. She couldn't bear the thought of giving it up now. 'I'm doing really rather well with the ARP. I'm helping protect our friends and neighbours. I want to make you proud, Tommy. I thought this would make you proud.' She was aware that she had become more animated as she was talking – the passion she felt for her volunteer role clearly coming to the surface. She hoped what she had said about their friends and neighbours might give him pause for thought. She knew how important other people's opinions were to him. Tommy's face remained stern as he listened to her.

'My mother's told me all about it, my love.' Something in the way he spoke told Dot that Beryl had been far from positive with her revelations. She wanted to get her own back by telling Tommy everything about Beryl stepping out with a man in secret. But Beryl had seemed convinced her new friendship would make Tommy angry, and the last thing Dot needed right now was for him to get heated.

'What do you think people will think of me if they see my wife off gallivanting with other men while I'm away defending the country? I must be a bloody laughing stock already.'

Dot wanted to scream in frustration. Why could nobody in this family see that she was simply trying to do her bit to help the country make it through this war? Why wasn't she allowed to spend time with other men without there being something more going on? She didn't want to push Tommy too far, but she couldn't give up on the ARP without at least trying to talk him round.

'I don't even patrol with other men, Tommy. I'm partnered up with another woman and—'

'I don't *care* who you roam the streets with!' Tommy cut her off to bellow. Dot caught Beryl flinching out of the corner of her eye. Tommy got to his feet and she braced herself. Surely, he wouldn't hit her in front of his mother? 'I don't want you doing it and that's the end of it! I'm the boss in this house and what I say, goes. Patrolling the streets as an air-raid warden is not a job for a woman, and certainly not a job for my wife. I want you here where I know you're safe.

You'll give it up immediately and everything will go back to normal. I won't have it, Dot. I just won't have it!' Dot waited nervously as he clenched and unclenched his fists. Then he abruptly sat back down beside her. 'Do you understand?' he asked quietly, staring into her eyes. Dot nodded silently, trying to stop the tears that had welled in her eyes from falling. She was devastated, but she didn't have a choice. She couldn't go against Tommy's wishes. He was her husband. Aside from the fact that she was frightened of what he might do if she refused to obey him, she was also aware of the fact that she had promised to do just that in her wedding vows. Love, honour and obey.

'I'll tell them this evening,' she said, lowering her gaze to her lap.

'What do you mean?'

'I'm due on duty soon. They're expecting me. I'll need to go in to explain—'

'You'll do no such thing,' he cut her off again angrily.

'But I can't let them down, Tommy. They've just lost one warden to the crypt bomb. They'll struggle without me there tonight, too.'

'Well, that just goes to show how bloody dangerous it is, doesn't it? For goodness' sake, Dot. I can't believe you've been putting yourself in all this danger and I had to find out about it from my mother.'

'But I've only just started. Last night was my first shift – I was going to tell you—'

Tommy held up his hand to silence her, then shook his head before taking a deep breath. 'Them being one down tonight is not our concern. It's a volunteer role – you owe them nothing. They've been sending you, a vulnerable young woman, out into a war zone night after night, expecting you to put yourself at risk and for what? No, Dot. You will not set foot back in there. I told you I want you here where I know you're safe and I meant it.'

Dot nodded her head again. That was it, then. She'd always known she was on borrowed time, but she had kidded herself that Tommy might somehow accept her warden work and even be proud of her for doing her bit. But he just wanted her at home – not so he knew she was safe – she wasn't stupid enough to believe that any longer. He wanted her here day and night so that he knew she wasn't talking to other men.

'And there will be no going back to that public shelter. I've heard about what happened there, and how many people died.'

'But, Tommy, it's the safest place to be,' Dot pleaded. She was now counting on going there tonight if there was another raid, so she could get a message to Peggy and Victor about why she hadn't turned up for her shift. It was bad enough that she was leaving them in the lurch when they were already a warden down, but she could at least give them an explanation. What would they think of her when she just failed to turn up?

'Don't be ridiculous,' Tommy scoffed, getting to his feet again. 'If there are any raids while I'm home, then we'll be bedding down together in the Anderson. I didn't spend hours out in the garden digging and building that blasted thing for you two to go and shelter down the road with all and sundry. I still can't believe you made my mother go down there. The indignity of it. Thank goodness she put her foot down last night and stayed here.'

Dot shot Beryl a look, but she was still refusing to give her eye contact. She gave herself away by squirming in her chair, though. So, she had told Tommy all about the ARP as well as the fact that Dot had been encouraging her to shelter at the crypt, which had now been struck by a bomb. As if Dot hadn't felt bad enough about that. But it was clear she'd only told Tommy all about Dot's misdemeanours in order to take the heat off herself. Well, if she was going to have to give up her beloved ARP, then she would make sure Beryl had to give up Jim, too. She had been willing to keep her secret before, but the gloves were well and truly off now.

'Did your mother tell you where she sheltered last night instead of going to the crypt?' Dot called after Tommy as he made his way towards the kitchen. He walked through the kitchen and put his hand on the back-door handle. Then he paused to answer Dot's question, still facing the door.

'She stayed in the Anderson, like you should have done,' he replied confidently. He turned around to face Dot again. 'Are you trying to make things worse for yourself, Dot? I think I've been very reasonable with you given the circumstances. You went behind my back to sign up for men's work, surrounded by men. I'm willing to let that go so long as you stop all this silly gallivanting, let go of all these ideas above your station, and get back to normal.'

Dot took a deep breath. She had nothing to lose now. She was going to enjoy this. She opened her mouth to tell Tommy all about Beryl's night with Jim, but, just before she spoke, her mother-in-law leaped out of her chair and flung herself across the room to the kitchen. Dot had never seen Beryl move so quickly, and the older woman's legs clearly couldn't cope with the exertion, because they buckled as she reached the kitchen. Beryl grabbed hold of the counter to steady herself, and Tommy rushed forward to support her.

'I just wanted to give you another hug, my dear boy,' she rasped, as she clung on to him.

'You nearly went over there, Mother, you must be careful,' he soothed. Any hint of the menace he had just shown Dot had disappeared, and he was now presenting as the kindest, most caring son.

'It's just so good to see you again,' Beryl whispered into his chest. Tommy kissed the top of his mother's head, then he looked at Dot again.

'This is why I need you at home. Can't you see she needs help? You can't be leaving her here all on her own, especially not overnight while the Germans are throwing everything they have at us.'

Dot wanted to laugh in his face. She wanted to tell him all about how capable Beryl really was. But, instead, she bit her lip and smiled weakly.

'I'm sorry,' she whispered. 'I just wanted to make you proud.' What was the point in trying to bring Beryl down with her? She would never break through their bond – Tommy would never side with her over his mother, no matter what the old bat did. And Dot was too scared and too weak to do anything but go along with what Tommy wanted.

'I'm going to go and make sure the Anderson is stocked with everything we need for the night. I expect the sirens will be going off soon enough, and I don't imagine you've kept it in order while I've been away,' Tommy said. He hadn't even acknowledged Dot's apology, let alone commented on the fact she had wanted to make him proud. Dot had never felt so miserable or worthless in all her life.

'I've got an awful headache. I think I need to go and lie down,' she whispered, fighting back tears. All she could think about was how disappointed in her her ARP colleagues were going to be for abandoning them this evening, and the fact she would never get the chance to patrol and help during raids again. If she was going to be stuck in the Anderson with Tommy and Beryl for the best part of the night, then she needed some time to herself now to come to terms with everything she had just lost and cry her tears in private.

Soon after, as Dot lay on top of the marital bed, huge sobs racked her body. She pushed her head into the pillow to try to stifle the noise she was making. When she heard footsteps, she quickly lifted her head and wiped her eyes and nose with her sleeve. She didn't want Tommy to see her in this state – he would never understand and he would just get angry with her. But the footsteps didn't reach the stairs. Instead, they stopped at the front door, and she heard the sound of a key turning in the lock. Tommy was making sure there was no way she made it out to her shift tonight. She was trapped here. Her ARP dreams were well and truly over.

22

When she spotted Viv working her way through the throng of people, Peggy started jumping up and down and waving her hands in the air. Viv saw her and slowly but surely nudged her way to her side, blowing her hair out of her face when she arrived in an exaggerated act of exasperation.

'I thought this was meant to be hush-hush,' she said dramatically as she looked around with wide eyes at the crowds of people waiting for the arrival of Queen Elizabeth and King George.

'Well, I suppose it's no surprise that news is spreading quickly at the moment, what with everybody being cooped up together for long periods of time with nothing better to do than to gossip,' Peggy replied playfully. She had heard her fair share of salacious chit-chat during her hours spent in the crypt and even she had grown bored of it. Everyone was desperate for something new to discuss, so Peggy wasn't at all surprised to see so many people out waiting to catch a glimpse of the royal couple. Their impending visit was the most positive and exciting thing that had happened in Chelsea for weeks. Life had turned into a constant cycle of air raids, death, and clear-ups, so it was little wonder that so many people were keen to get out and experience something different. And the fact that Buckingham Palace had been struck by bombs on a few occasions already made Queen Elizabeth and King George more relatable to the masses – it brought home the fact that it didn't matter how rich you were or how big your house was, you were still a target for the Germans. Everybody kept talking about how they were all in this together, and it was strong evidence to support the statement.

'Is Dot here yet?' Viv asked, looking behind her and then around at the other ARP workers.

'No. And she didn't turn up for her shift last night either,' Peggy replied.

'Maybe the previous evening caught up with her. It was a big one for both of you. I was surprised you both made it to my afternoon tea after everything you went through. I still can't believe you went back on patrol last night.'

'Victor tried to turn me away, but I need to keep busy. Honestly, I couldn't think of anything worse than being stuck in a shelter or the cellar at home with nothing else to do other than think about Lilli and how much I miss her.' The truth was, she had sat down to write a letter to Joan, to tell her about what had happened. She thought laying it all out for the person she felt closest to in the world would help her grieve, but she hadn't been able to do it. She'd agonised over what to write – where do you even start with something like that? And then the tears had started before she'd even got three words down. So, she had abandoned the idea and turned up for her shift early instead. She knew that refusing to face what she was feeling was the worst thing she could do, but it was so easy to get away with it at the moment while there was so much else going on.

Viv nodded thoughtfully to what Peggy had just said. Peggy thought she looked upset, and she was just about to ask if she was all right when she started talking again.

'I'm sure Dot will show up for this. She sounded really excited about it when we spoke about it yesterday.'

The three of them had agreed to meet at the crypt to see if they could sneak a peak of the royals as they came through when they had talked about the rumoured visit during their afternoon tea. Peggy hoped Viv was right and that Dot would turn up shortly, full of apologies for sleeping through her shift. Nobody would blame her for having done so, especially after the night they'd had.

But Peggy couldn't shake off the feeling that Dot was in some sort of trouble. She had to admit that she hadn't known her for very long, but she felt they had grown close enough for her to be certain that she wasn't somebody who just let people down. Worried about her friend, she had stopped by Dot's house on her rounds at the start of her shift the previous evening and found it in darkness. Of course, that wasn't unusual right now. But she suspected that if Dot had been asleep, then her incessant knocking would have woken her up. Neither her nor Beryl had turned up at the crypt when the sirens had gone off, which had worried Peggy further. Dot had seemed intent on continuing to use the shelter instead of their Anderson, and it had sounded as if Beryl felt the same way.

'Maybe Beryl's fancy man took her to another hotel,' Viv said playfully, pursing her lips, once Peggy had relayed her full fears to her.

'But what about Dot?'

'She might have decided to spend the night in the Anderson on her own, to make the most of not having her awful mother-in-law around. I know you don't think she would let you and the other wardens down, but this war is affecting us all in different ways. She could have just switched off for the night, without a second thought for anybody else – and, really, who could begrudge her that after everything she's seen and dealt with over the last couple of weeks? It's a lot to process. We found a woman wandering the streets during last night's raid. She was in a daze – lost all her family to a bomb a week ago and I don't think she had slept since.'

Peggy nodded her head thoughtfully. 'If she's struggling to cope with everything, that makes me even more worried about her,' she whispered. 'But what if she tried to get to the crypt and she was injured on the way? She could be lying somewhere in agony, or she could have been wiped out and we don't even know!'

'We work this patch,' Viv said calmly. 'All the wardens know Dot, and most of my ambulance colleagues do, too. If something had happened to her around here last night, then word would have reached one of us by now.'

Peggy felt a slight sense of reassurance, until another thought popped into her head.

'There's also the added threat of Stan. She stuck up for me after the crypt bomb, so he'll be after teaching her a lesson.' She realised then that, although she and Dot had told Viv about Stan's stealing, they hadn't gone into more detail about how awful he was in general. She quickly filled her in. Viv's expression changed from relaxed to concerned as she listened intently.

'Do you think he could have done something to her? Did you see him last night?'

'I saw him around a few times but, honestly, I don't know what he's capable of. All I know is that he was very believable when he cornered me and threatened me. And now we know that he steals from corpses. So, I don't think I'd put anything past him.'

Viv looked thoughtful, but their conversation was halted by a swell in the crowd. Everybody surged forward and people started shouting and cheering. Peggy went up on her tiptoes and caught a glimpse of a grand-looking hat slowly sweeping through the throng of well-wishers. She caught sight briefly of the Queen in between all the bodies, and she gasped at how resplendent she looked – her long, brightly coloured jacket and dress stood out amongst all the overalls and drab dresses she was surrounded by. She was able to see more of the King: tall and slim, he wore his military uniform proudly.

'They're here,' she cried. She had been so excited about the royal visit – the couple often stopped to talk to members of 'the people's army' as the volunteers were now being referred to. But now she was here without Dot, she found that her heart wasn't in it.

'I know you wanted your chance to talk to His Majesty, but I think we need to check in at Dot's again,' Viv said. 'Sooner rather than later.'

She held out her hand and Peggy took hold of it without hesitation. Viv pushed her way back through the crowds and when they emerged, they picked up the pace on their way to Lawrence Street. Peggy knew her friend could finally feel the sense of urgency and protectiveness that she had been battling since Dot had failed to show up for her shift.

Peggy felt anxious as they waited at Dot's front door after knocking. She knew how unpleasant Beryl could be, and she didn't much fancy trying to get anything out of her if she answered. But she might be their only option. Peggy listened out for any sound or movement from behind the door, but nothing seemed to stir in the house. She was just about to admit defeat when Viv made her hand into a fist and pummelled on the door so hard that the noise echoed down the street. Peggy looked at her in shock.

'We don't want to be in any doubt that we were heard,' Viv said with a shrug.

Peggy's hopes were raised when she heard a definite shuffling sound coming from inside the house. She grinned at Viv. Her insistence had worked. Muffled voices came next, and they both stood back, expecting the door to swing open. But nothing happened. Nobody answered the door. Peggy's hopes fell again.

'I'm certain I heard something going on in there,' she said. She checked the road and then walked into it and turned back to look up at the bedroom window. The curtains were open but there was no sign of any movement from the room. The curtains had been drawn the night before. The house had not stood empty between her visits – somebody had opened those curtains this morning, and they were still inside now, she just knew it. Frustrated, Peggy ran back to the front door and hammered on it. 'We know you're in there, Dot! We just want to make sure you're all right!' she shouted through the thick wood.

'Whoever is in there doesn't want to talk to us,' Viv said as she grabbed hold of Peggy's arm and stopped her relentless knocking. A woman from a few doors down had come out of her house to see what all the noise was about. Peggy didn't care if she was making a scene. She just wanted to make sure her friend was safe.

'But we can't just leave her in there. What if she's ill, or if she's hurt herself? She wouldn't just ignore us knocking at the door. She wouldn't do that to us. To me.'

'We can't break in. Perhaps she's decided the ARP isn't for her after all and she's too embarrassed to tell us.' Peggy threw her a look – she was too angry with the statement to respond. 'I know that's not likely. But I'm just trying to work out possible scenarios. Either way, we can't do anything more here now. Let's go away and take some time to think.'

'I'm sure she said she had a friend who lived on this street,' Peggy said, looking up and down the row of houses. 'If only I had shown more interest, we'd have somebody to ask. I think it was the woman who helped with her training exercise – I'd recognise her face if I saw her again. Maybe we could knock on a few doors, see if we can find her?'

'I think it's a little soon to be carrying out door-to-door enquiries, Peggy.' Viv sighed.

'Maybe we need to talk to Stan,' Peggy suggested. 'He might have threatened her or hurt her and that's what is keeping her hidden away. She might be too scared to get back to patrolling.'

'Surely he wouldn't just come out and admit to hurting her, if that's what has happened?'

'Oh, I don't think he would be able to help himself. If he's done something to her, I think he would enjoy gloating about it. But if not, he would certainly act in a way that would give him away.' Her blood was boiling now. She wanted to track down Stan and force answers out of him.

'Let's not be hasty,' Viv said calmly, running her hand up and down Peggy's arm soothingly. 'I can feel your rage, Peggy. It's seeping out of you. It will do us no good to confront Stan while you're this angry and upset. It will do Dot no good, either. Let's take some time to calm down and think about this properly. Hopefully Dot will turn up before we need to do anything drastic.'

Peggy left reluctantly with Viv. She wasn't happy about it, but she had to concede that no good would come of them spending the afternoon banging on Dot's door or laying into Stan. As they reached the end of Lawrence Street she turned back for one last glance at the house, hoping to see Dot finally answering the door with a smile on her face and an explanation for going MIA. Tears filled her eyes when her gaze took in the empty street.

23

It was the second time there had been a knock on the door since Tommy had locked them inside the house the previous evening. The first time somebody had knocked, the night before, Dot had suspected it was Peggy calling round to check on her. The timing was right – she would have turned up for her shift and found her missing, then gone straight to her house when she stepped out on her rounds. It was exactly what Dot would have done in the reverse. Dot had known that Tommy wouldn't answer the door, and that he certainly wouldn't allow her or Beryl to go to speak to whoever was there. So, she had stayed in bed and waited sadly for her friend to give up on her.

The thought of Peggy assuming that Dot had just thrown in the towel and walked away from the ARP without a word of explanation to anybody broke her heart. But maybe that was for the best. Even after Tommy had gone back, she couldn't return to the ARP. So, what would she tell everybody about her sudden desertion? She was too ashamed and embarrassed to admit to anybody that her husband had forbade her from volunteering. Perhaps it would be best if she told them that it had all become too much for her, and she was too shaken by everything she had already seen and dealt with to go through any more of it. She would still feel humiliated, but at least they would think it had been her choice to give up.

Tommy hadn't mentioned the knocking on the door the previous night when they had all gone to the Anderson after the raid had started. Dot hadn't dared to bring it up in case he started accusing her of having fancy men calling round for her at all hours. It had been an excruciating evening stuck in the small space with her husband and mother-in-law, but she had been grateful for the sirens saving her from sharing the marital bed with Tommy. He would surely be expecting her to carry out her wifely duties before he returned to service and, the longer she could put that off for, the better. For the first time since the war had started, she had found herself praying for the Germans to attack.

Now, as the second round of knocking continued – this time louder – Dot grew anxious. Had Peggy come back to try to speak to her again? She had been supposed to meet her and Viv for the royal visit. Her heart soared to think of her friend refusing to give up on her. She was sitting in the living room with Beryl, who had fallen asleep in her usual spot while doing some knitting. Tommy was out in the garden having a cigarette. More knocking came, and still Beryl didn't stir. Dot started to wonder if she could make it to the front door and back before Tommy came back inside. She just wanted to see Peggy and reassure her. She knew she would be worried about her. Maybe she could tell her she was poorly. She couldn't bring herself to admit she was leaving the ARP just yet. Besides, it needed to be a quick conversation and Peggy would only try to change her mind.

Dot stood up and crept to the hallway, but then all the nervous anticipation that had been coursing through her dissipated when she remembered that the front door was locked. Disappointment flooded her body and her shoulders sank. As she stood on the threshold between the living room and hallway, she heard two female voices outside. Peggy must have brought Viv with her! She momentarily felt happy at the thought of not one but two of her friends being outside, until she remembered that she wasn't going to be able to speak to either of them. Then she heard the back door closing.

'Who's that at the door? If that's a man knocking for my wife . . .' she heard Tommy raging as he made his way through the kitchen. Dot leaped back into the living room to try to stop him. She couldn't let him answer the door to her friends. What would he say? What would he do? She was too weak to stand up to Tommy, but she knew that Peggy and Viv would try to argue her case to stay on with the ARP, and she couldn't see Tommy taking too kindly to that.

'It's my friends. The women I met at the teashop yesterday,' she whispered urgently, blocking his path. 'They're probably worried about me after I didn't turn up for my shift last night.'

'Well, let me go and reassure them that you won't ever be back. And tell them to stop disturbing me during my leave.' He stepped to the right to try to walk around Dot, but she side-stepped to block his path again. She wasn't sure why she was acting so recklessly, but she felt so desperate to keep Tommy away from her friends that she found she couldn't stop herself. She would rather have them believe that she had abandoned them and the ARP than let Tommy loose on them. Tommy stepped to the left now and Dot jumped in front of him again. He took a step back and looked her up and down, anger and frustration spreading across his face. Dot wondered if he was going to shove her out of the way to get to the door.

'Please, they will leave soon and I'm sure they won't come back,' she pleaded. Just then, more knocking erupted – this time faster and even louder – and then she cringed as she listened to Peggy shouting that she knew she was in the house. They must have heard some of the commotion from inside. Tommy stepped forward and reached his arm out towards Dot, but she pointedly looked over at Beryl, who had finally started stirring. Dot had never been so grateful to see Beryl waking from a nap.

'What's going on?' Beryl muttered. Dot was hopeful again now. Tommy wouldn't shove her out of the way in front of his mother. If she could just keep them talking long enough so that Peggy and Viv gave up and left, then she could spare her friends from a confrontation with her husband.

'My friends have come to check on me because I didn't show up for my shift last night,' Dot explained quietly and slowly, trying desperately to bide her time. Beryl rubbed her eyes and sat forward in her chair. 'The ones from the ARP,' Dot added. If she could get Beryl moaning about the ARP, then she might be able to keep Tommy at bay for just long enough.

'Oh, those busybodies.' Beryl tutted, picking up her knitting from where it had dropped on her lap when she had fallen asleep. 'A right load of nosy parkers, that lot. I told you from the start you shouldn't be going around with that lot. I don't know what came over you, Dorothy.'

'I know. My place is at home.' It made Dot's blood boil to say it, but she needed to keep this conversation going for as long as possible. She had lowered her voice even more in the hopes that Peggy and Viv wouldn't be able to hear them anymore and would take the silence as a hint she wanted to be left alone. 'I just want them to go away so I can focus on enjoying this time with Tommy before he goes back,' she whispered now. She looked up at her husband and his face softened. She stepped towards him and put her arms around his waist. To her relief, he returned the hug. She braced herself for more knocking, but it was quiet again now as they held the embrace. Then, finally, she heard footsteps walking down the street and away from the house.

Dot spent the rest of the afternoon on edge, apprehensive about Peggy and Viv coming back to try to speak to her. Tommy was only home for one more night, but if she failed to turn up for duty again this evening, then she knew there was a good chance her friends would come knocking once more looking for answers. She couldn't bear the thought of Tommy answering the door to them. He had always been charming and kind to her friends – just like he'd been with her when they had first met. His charm had been one of the things to pull her in, and something she had always held on to, even when he was subtly controlling and bullying her. Of course, she hadn't seen it at the time, but now she thought back over their relationship it seemed obvious.

Dot knew there was a softer side to Tommy, and she realised now that she'd spent years chasing it, putting up with his horrible behaviour in the hope the man she had originally met and fallen in love with might return. But the way Tommy had looked when he had been making his way to the door earlier that day had worried her. His demeanour hadn't been one of somebody hoping to charm the people on the other side of the door into leaving them alone. The façade had dropped: he'd looked ready to give Peggy and Viv some choice words before sending them packing. He probably blamed her fellow female volunteers for leading her astray. She needed to keep them apart at all costs, but she didn't know how that was going to be possible when Tommy was keeping her hostage like this.

Following an early dinner, Beryl excused herself to her bedroom to rest. She had taken to retiring to bed before the sun had set the last week or so. Dot knew Beryl couldn't get a wink of sleep in the crypt or in the Anderson, so she could understand her getting a nap in before the raids started every night.

Dot was clearing the table and washing up when Tommy slid his hands around her waist and nuzzled his lips into her neck. She felt herself tense up at his touch, even though he was being loving. There was a time when she had felt like the luckiest woman alive to be the subject of this man's affection. Now it just made her feel nauseous. She couldn't bring herself to be loving towards Tommy when he had ripped away the only thing she had found joy from in her life in so many years. But she knew what he was expecting – especially as he was leaving again the next morning. If she could just hold him off until the sirens started . . .

'Why don't we go for a lie down before the Germans come,' he whispered in her ear.

'I have so much washing-up to do,' she said lightly, rinsing off the plate she'd just cleaned.

'That can wait,' he said firmly. His tone had turned from affectionate to irritated in a beat, and Dot felt cornered. She tried to keep her voice jovial as she replied.

'Just let me finish up here. I know you like things to be clean and tidy. I won't be long. You could wait upstairs for me, and I'll come and join you when I'm done.' If she could just get him to go up ahead of her, then she could stay downstairs until the sirens started – surely the Germans would be back before Tommy lost his patience. With any luck, he would fall asleep waiting for her. Then she could feign disappointment that they had missed their last chance at a full reunion before his return to duty. He wouldn't punish her in front of Beryl.

'How many times do I have to tell you, I'm in charge here,' Tommy said, his voice growing louder. He spun her round to face him.

'Please, I just want to get this finished then I promise we can have some time together,' she pleaded. 'I know how much you hate a messy kitchen.' She felt like she would do anything to avoid being intimate with him, and she was scared from the look on his face that if she went upstairs with him now, then he would force her. Dot yelped when Tommy grabbed her forearm and yanked her through the kitchen. Suddenly, her reluctance to stand up to him vanished. She knew where this was leading, and it was a step too far. She had put up with him controlling her life and stopping her from getting the independence that she wanted. She had even been willing to give up the ARP to avoid upsetting him. But if she let him take what he wanted from her now, then it would never stop. She couldn't live like this.

'Tommy, stop!' she shouted as he dragged her through the living room.

'Shut up or you'll wake my mother,' he hissed, then he turned around and the back of his hand flew into her face with such force that she fell onto the floor. The front-door keys, which he had kept stashed in his pocket since locking her in the previous day, fell to the ground first and she landed on top of them, wincing as they dug into her side. When Dot looked up, dazed, she thought she saw movement from the top of the landing but as she squinted her eyes to try to focus, she realised that she must have been mistaken. She had been hopeful that Beryl had come out of her bedroom just in time to witness what a monster her son really was. But she would still be in bed, fast asleep – the woman could sleep through anything.

'Look what you made me do,' Tommy roared, staring down at her. She cowered, terrified he was going to hit her again, or kick her as she was splayed on the floor. But he turned and stomped back to the kitchen. She heard the clink of a glass and the sound of liquid being poured. She grabbed the keys and tucked them into her waistband before slowly getting to her feet. Then Tommy walked back into the room holding a large glass of whisky. He sat down on the sofa and smiled at her smugly, which made her feel sick.

'You're going to go upstairs and get yourself ready, and I'm going to join you when I've finished this,' he said before taking a large gulp. Dot ran to the stairs and took them two at a time, holding the keys in place with one hand and making sure they didn't jangle or fall. She could hear Tommy laughing behind her. 'I knew you'd come around to my way of thinking,' she heard him say as she closed the bedroom door shut behind her. With the way he'd knocked back that first glug, she knew she didn't have long. She grabbed a suitcase from the bottom of the wardrobe and shoved in whatever clothes she could find. And then she retrieved her crumpled ARP uniform from the corner of the room where she assumed Tommy had chucked it on his return the previous day. She changed into it as quickly as she could, ignoring all the creases.

Tommy might have assumed she was rushing upstairs because she was doing as she was told. But she'd had enough of that. She knew now that she would never be able to stand up to him and he was never going to change – what he had just done had shown her that he thought nothing now of resorting to violence and force to get his own way. She had let him get away with too much already – this was where it was going to end because the alternative was just too much for her to bear. Dot had no idea where she was going or what she was going to do to survive. The only thing that she knew without a shadow of a doubt was that she couldn't stay in this house, or in this marriage, for one second longer. She would rather live on the streets than stay here. She was angry with herself for thinking they could make this relationship work. She had put up with his awful behaviour and lived in denial, making excuses for him, for long enough – and now she was finally going to walk away.

When she heard Tommy moving around downstairs, she took a deep breath, picked up the suitcase, and lugged it down the stairs with her.

'Is this some kind of a joke?' Tommy spluttered from the living room when he saw her in her uniform, suitcase in hand. His speech was slurring already from the drink. She noticed he had a full glass in his hand again – the noises she'd heard must have been him getting himself a refill. He started to laugh. 'If you walk out of that door, then you're never coming back again,' he said, sneering as he swayed from side to side.

'That was the plan,' Dot said proudly, surprised at the confidence in her voice and the bravery she suddenly felt.

'Oh, really?' he replied, smirking and reaching into his pocket. But his face fell as he patted around, searching for the keys.

'Looking for these?' Dot taunted as she held them up in the air. 'I'm going on duty, Tommy. And you're right – I won't be back.' He opened his mouth, but she carried on talking before he had a chance to say anything. She needed to tell him what she needed to say and get out before he tried to stop her. 'London needs me far more than you ever did – and a hell of a lot more than your mother does.' She turned and grappled for the correct key, shaking as she put it into the lock and turned it.

She could hear his footsteps approaching her along the hallway. Her heart raced as she pulled the door open and stepped out into the street. She turned and panic soared through her when she saw Tommy lunging for her. She threw the keys in his face, and she heard him cry out in pain and surprise as she ran along the street as fast as her legs would carry her. She didn't stop until she got around the corner. She leaned back against the wall and held her breath, listening intently to make sure she couldn't hear his footsteps. She hadn't thought he would follow her – he wouldn't risk anybody seeing him acting in that way, but she needed to be certain before she could relax. When she heard only silence behind her, Dot dropped her suitcase and slumped to the floor, with no idea what she was going to do next.

24

Arriving home that afternoon, Peggy's mind was still running over all the terrible things that might have happened to Dot to stop her getting to her shift. She wanted to be out looking for her friend, but she had been forced to agree with Viv that she needed to get some more sleep if she was going to be of any use. Viv was still convinced that Dot would turn up for her shift that evening. Peggy wasn't so sure, and she had made Viv promise that they would go to the police together if Dot didn't make it to the school for duty again.

'There's a letter here for you, dear,' Mrs Martin called out when Peggy walked into the kitchen to fetch a glass of water. Peggy's heart immediately lifted. What better way to take her mind off her worry over Dot than news from her family! She sprinted across to the post table full of anticipation, excited to see if the writing on the envelope belonged to one of her brothers, her sister Joan, their mother or their father. She was thrown to see large, messy handwriting that she didn't recognise. She stared at the envelope in confusion for a few moments before ripping it open, intrigued to discover the contents.

Dear Peggy,
Mummy is sick. Can you come home?
Love from Lucy

Tears filled Peggy's eyes as she stared at the loopy hand-writing and imagined her little sister trying desperately to pen the message to her. She was only six years old, and she had been struggling with her reading and writing when Peggy had left for London. She was amazed Lucy had managed to write the letter at all, let alone send it. She must have taken their mother's address book from the study without her permission.

Questions quickly flooded Peggy's mind. Why hadn't their mother written to her herself? Was she so poorly that she couldn't even manage a short note? Or had Lucy written to her without telling their mother? She was a very proud woman and Peggy knew that she would never ask for help, but she thought she must be in a bad way if Lucy had gone to all the trouble of writing her a letter and sending it. Maybe one of the evacuees had helped her – from what Peggy could remember they were a little older than her sisters. Another worry was who was looking after Lucy and Peggy's two youngest sisters and the evacuees while their mother was ill?

'Oh no. Not more bad news for you?' Mrs Martin said sympathetically. She walked over and placed her hand on Peggy's shoulder. Peggy felt overwhelmed. All this time she had been worrying about the safety of her father, Joan, and her brothers – and it ended up being her mother who was in danger. 'It sounds like they need you at home,' Mrs Martin added softly after reading the note over Peggy's shoulder.

'But I'm needed here, too,' Peggy whispered through sniffles.

'Nothing is more important than family,' Mrs Martin replied firmly. 'You get back there right away and see to your mother and those sisters of yours. London has coped well enough these last few weeks. It will still be standing when you return.'

Peggy sighed and wiped the tears from her eyes. She had to admit that she was grateful to have somebody to order her about. It was a difficult decision to make, and she wasn't sure if she would have been able to make it herself. She was still so worried about Dot, she felt as if she was being pulled in two directions.

Up in her room, Peggy pulled out her overnight bag and placed a change of clothes inside. She was feeling optimistic that her sister was overreacting, and she would find their mother in good health, upset at the fuss that had been made over her. She smiled to herself, hopeful that this would just turn out to have been a good excuse to have popped home to take some respite from what was happening in London. She went to lift the bag but found that she couldn't do it.

As much as she knew that she needed to be there for her mother and her sisters, she couldn't face leaving without making sure Dot was safe. She had arranged to meet with Viv the following morning to start a proper search and go to the police if Dot didn't show up at the school for duty tonight. Once the police were involved then she would feel better, and one more day wasn't going to make much difference to her mother, surely? She was friends with the local doctor's wife, so if she was in a very bad way, then she would be getting proper medical help, Peggy reassured herself. Lucy tended to go over the top about small matters, after all.

Pulling on her overalls later that afternoon, Peggy felt happy with her plan of action. With any luck, Dot would be back on duty and safe and sound by the time she travelled home. It also meant she would be able to warn Victor that she wouldn't be around for a shift or two. She knew he wouldn't have an issue with her taking the time off as he had been trying to encourage her to take a break after losing Lilli, anyway. She would also have a chance to explain her impending absence to Viv. She didn't want to just disappear off like Dot had done and leave her to worry. Maybe she could ask Bill to keep an eye on Dot for her and keep her away from Stan.

When Peggy walked into the school to clock on for duty, she immediately heard Stan's awful laugh echoing down the corridor. Her fears that he might have done something terrible to Dot rose to the surface and grew to absolute conviction that he was responsible for her friend's sudden absence. Images of him grabbing Dot off the street and hurting her flashed through her mind as she marched towards the canteen, ready to confront him and drag answers out of him however she could. She walked into the room and her blood boiled when she saw him talking animatedly to one of the young messengers. The last thing that poor boy needed was to be corrupted by such an animal. She stormed straight up to Stan and opened her mouth to shout, but then a shock of brown hair caught the corner of her eye, and she froze, gawping at the figure leaving the kitchen.

'You all right there, dear? I know I'm a looker, but nobody's ever been that bowled over by my beauty,' Stan declared, looking her up and down quizzically before roaring with laughter. Peggy ignored his comment and ran over to Dot, who had a mug of tea in each hand.

'You're here!' Peggy cried. She wanted to wrap her arms around Dot, but she didn't much fancy being scalded by hot tea.

'Last time I checked.' Dot laughed, looking uncomfortable at the attention. There were other wardens and messengers in the room – the afternoon shift was winding down and the evening shift was clocking on. Everybody had turned to look at the two of them after Peggy's outburst.

'We were worried sick about you.' Peggy's tone was hushed now as she realised how full the room was. She had been so intent on taking down Stan that she hadn't seen anybody else when she'd bounded in. She led Dot back into the kitchen for some privacy.

Dot placed both cups of tea on the counter and smiled at Peggy. 'The second cup is for you. I knew you'd be in soon.'

'Oh, thanks,' Peggy said. 'So, where were you last night? And, more importantly, what has happened to your cheek?' Peggy hadn't noticed it at first but now she could see that it was bright red and looked as if it was starting to bruise. It looked almost as if somebody had punched her.

'Oh, I took a stumble into a lamppost in the dark on the way here,' Dot said quickly. She touched her fingertips to the area tentatively and winced. It was as if she was becoming aware of the injury for the first time. 'I didn't realise it was noticeable,' she whispered, staring at the floor now and looking embarrassed. 'You know what it's like with the blackout,' she added, sounding overly light-hearted all of a sudden. 'Clumsy people like me are always walking into things!' She was laughing nervously now, and Peggy didn't buy her act one bit. Dot had never had an accident in the dark before; she was always so careful. Peggy decided not to push it, though. If Dot didn't want to tell her the truth about her face, then that was fine – maybe she would open up about what had really happened when she was ready.

Right now, Peggy was more concerned about her friend's disappearing act.

'So . . . where were you last night? Viv and I were going to draft the police in to search for you if you didn't make it in tonight.'

'You silly things.' Dot giggled, waving her hand dismissively.

Peggy frowned. All this laughing and giggling wasn't like Dot at all, and it made her feel as if her friend was trying to cover something up. 'I don't think we were being silly. There's a war going on – anything could have happened to you. Not to mention that brute, who has you on his hit list,' Peggy said, pointing angrily at Stan through the open doorway. 'We knocked at your house, Dot. There was no answer.'

Dot stared straight into her eyes, not saying a word. Then, suddenly, she started rambling. 'I'm so sorry. Beryl was poorly and I didn't want to leave her. She was too weak to get to the crypt, so we stayed in the Anderson. Maybe I was upstairs with her when you knocked? You can't hear a lot through her bedroom door. I know now how she manages to sleep through so much.' She was giggling nervously again.

Peggy didn't believe a word she was saying, but she was just relieved to have her back. Whatever was going on, she was confident Dot would tell her when she was ready. Right now, she had her own mother to focus on getting better.

'Well, please don't disappear like that again. You could have at least asked one of your neighbours to pass a message on at the crypt.'

'I didn't even think. I really am sorry. I'll keep that in mind in case anything like that happens again.'

'Forget about it. Right, let's drink our tea and then head out to check for lights.'

Dot was noticeably quieter than usual as they did their rounds. When the sirens sounded and they went to round everybody up and take them to the crypt, she seemed to drag her feet when they made it to Lawrence Street.

'Come on, Dot!' Peggy shouted back to her in between blowing her whistle and knocking on doors. 'Do you want to go and fetch Beryl?' she asked when Dot finally caught up with her.

'No, no, she'll stay in the Anderson on her own tonight.'

'But I thought she was terrified in there! I was surprised she made it through last night, but I suppose she had you with her. And is she not still unwell?'

'She doesn't hate it that much, and she can cope just fine on her own. Can you just leave it?' Dot snapped. She pushed past Peggy and ran ahead to help a woman who was struggling to get her four children out of the door with all the home comforts they wanted to take to the shelter.

Confused, Peggy followed after her. She was more than aware of the fact that Beryl was capable of looking after herself, but Dot's story about her being ill and not wanting to leave her on her own the previous evening conflicted with that. Now she knew for sure that her friend was lying to her, and she was worried about what was really going on. What could be so bad that she couldn't tell her? She was her friend – she would help her through anything.

As another bomb whistled down a few streets away, Peggy knew that now wasn't the time to try and get answers or offer any help. They needed to get through the night in one piece, and to do that they both needed to stay focused. She would wait and see what Viv thought when she met up with her in the morning.

25

Nestling down in the far corner of the room, Dot was surprised to find sleep taking hold of her almost immediately. She had been expecting to find it difficult to get any rest on the cold, hard floor. But as she felt herself relaxing into slumber, she reasoned that the relief of being free from her controlling marriage and miserable home-life must be cancelling out the uncomfortable makeshift bed she had hastily pulled together as well as clouding all her fears about what she was going to do next.

She had gone straight to Cook's Ground School after composing herself following the dramatic exit from her home – or, her former home, she supposed she should now call it. Not that the house on Lawrence Street had ever really felt like home to her. She had briefly contemplated knocking on Sally's door but thought better of the idea – that was the first place Tommy would check if he came looking for her. She also didn't feel ready to tell anybody about what had happened. She had planned on carrying out her shift and then finding a public shelter to take refuge in for as long as she could get away with. But when she had arrived at the school, she'd realised questions would be asked about her suitcase. So, she had sneaked in around the back and hidden it in one of the old classrooms where she knew none of the wardens ever ventured. That was when Dot had realised that she could probably get away with bedding down in the classroom at the end of her shift.

Dot had decided to leave her suitcase in the room and keep sneaking back in to sleep and change clothes whenever she needed to. It was the perfect base for her, so long as she kept out of the way of the rooms used by the other wardens. She would stay here until she had decided what to do next. It felt strange to her that she didn't feel more panicked, given the fact that she no longer had a home or even a family. Somehow, she felt lighter without those things – which just went to show how awful they had been. She had always believed having a home and a family was the best thing she could achieve in life, but now she knew she had been wrong. She felt a flutter of excitement as she imagined getting a full-time job once the war was over and finding somewhere to live on her own.

Peggy had asked a lot of questions about her absence the previous evening and it was clear she didn't believe Dot's lies. Dot wasn't surprised at that – she still didn't know why she had blurted out the fib about Beryl being poorly. Peggy knew how much Dot's mother-in-law despised her, so it was silly to expect her to believe that she would have let everybody down for Beryl's sake. But she had been so concerned with getting to her shift and finding somewhere to store her belongings that she hadn't even thought about the fact people would want to know why she hadn't showed up the night before. Leaving Tommy had been a split-second decision and she hadn't made any plans past getting out of the door. She wished she could swallow her pride and just tell the truth, but she hated the thought of people feeling sorry for her just as much as she hated the thought of people thinking her naïve for having married a bully and putting up with his controlling ways for so long. Her refusal to accept his behaviour for what it was meant that she hadn't even realised he was a controlling bully until now – how silly she would look!

They'd had a busy night on patrol after a row of houses were struck by a bomb. Thankfully, all the residents had been sheltering in public shelters, but it had brought home to Dot the fact that nowhere was safe during a raid. It didn't matter whether you sat it out in a public shelter, an Anderson, your cellar, the cupboard under the stairs, or if you simply stayed in bed like a lot of people had started to do – it really was down to the luck of the draw whether you survived the night once the Germans arrived. She had to admit that you probably stood more chance of making it out alive if you were in a cellar or shelter as opposed to lying in bed – but if a big bomb landed at the right angle, then you were for it no matter how far below ground you burrowed.

Dot had been relieved to find the crypt empty of Beryl and Tommy during her shift. Although she knew there wasn't much chance of them going there during a raid, she had naturally felt anxious about the possibility of bumping into them. Tommy had been drunk and angry when she had left, and she wouldn't have put anything past him. She laughed to herself when she thought about Beryl being forced to spend the night in the Anderson with her horrible son as he ranted and raved, his vile whisky breath filling the air as she jumped and screamed at every noise coming from outside. She wondered if her mother-in-law would have the gall to show her face at the crypt after Tommy's departure later today, or if she would force herself to spend future raids in the Anderson alone from now on.

*

Dot woke suddenly to the sound of a chair screeching across the floor. She must have fallen asleep a lot faster than usual. Rubbing her eyes, she looked to the side as her mind caught up with her. She had briefly forgotten where she was, but the pain in her back reminded her that she had slept on a classroom floor. She groaned as she moved slowly, trying to ease herself up to a sitting position. The jumper she had used as a pillow was flat now and had given her head hardly any support. She moved aside the blanket she had managed to squirrel away from the rest room as footsteps approached her from behind.

'Don't get up on my account,' Stan's unmistakable voice boomed out from across the room.

Dot's heart started to race. What was he doing here? How had he known where to find her? More worryingly – what did he want? She quickly scrambled to her feet and watched Stan make his way towards her, leering at her.

'This looks nice and cosy. Waiting for me, were you?' he said before breaking into his horrible laugh. 'My, my, what would the boss say about you using this place as a hotel?'

'Please don't say anything,' Dot spluttered, taking a step back and knocking against one of the tables. Stan clearly didn't understand personal space. He was standing right in front of her now, glaring down at her and looking pleased with himself. The table was digging into Dot's back. She didn't have anywhere to go.

'There's one way you can keep me quiet.' Stan laughed as he grabbed hold of her hand and thrust it towards his groin area. Instinctively, Dot's knee shot up and struck him there as she pulled her hand away. He obviously hadn't expected her to fight back as her hand came away easily and he doubled over, crying out in pain.

Panic surged through Dot as she grabbed her suitcase and ran out of the classroom. She kept checking behind her to make sure Stan wasn't following her as she sped along the corridor. Outside the back of the school, she dropped her suitcase and collapsed onto the ground herself.

Now, not only did she have no family and nowhere to stay, but she would have Stan waiting at every turn to get her on her own and make her pay for what she had just done to him. Big sobs racked her body as all the hope and positivity she had been feeling vanished and she realised she was in a lot of trouble.

When Dot felt like she had no tears left, she decided it was time to work out her next move. She had to accept that she needed help, but who could she turn to? She had been so foolish to push her friends away during the course of her relationship with Tommy. Of course, this was the result he had likely been after – if Dot had nobody to turn to, then he knew she would never leave him. He was probably sitting at home, expecting her to come crawling back to him any minute. And maybe under different circumstances she might have done. But Tommy hadn't counted on her meeting Viv and Peggy. Dot smiled through her tears now, confident that with the two women by her side, everything would be all right.

26

Viv checked the doormat hopefully when she emerged from her bedroom. She had given Johnny her address before he had left her at Café de Paris to return to Sussex, and he had promised to write to her as soon as there was any news on William. She knew it was silly to keep getting her hopes up like this, but she couldn't help it. She had to believe that William would turn up with some great story to tell about making his way back to base with the help of strangers having walked away from a plane wreck unscathed. The alternative was just too much to bear. And while there was no news to say that he had been killed, she was happy to believe that he was still out there somewhere, making his way back to her.

There was no letter waiting for her, and with a heavy heart she got herself ready to go and meet up with Peggy. They needed to find Dot today. Viv hadn't been too worried when Peggy had first told her of their friend's disappearing act; there was a lot going on and she could understand people wanting to retreat for a day or so to try and process what they were going through. But when she had learned about Stan and his possible vendetta, she had started to worry. Still, she was clinging on to the hope that Dot had just needed a break from it all and that they wouldn't need to go to the police today. She was beginning to see how much of an optimist she was becoming.

'Oh, thank goodness,' Viv sighed, once Peggy told her that Dot had turned up for her shift the previous evening. It had been a hectic night and Viv had been busy with casualties on the other side of Chelsea, so she hadn't seen Peggy and Dot. 'Can I go home and back to bed now, then?' She had cut her precious sleep short so they would have time to carry out another search and then report Dot missing to the police if they didn't find her. Now she knew Dot was safe and well, she was keen to get her head down again before the next air raid. 'What is it?' she pressed when Peggy grimaced. Something was telling her that she wouldn't be getting any extra rest today.

'I could do with leaving it at that, too; my mother isn't well, and I need to get home to check on her. But there was just something about the way Dot was behaving last night. I don't know what it is, but something isn't right.'

'Not another one of your hunches? Not twenty-four hours ago you were convinced Stan was holding Dot hostage somewhere and then she turned up safe and well. If she's back and she says everything is fine, then what can we possibly do?'

'I don't know.' Peggy shrugged. 'But there is more going on than she's letting on. She said she didn't turn up for her shift because Beryl was poorly, and she was busy looking after her. And she had a big red mark on her cheek, like she'd been smacked round the face. She told me she'd walked into a lamppost in the dark.'

'Well, that could all be true.' As soon as Peggy raised her eyebrows, Viv knew she was fighting a losing battle. 'So, what's the plan, then?' she sighed, trying hard to stifle a yawn. She knew Peggy well enough now to accept that she wouldn't back down once she had a hunch about something. And Viv wasn't about to let her go off and do whatever it was she was determined to do on her own. 'Are you going to force yourself into Dot's house and demand to see Beryl for evidence that she really is sick?' She had said it light-heartedly, but she suddenly realised that after seeing Peggy hammering on Dot's front door the previous day, she couldn't put that past her.

'I don't know. But something is up, and I need to check it out.'

'You could at least deny that you're going to force your way in to make me feel better,' Viv joked as the pair of them made their way back to Lawrence Street. 'Perhaps we could ask some of the neighbours if they've seen anything out of the ordinary going on,' she added, keen to steer Peggy away from pounding on the door again. If Beryl was truly poorly, then she wouldn't thank them for disturbing her a second time, and she would probably take out her anger on Dot.

When they reached Dot's house, Peggy didn't get a chance to knock on the door before it swung open in front of them. They were met by a tall and handsome man dressed in army uniform with a rucksack slung over his shoulder. He started when he saw them and took a step back into the house, but he didn't put his bag down. He had clearly been on his way out and he wasn't about to invite them in for a cup of tea. Viv assumed this was Dot's husband, Tommy. If he had come home on leave at the last minute, then that would explain why Dot had skipped her shift – she would have been desperate to spend time with him before he returned. But why wouldn't she have told Peggy that?

'Can I help you ladies?' he asked gruffly. He sounded impatient and Viv felt bad for keeping him from getting back to duty.

'I'm Peggy, and this is Viv. We're pleased to meet you. We're looking for Dot. Is she in, please?' Peggy said in an overly polite voice.

Tommy tutted and rolled his eyes before pushing his way past them both out on to the street. He slammed the front door shut behind him. 'Dot don't live here anymore,' he said coldly, turning to look at them with a definite sneer on his face. 'She's probably set up home with her fancy man. Shouldn't be too hard to track her down – he's one of you lot.' He looked them up and down – his face full of contempt. Peggy and Viv looked at each other in confusion. 'Now stay away from my house – my mother doesn't need you busybodies bothering her while I'm away.' With that, he stormed off along the street, with Viv and Peggy staring open-mouthed after him.

'I certainly wasn't expecting *that*,' Peggy muttered eventually.

'Your hunch was right, though. There is definitely something strange going on. Dot doesn't live there anymore? Since when? Fancy man? One of us lot? What on this earth could he be talking about?'

Peggy shrugged. 'I have no idea. I got the feeling from what little Dot has told me about her husband that things weren't great between them, especially with the way his mother treats her. But I just didn't have Dot down as somebody who would play away, no matter how bad things were at home.'

'Me neither. I mean, aside from anything else – when would she find the time?'

'Exactly.'

Viv checked back along the street to make sure Tommy was out of sight. 'Should we knock and see if Beryl can shed any light on this?'

'I wouldn't count on it,' Peggy said cautiously. 'She will have sided with Tommy over whatever is going on. She's a nasty piece of work, that woman.'

'Well, where do we start? We have absolutely nothing to go on, and we can't go to the police after what Tommy has said – they'll laugh us out of the station,' Viv replied, throwing her hands up in the air in exasperation. She felt useless.

'That's not strictly true. We have one lead.' Viv stared at Peggy, waiting for her to explain, because she had no idea what she was talking about. 'Tommy seems to think Dot has been up to no good with someone from the ARP, so we need to go to the school.'

Viv groaned with frustration. 'But she hasn't been having an affair. Why would she be there?'

'It's the only thing we have to go on,' Peggy snapped. 'Whatever is going on with Dot, it sounds as if it's connected to the ARP.' She paused and let out a loud sigh. 'Have you got any better ideas?'

Viv had to admit that she didn't, so they made their way towards Old Church Street.

'We could just wait until tonight's shift,' Viv suggested as they walked. 'Whatever is going on with Dot at home, we know she's safe and that she'll be back on duty later.' She felt as if they were searching for a needle in a haystack, and she was feeling uncomfortable about sticking her nose in too far to her friend's personal business; what if Dot had run off with somebody from the ARP? Viv would never judge her for that – she had too many of her own secrets to look down on somebody who had got themselves into such a sticky situation. But she wanted to respect Dot's privacy – if something untoward was going on and Dot didn't feel ready to share it with her friends, then they needed to respect that. She knew from her own experience the shame and embarrassment that Dot could be feeling. She didn't know how to voice that to Peggy without admitting to anything herself, though.

'I can't talk to her properly when we're on duty. We'll be too busy, and she'll just pretend everything is fine like she did last night. I'm certain that mark on her face was down to Tommy. I knew she was covering something up. And, besides, if she can't go home, then where is she? The poor thing could have been kicked out onto the streets for all we know. I don't care what she has or hasn't done – we're her friends and you support friends through anything. We need to find her.'

Viv's heart almost burst hearing Peggy saying that, but before she could respond, Dot came hurtling around the corner and almost ran into them.

'Oh! Thank goodness it's you two!' she exclaimed before checking back behind her and, on finding the street clear, dropping the suitcase she had been carrying and falling into Peggy's arms in tears.

'Let's get her back to my flat,' Viv suggested. 'Jilly is out with Ruth and Emily, so we won't be disturbed.'

Peggy nodded and started guiding a sobbing Dot along the street. Viv picked up the discarded suitcase and followed behind. Once at Viv's flat, Dot calmed down and told them everything that had happened over the previous few days.

'I'm proud of you for standing up to Tommy. Men like that don't deserve women like you,' Peggy announced passionately once Dot had finished. 'But I wish you'd told us sooner. You should have come to me straight away – you know where I live. And to think, you put yourself in danger with Stan. What were you thinking?'

'I felt ashamed,' Dot whispered, staring down at her lap. 'I married an awful bully and I put up with it for all these years, pretending to myself and everybody else that everything was fine and that I was happy. You must think I'm truly pathetic.'

'We think nothing of the sort!' Viv cried. 'I'm sure he wasn't like this when you met,' she added gently. 'Men like Tommy can switch on the charm to get what they want and then they show their true colours when it's too late. I know that better than most.' She had said it without thinking, and now both her friends were looking at her quizzically. She felt herself turning red with disgrace. Was this something she could share with them? She'd never told anybody. But how else could she explain her comment? She didn't want to lie to them. Besides, it might help Dot feel better about her own situation. Peggy's words about supporting friends through anything rang in Viv's ears as she started to speak.

'The truth is, I love William. I love him with all my heart and there is nothing I would like more than to marry him.'

'So, why did you turn him down?' Dot asked in confusion.

'I felt too ashamed of something I did before the war.' Viv took a deep breath. 'I had an affair with a married man.' She paused and thought about stopping there. But she had come this far – she might as well get the whole thing off her chest now. 'I fell pregnant, and he left me despite all his promises to leave his wife and set up home with me. He was only interested in me until he got what he wanted from me; he used me and then he completely changed, and he abandoned me. He abandoned us both. I was terrified but I decided to keep the baby and bring it up on my own.'

Her friends were listening intently now. She wondered if they were waiting for her to reveal that she had a secret little bastard child hidden away somewhere. Viv closed her eyes and tried to push away the image she had in her head of what the little girl would have looked like by now. She had been convinced it was a girl even though there had been no way of knowing, and she often taunted herself by thinking of what life would have been like for them.

'What happened?' Dot whispered.

'I lost the baby.' Her voice had wobbled with the words, and she cleared her throat before continuing. 'I'm certain that was my way of being punished for my actions.' Viv could feel tears running down her cheeks. She had tortured herself for so long over what had happened, but she had never spoken to anybody about it and saying the words out loud now made the pain feel fresh again. She was desperate to be a mother. 'I'm not worthy of somebody like William. How would he be able to love me if he knew the truth?'

'You mustn't talk like that,' Peggy whispered firmly. She threw her arms around Viv. 'People make mistakes every day. You can't let one slip-up rule your life. You're a good person, Vivian Howe, and you go out onto the streets of London every day and put your life at risk to save others. How could you ever be ashamed of yourself? I bet that man isn't beating himself up like you are.'

'She's right,' added Dot. 'You must move on from the past. You could have a wonderful future with William if you just forgive yourself.'

'Well, it might be too late now, anyway.' Viv freed herself gently from Peggy's embrace and retrieved her compact mirror from her handbag. She topped up her make-up and reapplied her lipstick while her friends waited patiently for an explanation. She wanted to stay strong when she told them about William and redoing her make-up was her way of resetting her emotions. 'William is missing in action,' she said tightly with a nod of her head. She hoped she had managed to hide the wobble in her voice when she spoke.

'I'm so sorry,' Dot replied.

Viv needed to change the subject quickly. She couldn't have Dot and Peggy feeling sorry for her because their sympathy would cause her mask to slip, and she would get upset again. She was so grateful to them for making her feel better about her secret, but she wasn't normally one to show her emotions and she didn't want to do it again.

'Whatever happens I'll be fine. It's you we need to look after, Dot – I'm sorry for taking over for a minute there. I just wanted you to know that you're not the first woman to be fooled by a handsome man's charms and you certainly won't be the last.'

Dot smiled gratefully. 'I still can't believe I walked out on Tommy. I think joining the ARP gave me the confidence and independence I had been lacking after marrying him. Doing something for myself made me realise how badly he'd been treating me. I just feel so silly for not seeing it before.'

'Well, you mustn't,' Viv said firmly.

'It sounds as if you gave Stan a good hiding, too.' Peggy giggled.

Dot groaned. 'Do you think I've made things worse for myself with Stan? He'll be really angry after what I did.'

'I don't think you need worry about him, my dear.' Peggy smiled. 'I'm confident he won't try anything else with you after the way you hit back. Remember, he's a bully who picks on the weak. You've just shown him you are in no way weak. Just like you showed Tommy and Beryl.'

'I hope you're right,' Dot muttered.

'It wouldn't do any harm to keep avoiding Stan, just in case. And we need to focus again on exposing him as a thief to get him out of our hair once and for all. But first I need to get home for a day or two.'

'Oh yes, what's wrong with your mother?' Viv asked. She felt bad for not having asked previously, but there had been a lot going on.

'I'm not entirely sure. I'm hopeful it's something about nothing but I need to see her for myself to put my mind at rest. Can I leave you two to it?' Viv and Dot smiled and nodded.

'Dot will stay here with me for as long as she needs,' Viv said confidently.

'Are you sure? What about Jilly?' Dot asked cautiously.

'She won't be a problem.' Viv knew that Jilly would welcome Dot with open arms.

'Great. Now I know you're sorted, I'll go and fetch my bag and then I'll pop into the school to let Victor know I won't make my shift this evening.'

'Good luck,' Viv and Dot said together as Peggy left the room. Viv crossed her fingers that after everything Peggy had been through losing Lilli, she wasn't about to suffer more heartbreak.

27

Peggy couldn't stop thinking about Dot on her journey home to Sussex. If that was what married life was like, then she would quite happily live out the rest of her days as a spinster. She found it upsetting to think about everything Dot had been through since marrying Tommy but doing so stopped her from fretting about her mother and getting upset with herself for delaying her trip home. What if those twenty-four hours had made the difference between life and death? She had let Lilli down and now her own mother. She shook her head, attracting a worried look from the man sitting opposite her on the train. She couldn't think like that. Her hunch about Dot had been correct, after all. She had done the right thing staying to look for her. The alternative didn't bear thinking about.

Goodness knows what Dot would have done if Viv and Peggy hadn't found her after her run-in with Stan. She had been so desperate and frightened that she might have even gone back to Beryl to ask for help. Peggy physically shuddered at the thought, and the man opposite her tutted, placed his hat back on his head, and moved seats. Peggy smiled to herself. He must think her quite mad, but at least she now knew how to get a row of seats to herself on public transport.

When the train started chugging through fields and open space as far as the eye could see, Peggy began feeling anxious. She was nearly home, and she had no idea what she was about to walk into. Had her mother been so poorly she hadn't been able to look after her sisters and the evacuees staying with them? What kind of a state would the house and everybody staying there be in? Her family home was about a mile from the train station, and she found herself running the whole way, powered by nervous energy and angst.

Pushing the front gate open and making her way up the long path to the house, relief flooded through Peggy when her three youngest sisters rushed out of the front door towards her. She took a moment to look them over and they all looked excited, happy, clean and healthy. That was a good sign. Peggy stumbled backwards as they threw themselves into her, and they landed on the cold, damp floor in a giggling heap.

'You came!' Lucy cried. Peggy gently eased each of her sisters off her and they all got to their feet.

'I had to come after I got your letter,' she said quietly while they all brushed themselves down. She looked up to see two older children emerging from the house.

'This is Phillip and Sarah,' Lucy explained. 'Their mummy and daddy are still in London.'

Peggy felt a pang of sympathy for the two of them. They only looked a few years older than her sisters and they had been torn away from their parents, knowing how much danger they would both be in staying in the city. She made a mental note not to talk about how dreadful the bombing raids had been. She knew from her mother's letters that they weren't getting the full picture out here of what was happening in

London from the news, and she suddenly understood why that was for the best. She was happy for them to stay in the dark. Who even knew if their parents were still alive?

'It's nice to meet you,' Peggy said. 'I hope these three darlings are looking after you.' Phillip and Sarah smiled and nodded, and Peggy felt guilt now – because these children had been sent here to be cared for at a terrifying time, and she wasn't sure if her mother had been capable of doing that. The thought reminded her of the reason for her trip.

'Where can I find Mother? How is she today?'

'We're really worried about her,' Lucy explained as Martha and Annie's faces both dropped. 'She keeps stopping and putting her hand to her chest, and she's so tired all the time. She says there's nothing wrong but she's not herself. She's been in bed all morning.'

The insistence that nothing was wrong sounded like their mother – she would be too proud to admit that she was suffering, especially right now when so many were off fighting to save the country and she had children relying on her. But the rest made Peggy uneasy. Her mother was always so full of energy. And why was she clutching her chest all the time – was there something the matter with her heart? The thought made Peggy's own heart race.

'If Mother is so poorly, then who has been looking after you all?' Peggy looked her sisters up and down for a second time since seeing them and noted with relief that they looked clean and well fed. 'And has Dr Brady been informed of her condition?' The local doctor's wife, Patricia, was one of her mother's best friends – surely he would have checked her over by now.

'We didn't want to tell anybody else because we don't want to be sent away,' Lucy said quietly. She was getting emotional now. 'That's why I wrote to you.' She sniffed. 'Phillip and Sarah have been helping around the house. They're really good at cooking.'

'We're happy here,' Phillip chipped in, giving Peggy a nervous smile. She knew that they must all feel nervous about being sent to another family if her mother was poorly, but she would need to get her medical attention if she needed it.

'Don't worry, you won't be sent away,' Peggy said resolutely. She wasn't sure why she was making a promise that she wasn't certain she would be able to keep. But then, maybe she would end up having to come back from London for a time to help out until her mother was better to keep her sisters together. Or Joan could help. Between them they would find a way to keep their sisters at home. But, for now, she needed to see her mother and get her the help she needed. 'Why don't you all go to the playroom, and I'll go and have a talk with Mother,' she suggested lightly, trying to hide the fear in her voice. She wasn't sure that she was ready to see her normally bright and vivacious mother weak and feeble. But when Peggy walked into the house, she immediately heard her mother's beautiful voice ringing out from the kitchen, singing 'Danny Boy'. She had sung it to Peggy's brothers before they went off to war, and hearing it again now gave Peggy tingles down her arms.

Peggy thought back to that final afternoon they'd all spent together as a family. They had just enjoyed a picnic in the garden when their mother swept both her sons into her arms and started singing to them. Despite their size and obvious desperation to appear manly and brave, the two of them had wilted in her arms and embraced the moment. Peggy had seen then how terrified the two of them were about going off to fight, despite their bravado. She wiped away a tear and stopped in the doorway to watch her mother. She was gliding around the kitchen, moving so smoothly as she picked up dirty dishes and washing them, that it was almost like some kind of clearing-up dance. It was enchanting to observe. Peggy had always enjoyed watching her mother at work; she seemed to be able to make any chore into a dance.

'Well, you certainly don't look as though you're at death's door,' Peggy declared with a laugh. Her voice made her mother start and she instantly regretted what she had done – fancy creeping up on somebody who was having heart issues. But after jumping and turning around to face her, Peggy's mother's face lit up and she bounded over to sweep Peggy up into an embrace.

'My darling girl!' she cried, pulling back to run her fingers through Peggy's hair and look her in the face. It was almost as if she was checking she was real. 'You're really here! What brings you? Do you have news?' She pulled out a chair from the kitchen table and eased Peggy onto it before sitting down beside her and taking both her hands in her own. She squeezed them and grinned at Peggy, waiting for her answer. Then her eyebrows lifted as if she had just remembered something. 'Death's door?' she asked.

'Lucy wrote to me.' Her mother's face screwed up in confusion. She was obviously as perplexed as Peggy had been about how Lucy had managed such a task. She would have to remember to ask her how she had managed to write and post the letter before she left. 'She didn't say much, but it was enough to get me here. And before you say what I was thinking – it wasn't just a ruse to see me. I've just spoken to her, and she's really worried about you. And so am I now.'

'But there's nothing wrong with me,' her mother said with a laugh.

'It looks that way to me. But Lucy says you've been having issues with your heart.' Her mother tutted and waved her hand at Peggy dismissively. 'I know Lucy can be dramatic, but I don't think she's making it up. She told me you keep clutching your chest. You need to tell me if you need help. I can come back. We can get you better.'

'You'll do no such thing! I'm proud of our family doing their bit. I wouldn't dream of dragging you back from such important work just because I'm suffering with a bit of indigestion.'

'Indigestion?'

'Yes, you silly girl!' Everything clicked into place for Peggy. Her mother had been slowing down and clutching her chest because she was fighting indigestion – not an imminent heart attack. 'You know Lucy has always had a vivid imagination. I'm sure I've even told her it's indigestion. It's probably this rationing wartime diet I've been forced to stick to.' Peggy took a moment to process this explanation. Was her mother covering up the fact she was very ill, or was she telling the truth? 'You've seen the girls and they look happy and healthy, yes?' Peggy nodded her head. 'Right, well, that wouldn't be the case if I was laid up at death's door now, would it? And you know Patricia would never let me get away with ignoring something like that. She'd have Dr Brady round here as quick as a wink.'

Peggy laughed. Of course, her mother was right – how had she ever thought she would be left to languish with a doctor's wife as a best friend?

'I think the lack of sleep and stress might be getting to me.' She sighed. 'I'm sorry for doubting you.' As her mother looked into her eyes, Peggy felt herself crumbling. Without warning, all the grief and pain she had been bottling up since losing Lilli tumbled out of her. Her mother held her as she wept and then she stroked her hair as Peggy told her about what had happened. When she was finished, she felt a release. She hadn't realised how much she had kept inside.

'It sounds like Lucy did the right thing in bringing you home, after all,' her mother whispered into her ear. 'Only it's you who needs the looking after, my darling.'

Peggy felt more tears stinging her eyes. She had missed home and her mother so much. She had missed her whole family. She was suddenly overwhelmed with relief that her mother was healthy and happy and that she was sitting next to her again, instead of staring out at her from a picture frame in her bedroom.

Her mother smiled. 'You go to your room and have a lie down. Once you've rested, we can have a lovely time catching up with everything, and we'll send you back to London tomorrow refreshed and with a full belly and an even fuller heart.'

Peggy wiped away the tears that were now flowing down her face. She couldn't think of anything she would like more.

28

When Viv turned up for duty, they were already five ambulances down. While her colleagues explained all the places that had been hit so far, she could hardly hear them over the sound of the deafening gunfire. Bombs were landing with hardly any let-up and Chelsea was experiencing one of its worst barrages of the war. She already knew about fires at Harrod's Depository and Chelsea Library. It seemed as if the Germans had forgotten about the rest of London for an evening.

'It's going to be a bad one tonight,' Station Officer Spencer declared solemnly as the office phone started ringing once more. Viv thought it was a silly statement – it was already an awful night. The room had been shaken by a falling bomb not minutes before, and Viv had come in to see her boss in anticipation of the next job. Station Officer Spencer had only just sent extra crew members – including Paul – out to a fire at Peabody Buildings. Apparently, the whole top floor was alight. Normally Viv would have expected to be sent out with somebody else when Paul was elsewhere, but they were short-staffed tonight and Station Officer Spencer had already warned her that she was likely to be going it alone for the evening. It felt strange to be waiting for the incident details in the office instead of sitting in Hudsy ready to go while Paul picked them up and dashed to join her. She felt a rush of anxiety at the prospect of driving out into the thick of it all on her own. Paul was her extra pair of eyes when it came to navigating the debris on the burning streets and he had become like a security blanket. When Station Officer Spencer thrust something at her, Viv dismissed all her worries, grabbed hold of the scrap of paper and ran out of the room. There wasn't time for feeling fearful.

'It's a boarding house so make sure all residents are accounted for!' Station Officer Spencer called out after her. Viv raised her hand in acknowledgment. It wasn't until she was in Hudsy that she looked at the piece of paper in her hand.

'Bramerton Street,' she muttered to herself, crumpling it up and throwing it into the passenger footwell before starting up the engine. The name had triggered something within her. She knew somebody who lived there but she couldn't quite put her finger on it. It certainly wasn't Dot – she had visited her house enough times over the past few days to know exactly where that was and, besides, Dot was bedding down with her now anyway.

Viv didn't know many other people in London well enough to be aware of their address, so the chances were that it was ringing a bell because it was where the other person closest to her at the moment lived – Peggy. Pulling out onto the road, Viv breathed a sigh of relief that her friend had travelled back home to Sussex the previous day. If the bomb had fallen anywhere near Peggy's boarding house, then thank goodness she was miles away. She might even end up putting her up as well once she returned to London. She knew Jilly wouldn't mind. Everybody was pulling together through this terrible time and her roommate was no exception. She hadn't even batted an eyelid when she had come home to find Dot sleeping on their sofa.

Making her way to the incident, Viv couldn't help but stare in awe at the red glow that was covering the skyline. It would have been beautiful if it wasn't for the fact it had been caused by bombs and gunfire. There were so many blazes burning around her, Viv felt hot despite the cold winter evening air. It was a bizarre feeling and one she wasn't sure she would ever get used to.

Viv winced every time a bomb whistled down from the sky. But there wasn't time to worry about where each of them landed or who they might hurt as she tried to stay focused on getting to the people who were waiting for her help. She would feel inadequate turning up alone. It was hard enough for her and Paul to cope with all the casualties when they were on duty together. She hated having to decide who to treat first and who to leave waiting, suffering and in agony. It was like they were playing God with people's lives, but it was just the way it had to be when the number of people injured was so high and the number of medics was so desperately low in comparison.

She navigated her way through the eerie streets as quickly and as carefully as she could. Driving past what remained of a row of shops, she peered in through the blown-out front of the greengrocers and she shook her head sadly at the group of people grabbing items off the shelves at the back of the store. They were risking their lives for the sake of some eggs and bread, but this was what it had come to now. Viv turned her attention back to the road just as the car started shaking violently. Panic surged through her as she held tight to the steering wheel and tried to keep it straight while it pulled the car to the left. She came to a stop and breathed a sigh of relief that she hadn't been able to drive any faster – it felt like the tyre had blown out and she could have been in a lot of danger if she had been driving at speed.

Viv got out and checked the front passenger-side tyre. There was a gaping hole about two inches wide staring back at her. Her heart started racing as she panicked. It was possible she had driven over something to damage the tyre – it happened a lot during the blackout with all the rubble they had to get through. But she also hadn't carried out her usual vehicle checks on Hudsy before heading out. Everything had been such a rush this evening and she had been out of her normal routine without Paul by her side. The reminder that Paul wasn't with her made her panic rise even more – she always relied on him to change the tyres when they were damaged. She had been shown how to do it as part of her training, but she'd never quite got the hang of it, and then with Paul always being on hand to help, she hadn't had any reason to get to grips with it.

Viv cursed herself for being such a fool. She normally prided herself on being a strong woman who didn't need a man but now, here she was, stuck, because she needed a man to help her. Paul was always telling her to pay attention while he was changing the tyres. She could kick herself. Instead of kicking herself, she kicked the damaged tyre. What was she going to do now? There were casualties waiting for her. She was only a couple of streets away, but she was no use to anybody turning up without her equipment or a form of transport. Maybe she should have listened to William and run home to the safety of the countryside when he had suggested it. She was no good to anybody here. Her heart dropped at the thought of poor William, and then she kicked the tyre again in frustration, before yelping in pain and grabbing her foot.

'Hey! Leave poor Hudsy alone – what's he ever done to you?'

Viv turned around and relief flushed through her when she saw Dot walking towards her. But then her joy turned to sadness when she realised her friend wouldn't be able to change the tyre, either.

'Are there any other wardens around? My tyre's blown and I need to get to my next job.' They both ducked down beside Hudsy and covered their heads with their hands as a bomb whistled overhead and the gunfire intensified. When the coast was clear again they got to their feet.

'Why are you after other wardens?' Dot asked now, walking round to the back of Hudsy. 'Here, clear this equipment out of the way so I can get to the spare tyre, will you?'

'But . . .'

'But what? We don't need a man, Vivian. I'm more than capable of changing a tyre!'

Viv rushed forward to do as she was told, and watched in wonder as Dot swiftly jacked up Hudsy and pulled the damaged tyre off before replacing it with the new one.

'Where did you . . .?'

'My father ran Tommy's garage before he passed away. I used to work on the reception there, but I picked up a few things along the way. My father used to let me help him work on the cars after school when I was younger. Of course, it all changed when Tommy took over, but I can still remember the basics.'

'You put me to shame,' Viv said, shaking her head.

'Anyway, where are you heading? I was just rounding up stragglers. I was about to yell at you to get to a shelter until I got closer and recognised you.'

'There's been a bomb at a boarding house on Bramerton Street. I don't know any more than that,' Viv explained as she climbed into the driver's seat. 'I best not leave them waiting any longer.'

Dot's face fell and she pulled open the passenger door. 'That's where Peggy lives,' she said, her face ashen as she sat down next to Viv.

'I knew I recognised it! Good job she's at home with her mum and sisters tonight, otherwise I would have been really worried.' Viv had started driving again now, as it seemed clear that Dot was coming along with her.

'She's not in Sussex,' Dot whispered, staring out at the road ahead.

'What? Well, she must be out on duty, then?' But she knew the answer before Dot said anything. Her stomach lurched as she realised what this meant. If Peggy had been on duty, she would have been with Dot. The two of them always patrolled together. So, if she wasn't in Sussex and she wasn't on duty, then that meant . . .

'I've just been to the crypt. She's not there. She's just managed to persuade her friends at the boarding house to shelter in the cellar again,' Dot whispered. 'We need to get there. It might already be too late.'

29

Dot had just enough time on the way to Bramerton Street to explain to Viv that Peggy had returned from her family home earlier than expected. Finding her mother in good health, she had come back to London after just one night away. She had wanted to get straight back out on duty tonight, but Victor had turned her away and told her to get some more rest.

'She was so disappointed, but she looked utterly exhausted. I know we all are, but she truly looked like she could fall asleep standing up. I told her Victor was right. Why did I do that? I sent her off to get blown up!'

'It's not your fault,' Viv said firmly. 'You could just as easily have taken her along on patrol with you, only for you both to get injured during the course of the evening. We're all targets, no matter what we're doing, so you can't think like that. We all need to stop blaming ourselves for the actions of the Germans.'

Dot nodded. She appreciated Viv's support, but it still didn't stop the guilt from encompassing her. She had shown the same support to Peggy after what had happened to Lilli, but now she understood just how awful the feelings were in this kind of situation. There really wasn't anything anybody could say to make it better. She closed her eyes and prayed that Peggy wouldn't end up going the same way that Lilli had.

They turned into Bramerton Street and Dot's heart sank even further. All that was left of Peggy's boarding house was a huge pile of bricks, wood and debris. The sky's red-and-orange glow illuminated broken pieces of furniture. There was only half of the house next door left. An elderly gentleman was standing in the road, staring at the devastation. Viv parked as close as she could manage, and they both ran towards what was left of their friend's home. Dot had to believe that Peggy was in the cellar, and that they could get her out. It had been done many times before – Peggy had even told her about the time she and Viv had rescued a group of women and a baby from a cellar when the rest of the house had collapsed above them.

But first, they needed to deal with this man while they waited for the rest of the emergency crews to turn up. Dot knew it was a busy night, but she hadn't expected to be first on the scene, especially not after their hold-up with Hudsy. When they reached the man, he didn't seem to notice them. Dot gently placed her hand on his shoulder, but he didn't even flinch. There were tears running silently down his cheeks, cutting through the dust and muck the explosion had left on his face to reveal a line of his skin through the mask of grime.

'Do you think he's in shock?' Dot asked.

Viv nodded sadly before rushing back to Hudsy. Seconds later she was back with a blanket. She wrapped it around the man and, together, she and Dot guided him a little further along the road and eased him down to sit on the kerb. She was desperate to start searching for Peggy, but there was nobody else here to help this poor man – or to help her and Viv.

'Where is everybody?' Viv asked desperately. 'Normally by the time I get here, the rescue teams are heading in, and wardens are guiding out the injured. And I was delayed because of the tyre. How have we managed to be the first ones here, I don't understand?'

'There's just been too much to cope with tonight,' Dot replied. 'I'm sure they'll be drafting in backup from other areas that haven't been hit as hard, but it will take time.' All her colleagues had been sent out in the first hour of the raid. She had wanted to stay at the school to take the next job, but Victor had insisted she head out to make sure as many people as possible were in the shelters – either public or their own. But she knew as well as he did that there was a large number of people who couldn't be convinced to leave their homes anymore. She looked at the man on the pavement next to her and wondered if he was one of them, or if he'd simply been on his way to a shelter when the bomb had landed.

'I couldn't get her out,' the old man whispered out of nowhere. Dot and Viv both turned to look at him. He was still staring at the half-house next to the rubble of Peggy's boarding house. Fresh tears rolled down his cheeks, but he made no move to wipe them away.

'Is that your house?' Viv said urgently now. 'Is there somebody in there? Is it your wife?' Dot could feel her friend's sense of urgency. If there was somebody trapped in the wreckage, then time was of the essence – they needed to try to get to her.

'She's gone.' He didn't move his focus. 'I'd nipped off to the lav, couldn't hold it any longer. Vera was in bed when the bomb landed. Her one wish was that we left this world together and I let her down.' Dot slowly turned to look at the house again. 'Everything caved in on her. I could see her foot sticking out, but I knew I'd lost her. I couldn't even get to her to bring her out. I can't stand to think of her buried in there still.'

'Is she definitely gone?' Dot asked carefully. Even if he thought that she was, they would have to check. She'd heard of people surviving for days buried deep in the rubble – they couldn't leave the poor woman where she was if there was a chance that she might survive. They had to try. But, what about Peggy and all her friends? They needed to try to dig down to the boarding house cellar, too. She looked around them frantically, hoping to conjure up some more manpower. Just then, a fire engine turned into the road.

'Thank goodness,' Viv said at the same time that Dot made the same grateful exclamation. Together, they ran over to greet the crew and they quickly explained the situation.

'I don't think we're going to see a rescue team for a while,' the chief fireman told them, rubbing his chin and taking in the scene in front of him. 'We've just come over from Beaufort Mansions. We got the fire under control but it's going to take them a long time to get the survivors and the bodies out. We'll have to do what we can here, but I've only got one crew. We'll start with the lady in the next-door house as it looks like the rest of the building could collapse at any moment.'

Tears filled Dot's eyes. The thought of Peggy trapped in the cellar just feet away and waiting for her friends to rescue her broke her heart.

'We can start clearing a path to the people in the cellar,' Viv offered confidently. Dot's mouth fell open. The fireman looked between them quizzically. 'I've done it before,' Viv added loudly.

'But . . . didn't you and Peggy have help when you did it? I thought they had already cleared a tunnel and you went in to help everyone out?' Dot thought she was probably just as desperate as Viv to get to Peggy, but this sounded like a suicide mission – how could they possibly clear a safe path through all the rubble when it was just the two of them? What if they brought it all down on top of them – they could kill themselves along with everybody sheltering in the cellar.

'You'll have help this time, too,' a man's self-assured voice boomed from behind them. Dot turned around and was shocked to find Bill and a group of men in similar-looking clothing standing with him. She hadn't even realised anybody else had turned up, and she was certain that Victor had told her it was Bill's night off – she definitely hadn't seen him when she'd turned up for her shift that evening. 'We were just clocking off at the docks when the raid started,' he explained. 'When I realised how bad things were getting, there was no way I could go to a shelter for the night. And this lot wouldn't let me come out to help on my own.' He gestured to the group of men who were obviously his co-workers from the docks.

'That's that sorted, then,' Viv said victoriously. 'Let's get you chaps digging.' She led them to what was left of the boarding house and Dot followed along as the fire crew set off towards the house next door. Bill looked over and caught Dot's eye and she suddenly felt certain that they were going to get to Peggy in time. Bill had a comforting and reassuring air about him, and she realised that she had never been as relieved to see somebody as she had felt when she had turned around and spotted him.

She looked over to Viv and smiled when she saw her reach for her lipstick. But her friend stared at the stick of make-up sadly before putting it back in her pocket. She caught Dot's eye.

'Things feel a little too serious this time, even for this,' she whispered. 'I'll save it for the celebrations once we have Peggy safely out of there,' she added.

Dot nodded her head and pushed back the tears that had started welling in her eyes. 'Let's get Peggy,' she declared positively, and they set to work helping the men clear a tunnel to the cellar.

30

Peggy shivered despite the heat that was emanating from all the other bodies huddled up around her, and she drew her knees up to her chest. She was stuck in a tiny space down in the cellar with ten other residents from her boarding house. After the bomb had hit the building, part of the cellar ceiling had collapsed, crushing Mr Moore, Mrs Steel and Mr and Mrs Jeffries. Peggy and the others had called out for them for what had felt like hours, but they had now finally accepted there was no hope for the four of them. Peggy was happy that Mr and Mrs Jeffries had died together. It felt like a terrible thing to think, but she couldn't imagine how painful it would have been if one of them had survived and left the other behind. She could at least believe that they were at peace together now.

Through a complete stroke of luck, a huge beam had fallen and landed just to the left of where Peggy had been cowering when everything collapsed around them. It had saved their corner of the cellar from caving in, and now they were all huddled close together, waiting for some-body – anybody – to come and try to rescue them. Not that Peggy was pinning all her hopes on that. Even if the best rescue team came to their aid, there was still a huge chance that the mission could go wrong. They were safe for now, but everything could come crashing down on top of them and crush them all at any moment. It was just a waiting game, really.

'What if they're alive but we just can't hear them?' Mr Griffiths exclaimed suddenly.

Peggy sighed.

'We've already agreed it's too risky,' Mrs Martin replied firmly.

'But . . . we need to try! I need to do *something*! I can't just sit here waiting to die!' Mr Griffiths started crawling towards the beam and, just as quickly, Ralf scrambled after him. Ralf was a refugee who had arrived with Lilli. His English wasn't very good, but he had been out most nights helping the rescue teams and Peggy had noticed how strong his body was becoming because of all the heavy lifting. She was grateful for that now, as he pinned Mr Griffiths to the floor. The older man sobbed, but Peggy was all out of comforting words. Just then, there was a creak from overhead, and suddenly it sounded as if the whole building – or what was left of it – was groaning in protest at the sudden movement. There were yelps and tears as everybody braced themselves for the inevitable. But then it all went quiet again.

'We really must try to stay as still as we can until help arrives,' Peggy whispered through the darkness. She could just about make out Mrs Martin's face next to hers, and she smiled when the older woman took hold of her hand and squeezed it reassuringly. Peggy may have been coming across as calm and collected, but that was just the air-raid warden in her kicking in. She was saying all the right things to try and make everybody else feel less pan-icked and frightened, but underneath it all she was just as petrified as the rest of them. And Mrs Martin would know just how terrified she was after all the conversations they'd had when Peggy had confessed her true feelings and fears about what was happening in London. The truth was, Peggy was probably one of the most panicked people in that cellar right now.

But at least she was in the cellar, she thought to herself, as visions of the residents who had refused to join them flashed into her mind. There had been at least twenty men and women bedded down in the main part of the house before the bomb hit. Peggy had tried with all her might to convince them to go down to the cellar with her and the rest of her group when the sirens had started up, but they wouldn't hear a word of it. Of course, some of them would have perished down here anyway – as they all still might – but she couldn't help but feel disappointed at the needless waste of life.

Everybody was silent now – so quiet that Peggy could hear people's breathing. She wondered if they were all, like her, listening out for the creaks and groans from the timber struggling to stay in place and keep them safe. She found herself flinching every time she heard even the slightest noise. Maybe it would have been better to have been wiped out upstairs with the others, after all. If she was going to die anyway, it would have been preferable to just go without all this lead-up and time to think about it.

'I suppose we did well to last this long,' a voice sighed through the blackness surrounding them. It sounded like it had come from opposite Peggy. She couldn't be sure, but she thought the voice might belong to Mrs Glenn, a widow who had moved in only a few weeks before. 'The rest of my family have seen the end already because of this blasted war. And what about those poor bastards upstairs. I don't suppose any of them have survived.'

'I think I might have preferred to have been blown up along with them,' a man's voice chipped in. 'It would have been over quickly up there. I can't see anybody managing to get us out of here in one piece, so we're going to be forced to sit here and wait for the inevitable. Maybe we'll even suffocate in the end.'

Peggy was just about to cut in and try to bring the topic of conversation to something more positive, but Mrs Martin beat her to it.

'If this is the end, then I'm happy with the way I lived my life,' she declared proudly. She gave Peggy's hand another squeeze before continuing. 'I brought up two wonderful daughters, who now have beautiful children of their own. And I told my husband that I loved him every day until he died. He left this world knowing he was truly loved, and I will leave the same way. I'm grateful for that.'

The room fell silent again, but Peggy wanted to keep the momentum going before anybody started getting morose again.

'I'm grateful for the love I've had from my family.' She felt her voice quiver with emotion as she thought about her brothers and sisters and their mother and father. 'They are the best I could have wished for, and nothing can take that away. If the rescue teams don't get to us in time, then I will die with a smile on my face because I know I was loved.' She was glad the others wouldn't be able to see the tears running down her face. She wasn't sure how her little sisters were going to cope without her, and she was trying to banish from her mind the thought of them receiving the news that she had died in London the very same day she had waved them goodbye.

'I had a good life, I suppose.' Peggy recognised Mr Bowler's voice straight away and she smiled at the gruffness of it. He'd hardly spoken all evening and she was amazed at how happy she was to hear his voice. 'My sons are off fighting for our country, and the last time I saw them I told them how proud I was of them.' Peggy was surprised. Mr Bowler didn't seem like a man who liked to show emotion. 'They almost fell off their chairs to hear their old man being sentimental, and of course they laughed at me for being soft, but I'm glad I did it. Now they'll always know.'

'You can tell them again the next time you see them,' Mrs Glenn said firmly, and Peggy could hear the smile in her voice.

Soon enough, everybody was joining in, sharing everything they were grateful for in their lives. Peggy enjoyed listening to all their stories, especially as it distracted her from the dark thoughts of death, and everybody she would leave behind that kept trying to push their way to the front of her mind. Once they had all had a turn, a hush fell over the space between them again. Peggy could feel the atmosphere becoming negative once more. Then, from beside her, came a beautiful sound that had her instantly transfixed.

'We'll meet again, don't know where, don't know when . . .' As Mrs Martin's soft voice drifted around the small space that was left of the cellar, a calm descended upon Peggy. 'But I know we'll meet again some sunny day.' There was a pause, and Peggy found herself desperate for her friend to continue. Just as she did, more voices from opposite them joined in.

'Keep smiling through, just like you always do . . .' Peggy couldn't help it now. She joined in, and as soon as she started singing, she felt her spirits lifting.

''Til the blue skies drive the dark clouds far away.' Soon enough, it sounded as if they were all singing, and Peggy felt overwhelmed by the emotions that she could feel pouring out of everybody. They got louder and louder as their feelings of fear and sadness took over, and she stopped worrying about the vibrations from their voices shaking the foundations and moving the rubble dangerously. If she was going to go, then this was the perfect way. She closed her eyes and let herself get lost in it as they sang the song over and over, getting louder and louder. Hitler wasn't going to win – they were going to leave on a high.

But they all came to an abrupt halt when a pile of dust and debris suddenly covered their heads. Instinctively, Peggy lowered her head between her knees and put her hands over her head. But she was ready for whatever was coming. She felt more heavy objects glance off her hands as she waited for the bricks and beams above her to collapse and crush her. Something must have shifted the rubble to dislodge a load of dust and debris like that. She took a deep breath and silently said goodbye to her family. But instead of more bricks falling, Peggy suddenly heard voices coming from outside.

'They're coming for us,' she whispered, tentatively looking up and around. There was a scraping sound, and then suddenly a glimmer of light shone into the space they were occupying. They must have been singing so loudly that they hadn't even heard the rescue workers digging a tunnel towards them.

'Thanks for guiding us in with your wonderful voices,' she heard a familiar voice say with a laugh. 'Now, let's get you all out, shall we?'

A large piece of rubble was pulled away and they all squinted at the light suddenly pouring in from the full beam of the flashlight. As she caught Dot's eye, she saw relief wash over her friend as she registered the fact that Peggy was still alive.

'There's one other thing I'm truly grateful for that I forgot to share with you all,' Peggy said before they all started scrambling to the newly created exit. 'My amazing friends.'

31

Settling down on Viv's sofa with a blanket and a cup of tea, Dot closed her eyes and took a deep breath. She was desperate for sleep, but she knew that she needed to process everything that had just happened before she would be able to relax into any kind of slumber. The sofa wasn't very comfortable, but she knew she would be able to sleep with no problems – if she could get through a night on a cold, hard, classroom floor, then this lumpy sofa would feel like luxury in comparison.

Jilly had been so welcoming to both her and Peggy – who, of course, was bedding down at the flat too following last night's events. Jilly had given her bed up for Peggy to sleep in this afternoon while she was off volunteering at the rest centre. Peggy had offered to share the bed with Dot, but Dot hadn't wanted to hamper her friend's chances of recuperating, so she had insisted on taking the sofa instead.

Dot finished her tea and smiled to herself when she heard Viv snoring in the room next door. Her glamorous friend was the last person in the world she expected to be a snorer but then everybody was so exhausted at the moment, she reasoned, that even the quietest and lightest of sleepers were probably starting to fall into deep and noisy snoozes whenever they got the chance to rest. She'd seen people fully passed out on buses recently, having to be shaken awake when they got to their stop.

Lying down and snuggling under the blanket, Dot thought back to the moment she had seen Peggy in that tiny space in the cellar. She and the other surviving residents had been crammed into such a small area, Dot had been surprised they hadn't struggled for air down there. Dot, Viv, Bill and his men had been working for hours trying to dig a path through the rubble and down into the cellar without disturbing too much of the rubble and bringing more down. They'd had no idea if there were any survivors down there or even whereabouts they were, and it was only when the singing had started that they had been able to pinpoint exactly where they needed to dig. When they had eventually led everyone out, they had all stared back at the boarding house in a daze.

'How did we survive that?' one of them had whispered. Dot hadn't been sure how to answer – still unable to believe it herself. One huge beam had fallen in just the right place to protect them all from terrible deaths. Viv had checked everybody over while Bill and his men had started the awful job of trying to retrieve the bodies of the residents who had sheltered in the dining room. There was no lucky beam for them – they hadn't stood a chance when the bomb struck.

Incredibly, none of the survivors had suffered serious injuries. So, after cleaning up various wounds, Viv had driven them all to the nearest rest centre, keen to get them away before the bodies of their friends were pulled out of the wreckage. As she had driven off, Bill had come over to let Dot know the old lady from the house next door had been rescued while they had been busy digging a tunnel to Peggy. Her leg had been completely crushed, but it sounded hopeful that she was going to make it. Dot had felt relieved for her husband, who had been so convinced he'd lost her. The only boarding-house resident who had stayed behind with Dot and Peggy was Mrs Martin, who Peggy refused to send to the rest centre. In the end, Viv had taken her to Ruth and Emily's flat, and the two girls had been more than happy to take in the older woman for as long as she might need.

Now, as sleep started to envelop Dot, she felt grateful for her friends. The war had already taught her how precious life was, but the last few days had certainly hammered the message home to her. She now knew how important it was to look out for the people she cared for and that it was all right to walk away from those who hurt her. She was startled to by a knock at the door. Sitting up, she waited for Viv to go and answer it. But despite the disturbance she could still hear her friend snoring. Another knock came, and still there was no movement inside the flat. Dot wasn't surprised that Peggy hadn't stirred either – she supposed it would take an awful lot to rouse her after everything she had been through the previous night.

When the third knock rang out around the room, Dot decided this visitor was not going to go away any time soon and that she had better go and see to them. She felt bad answering the door when it wasn't her home, but it didn't seem that she had a choice. She would take a message from whoever it was to pass on to either Viv or Jilly. But when she opened the door, she had to take a second look at the figure standing in front of her. It was the last person she expected to see.

'Beryl?' she whispered, confusion running through her. She thought maybe she had managed to fall asleep, and this was a bad dream. She was tempted to slap herself on the face to try and wake herself up.

'Oh, don't look so shocked. You weren't that hard to find.' Her mother-in-law tutted. 'Now, are you going to let me in?' It was the last thing that Dot wanted to do, but she found herself stepping aside as Beryl nudged her way over the threshold.

'It's not the fact you've found me that's surprised me,' Dot said as she followed the older woman into the living room and watched as she pushed her blanket and cushion to the side to make some space to sit down. *Make yourself at home*, she thought to herself. 'I'm just at a loss as to *why* you would want to find me in the first place.' She purposely remained standing. She wasn't intending on Beryl staying very long, so there didn't seem much point in joining her on the sofa. Plus, standing made it clear that she wasn't planning on this being a long visit.

'We'll get to that. Is there any tea left in the pot for me? I'm gasping after tracking you down,' Beryl said, pointing at Dot's empty mug on the coffee table.

Sighing, Dot picked up the mug and took it to the kitchen. She supposed the best way to get rid of Beryl was to listen to what she had to say. No doubt she would be here grovelling on behalf of Tommy. He wouldn't be able to stand the shame of his wife walking out on him, but the shame of having to ask her to come back would be even worse. Dot couldn't wait to tell Beryl she was done for good with her horrible, abusive son and to send her away with her tail between her legs. She had put up with so much from the pair of them for so long that this new, stronger Dot was going to come as a surprise – and Dot couldn't wait to see Beryl's face when she gave her a piece of her mind.

After making a fresh pot of tea and building up her confidence by reminding herself that she deserved much better than Tommy, Dot brought in two steaming mugs and placed them on the coffee table. She sat down next to Beryl, turned to face her and declared defiantly:

'I'm not coming back.'

'I shouldn't think so, too,' Beryl replied quickly and just as firmly, holding eye contact.

Dot rolled her eyes and looked away, laughing to herself. If Beryl was here to gloat about how she had won the battle for Tommy's affections and tell Dot she would regret leaving him, then she wasn't interested in hearing a word of it. She was about to stand up and ask her to leave, when Beryl spoke again.

'I don't know 'ow you put up with him for so long, but I just wanted you to know that you're better off out of it, and that I hope you one day manage to find the happiness you deserve.'

Dot's head was spinning now. Was this some kind of a joke? Or had Beryl been knocked on the head during one of the raids? What was happening?

'I don't understand. You've always hated me. I thought you'd be glad I'd left him.'

'I've never hated you, dear.' Beryl sighed. 'I just wanted better for you.'

Dot was now dumbstruck as well as confused, so she waited patiently for Beryl to elaborate. Beryl sighed again and fiddled with her hands in her lap. It was clear that being contrite didn't come easily to her.

'The thing is, I've always known my Tommy was a bad egg. I tried and tried with him when he was little, but I just couldn't do anything to take away that nasty streak that seems to be embedded in him. I'm his mother, so, in the end I accepted it as a part of him. I've done my best over the years to stop people getting too close to him – as a way of protecting them. I've seen off quite a few young ladies who were swept away by his charms but who I knew were too weak to cope with him at his worst.'

It was all falling into place for Dot, now. Maybe Beryl hadn't been mean to her all these years because she didn't like her – maybe she'd been trying to drive a wedge between her and Tommy to make her leave, because she knew how awful he really could be.

'You were different,' Beryl continued, looking up at Dot again now. 'As much as I tried to get between the two of you, you just kept coming back. I realised that you must really, truly, love my boy to put up with all my nonsense. And it showed that you were a strong woman. I thought that love and your strength might be enough, that maybe you two could make a go of things. I've always stood up to Tommy and he's never bullied me. I thought if he had a wife who was tough enough, then he might treat her right.'

'But then I got weak,' Dot whispered.

'I hated the way he beat you down like that. He slowly chipped away at your self-worth and confidence until you were stepping on eggshells around him, desperate to please him.'

'But you joined in,' Dot replied. She was trying to keep her voice even, but she could feel the emotion – the anger – creeping out.

'He's my boy, Dorothy. I didn't want to admit to anybody else what a monster he was, and I knew he'd never forgive me if I made you see what he was doing and leave us for a better life. I was always happy to stand up to him myself, but I was too scared to stand up to him on your behalf. And I couldn't bring myself to betray him like that. But if you did it off your own back . . .'

'So, you made my life hell for my own good?'

'I can see now that it wasn't the best way to go about things, being so mean to you in the hope I would drive you away. But once I'd started it was difficult to go back. I kept thinking that if I just kept going for a little while longer, you'd finally have enough and walk out, but you kept putting up with it. And then I suppose I got angry with you for sticking around and wasting your life. I'm his mother – I was stuck with him. But you could have done so much better.'

Dot took a few minutes to take in everything Beryl was saying while they both drank some tea. She wanted to be angry with her but, in her own strange, misguided way, it seemed as if Beryl had been trying to protect her.

She found that she couldn't bring herself to feel anything but pity for the woman who had helped make her married life a misery. Beryl knew her son was a monster, yet she was too weak to stand up to him when he was treating other women badly, and she had spent her life trying to scare admirers away for their own good. And now she was going to be stuck with him in that house. But that thought made her think back to something Beryl had just said.

'You said you *were* stuck with him. Does that mean . . .?'

'I've told him not to come home,' Beryl said boldly. Her voice was firm, and she was holding her head high, but the tears in her eyes gave her away. She was devastated. 'I've let so much slip over the years, but when I saw him lashing out at you, I had to say enough was enough. It's broken my heart to throw him out; he's my flesh and blood and I've always loved him no matter what. But I can't abide violence. It's my house and I won't tolerate it.'

Dot was lost for words. She'd had no idea that Beryl had even seen their altercation in the living room on the night she'd walked out. But then she suddenly remembered the flash of movement she'd spotted at the top of the stairs just after Tommy had struck her. She'd thought she was imagining things and dismissed it at the time, but Beryl must have seen him strike her, after all. The fact it had led her to finally accept that her son didn't deserve any more excuses after she had let him get away with so much was a little more than Dot could handle.

'I heard raised voices and came out of my bedroom,' Beryl explained. 'I got out on the landing just in time to see Tommy hitting you. I was so appalled, but I didn't know what to do. I wanted to help you, but then you ran away from him, so I ducked back into the bedroom. I waited by my door until you left – if he had tried to get into your bedroom, then I swear I would have stopped him.' Somehow, even after everything Beryl had let her son get away with, Dot believed her on this. 'When I heard you leaving, I felt proud of you. You finally stood up to him.'

'I think it was joining the ARP that gave me the strength.'

'Yes. I should apologise for my behaviour about that, too. I was only so against it because I knew how angry it would make Tommy. I actually think it's brilliant that women are doing their bit like that. But I'm afraid I tried to stop you joining to save us both the hassle of his reaction.'

'Well, now he's gone, maybe you can start showing your support to the ARP?' Dot knew she was pushing it, but she wanted to see just how sorry Beryl was.

'I will, I promise.'

'Where will Tommy go when he comes back?'

'I don't know, dear, but a man like Tommy can look after himself. It won't take him long to wheedle his way into another woman's affections. And I'm afraid I'm too old and too worn down to try and stop it this time.'

Dot felt bad thinking about the poor woman he would pick on next. But she couldn't let that be her concern – she was free now. And Peggy had been right about bullies getting their comeuppance.

'I imagine he wasn't best pleased when you told him he couldn't come back?'

'I waited till his head was banging from the whisky the following morning and he was on his way out. He didn't have time to argue, and I think he was so shocked that he wasn't able to, anyway.'

Dot laughed at that. She liked the thought of him suffering from the hangover and then getting that extra blow from his mother. Viv and Peggy standing on the doorstep and asking after her as he tried to leave the house would have been an extra punch to the stomach. No wonder he'd told them not to disturb his mother – he didn't want them finding out the truth about her kicking him out.

'So, what's next for you? Surely you can't sleep on this sofa forever?' Beryl asked, looking at the blanket and the cushion she had shoved to the side.

'I'll work something out.' Dot shrugged.

'Well, you're welcome to come back home.' Dot's eyes widened in shock. The two of them might have reached some kind of understanding now that Beryl had explained her past behaviour and finally put her son in his place, but she couldn't see how they could ever live together again – not after what Beryl had put her through. 'Think about it,'

Beryl added softly before pulling out a pocket watch and checking the time. 'I'd best be off – I'm to meet Jim for some lunch if we don't get another raid this afternoon.'

'Wait,' Dot cried, grabbing at Beryl's hand before she could put the pocket watch back.

'Whatever's the matter, dear?'

'That watch – can I take a closer look?'

'Yes, of course.' Beryl handed her the pocket watch with a proud look on her face. 'Beautiful, isn't it? A present from Jim. He certainly knows how to treat a lady.' She smiled, staring off into the distance, as Dot turned the device over in her hands.

'Where did he get it?'

'What do you mean? Why would I know where he got it from? It was a present.'

'It's stolen.'

Beryl's head snapped back to look at Dot. 'What do you mean? My Jim isn't a thief.'

'I know that. And I know that because I know exactly who stole this watch.' It was too much of a coincidence to not be true. Charles's body had been amongst the dead bodies that Dot had seen Stan stealing things from. The watch had been in Charles's pocket the night he'd died – he'd showed it to Dot that evening and he'd even told her that he always kept it with him. There was no other explanation: she hadn't just witnessed Stan stealing from corpses that night – she'd seen him lifting Charles's most treasured possession from his body before it was even cold. 'It belonged to one of my colleagues,' she explained now. 'You see this dent in the back?'

'Yes, I knew it was second hand – it added to the charm of it,' Beryl said quietly.

'Well, that dent came from a bullet. My colleague had this watch in his breast pocket when he was fighting during the Great War. The bullet hit the watch and stopped him from being killed on the battlefield.'

'I don't understand, Dorothy.'

'The man this watch belonged to is dead. It didn't save him a second time unfortunately. But I watched on as another of my colleagues snatched it from his dead body.' Beryl gasped and put her hand to her mouth. 'Beryl, I need to have a word with your fancy man. He's going to help me bring down a corrupt ARP warden.' Excitement suddenly gripped Dot: one bully had been served their just desserts and now it was time to hand some out to another. The two women stared at each other in silence before Dot added defiantly, 'And you really must start calling me Dot from now on.'

32

Viv woke to the sound of raised voices. She rubbed her eyes wearily and reached to the bedside table for her watch. When she finally laid her hands on it and brought it to her bleary eyes, she saw that she hadn't been asleep for very long. The temptation to throw the blanket over her head to block out the noise and try to go back to sleep was strong – but she knew that wasn't going to happen no matter how tired she was. For one thing, she was far too nosey. She was already desperate to know who was having a tiff and why. Groggily, she got herself up out of bed and shuffled her way into the living room.

'Will you please tell Beryl that she needs to find out who her boyfriend bought this watch from?' Dot blurted loudly at Viv as soon she entered the room.

'How many times do I have to tell you – he's not my boy-friend!' Beryl shouted in response.

'Probably as many times as I've had to tell you to call me Dot instead of Dorothy,' Dot shot back, clearly shocking the older woman.

'Pause for a moment, please,' Viv pleaded, holding her hands in the air and trying to collect her thoughts. She hadn't had a chance to wake up properly yet and she was so tired that her head felt heavy and woozy, almost like she had enjoyed too much liquor the night before. 'Can you both please calm down and tell me what's going on?' She rubbed her eyes before adding in a whisper, 'And do it quietly – you've already woken me up so let's try not to disturb poor Peggy, too.'

'Agh, sorry.' Dot winced before launching into detail about how she and Beryl had 'kind of' made amends and eventually getting on to the fact that Beryl's boyfriend (or gentleman-friend, depending on which one of them you believed) had bought Charles's pocket watch for her as a present and so should be able to help them expose Stan's stealing from dead bodies.

'He's our best hope. Only Beryl is refusing to help us,' Dot added bitterly, looking over at her mother-in-law with a scowl on her face.

'I want to help, Dorothy.' She put her hands up defensively. 'I'm sorry – I mean Dot. I just feel uncomfortable asking Jim where he got it from. I don't want him to think I'm accusing him of anything untoward, or that I'm ungrateful for his present. He's a good man. I'm sure he didn't realise that he was buying stolen goods. I don't want to get him into trouble.'

Viv wasn't sure she believed that this Jim hadn't realised he was buying a stolen watch, but she wasn't going to say anything about that to Beryl.

'He won't get into any trouble. We're not interested in shopping him to the police for handling stolen goods,' Dot stressed. 'Our only concern is that we get an independent witness to back up the fact that Stan has been stealing from dead bodies and selling the items on. We need to get him stopped.' Beryl was wringing her hands now with a pained expression on her face.

'Right, where does this Jim fella live? We'll go and ask him ourselves; save you the hassle,' Viv declared. She was fed up with this now. She was too tired for all this mucking about.

She pulled a big jacket on over her nightclothes – nobody would be able to tell.

'Wait!' Beryl cried, holding out her hand. Viv turned and looked at her expectantly. She had hoped calling the older woman's bluff would do the trick and it looked as if it had. 'He won't be able to help because he didn't buy it from your colleague.'

'What do you mean?' Dot asked. 'It's Charles's watch, and I saw Stan stealing from bodies right where Charles's body was laying after the crypt bomb, waiting to be taken to the morgue. I would bet my life on the fact he stole it from Charles.'

'Yes, but people like that aren't silly enough to keep hold of the goods for very long. Think about it. They don't want to get caught carrying stuff like that around. And they can't very well go offering them to people in broad daylight. So, they give them to a middleman to sell for them.'

Viv nodded. That made sense.

'Oh! I've heard of those,' Dot said suddenly. 'What is it they call them?'

'Spivs,' Beryl answered, looking down at the ground. 'They operate mostly out of the back of pubs where they won't get spotted by the wrong people. I can't see the problem myself. People are happy enough to buy things from them when no one is looking, but they all look down on them if they spot them out in public. They've got to make a living, though, just like everybody else. This war has thrown up a great number of hypocrites, if you ask me.'

'You seem to know an awful lot about it,' Viv said suspiciously. Beryl was being rather defensive all of a sudden. 'Anyway, Jim can tell us who the spiv is he bought the watch from, and then we can go and have a chat with him,' she added, buttoning up her coat. 'Come on, let's get going and we might catch the rascal before the pubs open and he starts his illicit trading.'

'He's just trying to make a living. You don't know how hard it is for the men left behind – no work to be had and they can't get out and help defend the country because of some silly injury.'

'It's Jim, isn't it?' Dot said, her face suddenly lighting up. 'Jim's the spiv! You're dating a criminal, Beryl. No wonder you didn't want Tommy finding out about your new man!'

Viv knew how much her friend would be enjoying this revelation; her mother-in-law stepping out with a wrong-un after all the hassle she had given her over the years. They might have made amends, of sorts, but Viv could tell from Dot's face and delighted tone that she was relishing this.

'He's not a criminal,' Beryl snapped. 'I've already told you that Jim is not a thief.' She paused and stared at the ground before adding, 'He's not a proper spiv.'

'But he's buying stolen watches from dishonest air-raid wardens! And I'll bet he would have sold this on for a fair whack had he not decided to try to woo you with it,' Dot exclaimed, waving the pocket watch in the air.

'He won't have known it was stolen. I can guarantee that,' Beryl said firmly. 'He's not a villain.' She sighed and sat back down on the sofa. Viv didn't move to take her coat off. She was happy to listen to Beryl's excuses for Jim, but as soon as she was finished, she was heading out to track him down – with or without Beryl's help. She'd trawl all the pubs until she found him. It wouldn't be hard. 'He's a pawnbroker. He used to own a pawn shop, but it got bombed. He lost everything. So now he has no choice but to trade on the streets to keep a roof over his head. He's going to get his business back as soon as the war is over.'

'That's a very sad story, but it doesn't explain how he came into possession of a watch that had been stolen from a dead man,' Viv said impatiently. She thought that either Beryl knew Jim was a spiv but was just too ashamed to admit it, or he had spun Beryl a line and she had fallen straight for it. Viv hadn't heard of any pawn shops around here getting hit since the raids had started. She would have felt sorry for Beryl had she not been so awful to her friend previously.

'Well, that must have been a mistake. He doesn't buy stolen items; he only buys items from the owners. Then he holds on to them in case they want to buy them back and if they don't then he sells them on. A pawnbroker – but without a roof over his head. Maybe your corrupt warden tricked him and told him that the watch belonged to him? He's the one in the wrong here, not Jim.'

'Yes, let's go with that,' Viv said, clapping her hands and gesturing for Beryl to get to her feet. 'Now, let's go and have a little talk with Jim and see what else Stan has sent his way. I've a feeling he might be a regular customer, in which case Dot's boss will be needing a word with your fancy man, too.'

33

Dot had to admit that she'd enjoyed discovering Beryl's new boyfriend was a spiv. She could deny it all she liked but the truth was obvious. The two women may have called a strange truce, but she hadn't been able to help revelling in the fact – especially when Beryl seemed so ashamed of it. But Dot knew better than most people that you couldn't help who you fell in love with, and so she had eased up on her mother-in-law once they had left Viv's flat in order to track down Jim. Beryl was still insisting that Jim wasn't a spiv, and he was simply a pawnbroker operating out of a suitcase. Dot was happy to go along with that – on the condition that he helped them expose Stan.

It had been gone lunchtime by the time they had left Viv's flat in the end, and so Beryl had told them the best places to try were the local pubs, as Jim probably would have started 'working' already.

'If he's a law-abiding pawnbroker, then I do have to wonder why he's trading out of the back of pubs,' Viv mused. They had already tried two and were on their way to a third. Dot shot her friend a warning look. She knew Viv was only teasing Beryl in solidarity with her, but she felt like they had taken things far enough now – and she didn't want Beryl to get upset and change her mind about helping them. She knew all too well how stubborn she could be. Viv returned

Dot's glare with a knowing nod, and Dot felt grateful that she had obviously understood what her look had meant.

Beryl went into the pub ahead of Viv and Dot and had a quick conversation with the man behind the bar, as she had done in the previous two pubs. Dot watched on from the doorway in wonderment as her mother-in-law joked and laughed with the landlord, obviously at ease in surroundings she was used to. The fact Beryl clearly regularly frequented places like this was still a massive shock to Dot. She had always been under the impression that Beryl sat around at home all day waiting for Dot to cook dinner for her and carry out all the housework. She wondered if her mother-in-law had started slipping out of the house to socialise whenever Dot had been out herself. It seemed that Tommy being away had brought new opportunities for both of them. Dot made a mental note to ask Beryl about that when the time was right.

'He's here,' Beryl shouted back to them, waving them over to the bar. They joined her eagerly. 'He's in a corridor out the back. I'll take you there and introduce you, but I won't stick around. I want him to be able to talk to you freely, and I don't think he'll do that with me there because he's a gentleman and he won't want to upset me.'

Viv and Dot exchanged a knowing glance. Dot was certain that Viv was thinking the same thing that she was – that Beryl knew full well that Jim was a spiv, but she could carry on pretending that wasn't the case if she didn't hang around to hear him talking about it.

'That sounds like a good idea.' Dot smiled. If Beryl was happy to feign ignorance, then she wasn't going to stand in her way. She had lived in denial about her own relationship for long enough. Beryl led them through the pub, which was already busy despite the early hour, and through a door at the back. At the far end of the corridor, she could see a man in a long jacket wearing a trilby hat. He had a suitcase open on a small table next to him and he was shaking hands with another man while putting a wad of notes he had just accepted from him inside his jacket pocket.

'I'll let you know how I get on with them, Jim. Good man, see you tomorrow,' the man said before turning and spotting the three women walking towards them. He gave them a friendly nod and then dashed out of the back door leading to the yard outside the pub.

'My dear Beryl! You bringing me new custom? What can I do for you, ladies?' Jim called out, taking his hat off and bowing his head while giving them a cheeky grin. When they reached him, he hugged Beryl and kissed her on the lips but she pulled away sharply, looking embarrassed.

'They're not here to *pawn* anything, Jim,' she said sternly. 'Because that's what you would normally come to a pawnbroker for,' she added, holding eye contact with him until realisation flooded his face and he slowly nodded along with her.

'Ha ha, yes, but of course! Just a regular pawnbroker, me. Well, how can I help?'

'This is my daughter-in-law, Dot.'

'Oh yes, the famed ARP warden! Lovely to make your acquaintance at last. I've heard ever so much about you.' He took hold of Dot's hand and kissed it, giving her a mischievous wink. Dot found herself warming to him immediately despite her misgivings about how he chose to make a living. He was certainly a cheeky chap, and he had a heap of charisma. Beryl had always been so straight and serious, but Dot was beginning to understand how even she could fall for the wily ways of somebody like this. She really was learning a lot about this woman since walking out of her life.

'They think one of their colleagues might have pawned something with you. Only it might not have been his to pawn.'

'I see,' Jim said, slowly nodding his head, his eyes wide in exaggerated acknowledgement.

'I'll leave you three to talk. I'll be back for our lunch later, Jim.' Beryl left through the same door as Jim's previous customer while Dot tried to get her head around the thought of her mother-in-law drinking in a pub like this. There was no way Tommy would allow it if he was at home. She was starting to wonder if his bout of violence towards her was going to end up working well for Beryl – now she had thrown him out of the house she would be free to continue this new life she had started up on the sly in his absence.

'I suppose you're here about Stan?'

'How did you know?'

'He's not very subtle about what he gets up to. I've told him not to come to me wearing his uniform, but he carries on regardless. It's hard enough for me to do what I do without people like him drawing attention to it.'

'So, you *are* a spiv?' Dot asked cautiously. She didn't want to offend him, but everything seemed to point to it.

'Listen, I know Beryl likes to defend me and tell everybody that I'm a down-on-his-luck pawnbroker, but I think we all know the truth here,' he replied, gesturing to his suitcase on the table and then holding open one side of his coat to reveal a wad of cash and coupons for clothes and petrol. 'Beryl likes to think I'm a good man fallen on hard times but, to be honest, backstreet dealings is all I've ever known. As much as she can't accept it, I'm a spiv. I ain't proud of it, but sometimes you've just gotta do what you've gotta do and I've got the love of a good woman there. If she feels better convincing herself that I'm all above board, then where's the harm in going along with it?'

Dot smiled. She was surprised to find that she was feeling happy for Beryl. She had realised today that her mother-in-law had spent just as long as she had done feeling miserable. Yes, things could have been a lot different if Beryl had decided to support her through her marriage with Tommy instead of turning against her in a vain attempt at helping her see the light and leave, but she had dealt with the situation the only way she knew how to and she had simply been trying to help her.

'So, what is it that Stan's up to?' Viv asked.

'He's pinching stuff from bombed-out houses and shops and bringing them to me to sell on, ain't he? And, yes, I know I'm an awful person for taking the stuff off his hands but I'm just trying to make a living as best I can in these circumstances.' He gently closed the suitcase when he looked up and saw Viv peering into it. 'He's been coming to me for a few weeks now. It started off with a few things here and there but recently it's got out of hand. I've told him to slow down – I've gotta stash it all somewhere and if I get caught with too much I could get in real trouble.' Dot furrowed her brow in confusion. 'The cops will let go a little bit here and there – they've got enough on their plates without having to worry about petty criminals like me. But he's been rocking up with bags full of expensive jewellery that'll get me slung in the clink if I'm caught with it all.' Jim checked his watch – Dot wondered if it had been stolen from a dead person, too – and peered along the corridor behind them before continuing.

'I've asked him to dial it back a bit but he got pretty nasty with me.' He checked along the corridor again before rolling up his coat sleeve to reveal a huge bruise on his arm. 'He's a big lad and to be honest I'm scared of him. And I operate on the sly so there's never going to be anyone around to jump in and help me if he goes for me again.'

'So, why keep buying from him?' Viv asked.

'This is what he did to me when I asked him to bring me less stuff – imagine what he'd do to me if I told him I wasn't going to deal with him anymore,' he said before rolling his sleeve back down. 'And, look, if I don't buy it from him, then he'll just go to another spiv – he's still going to profit from what he's doing, so why shouldn't I get to share in that?'

'Because it's wrong,' Viv scoffed.

'Hang on a minute,' Dot cut in gently. 'We're not here to admonish you or judge you, or even to try to get you to stop what you're doing.' They needed to keep Jim onside if he was going to help them, so she wasn't sure why Viv was trying to start an argument with him. 'It's just that, well, Stan isn't the most pleasant of people to work with, as I'm sure you can understand,' she added, gesturing to Jim's arm, which he was now rubbing. 'He's a bit of a menace in all honesty, and now we know he's stealing jewellery from dead bodies we think it's probably best he's stopped.'

'What?' Jim's eyes widened and he looked genuinely shocked. 'I knew he was looting homes and businesses after the fact, but I had no idea he'd been lifting stuff from corpses.' He scratched the back of his neck and looked quite distressed by the thought. 'How do you want me to help?'

'We just need you to come and tell my boss, Victor, what Stan has been bringing you. We can't turn him in without evidence and, well, you're the only evidence we have.'

'But what if he gets the bobbies in? I'll be implicated – I can't risk it, girls, I'm sorry.'

'He won't involve the police.'

'How do you know?'

'Because Stan is his brother-in-law. You think his wife is going to be happy with him for getting her brother thrown into jail? Victor is a man of principles, so we know he won't keep him on the ARP team, but he'll let him go quietly so as to not cause any gossip that will upset their family. That will work for all of us.'

'The fact that Stan is Victor's brother-in-law means we need evidence from somebody like you. He won't be willing to accept it if we tell him Stan's been looting on the job with nothing to back up our claims,' Viv explained.

Jim rubbed his chin thoughtfully. 'And it won't come back on me? I mean with Stan. Like I told you before, I'm not ashamed to admit that I'm frightened of the man.'

'We'll make sure your name isn't brought into it,' Dot assured him. 'We feel the same way – the last thing any of us needs is that horrible man gunning for us. But I know Victor and I know that if I ask him to leave our names out of it, then he will. He could say someone in the pub saw him doing a deal and dobbed him in.'

'All right, ladies. I'll help.' Jim checked his watch again. 'I'm just waiting on one more customer and then you can take me to this Victor chap so we can get it done before I change my mind.' Viv and Dot smiled at each other, victorious. 'Meet me out the front in ten minutes.'

34

Peggy woke with a start, waving her arms in the air and struggling to breathe. Sitting up straight, she looked around the room slowly, trying to work out where she was. In her dream, she had been stuck in the cellar of her boarding house with Mrs Martin and some of the other residents. The beam protecting them all from the foundations of the building collapsing on them had groaned loudly and snapped, bringing everything down on top of them. Peggy had woken up believing she was there, trying in vain to stop bricks and concrete landing on her and crushing the life out of her.

As she worked to calm her breathing, she remembered she was in Viv's flat. She had made it out – they all had, thanks to her amazing friends. She smiled to herself, thinking about how lucky she was to have Dot and Viv to look after her. Her thoughts tried to wander to the group who had insisted on sleeping in the main part of the house, and those who had been unfortunate enough to be sitting on the other side of the cellar, but she shook her head and stopped them. It wouldn't do her any good to dwell on that. She would never make it through a day if she allowed herself to get caught up in the feelings of grief that tried to bubble to the surface every time she thought about the people who had fallen victim to this war. And it was only going to get worse. She needed to focus on the positives and keep going.

She thought about her new friends and smiled. She knew that Dot and Viv would have pushed to dig a tunnel to the cellar as soon as they realised it was her boarding house that had been hit. She didn't want to think about what might have happened if they had ended up at different locations the night before, not knowing about the Bramerton Street bomb. Would other wardens have looked at what was left of the building and just assumed that nobody would make it out alive? Peggy was certain the beam protecting her and the other residents would have given way sooner or later.

Looking at her watch she realised she had been asleep for most of the day. She groaned and stretched out, feeling all the muscles in her body tensing. She wasn't sure how long she had been stuck in that cramped space, but her body was certainly letting her know about it now. A brisk walk around the neighbourhood would help her muscles feel better, she decided. She was disappointed to find the flat empty – she had hoped her friends would accompany her on her walk.

Peggy looked at her watch again. It was too early for them both to head off for their shifts. Maybe they had gone out to avoid disturbing her. She smiled gratefully when she remembered how Dot had forbidden her from trying to clock on this evening. Peggy had been certain when she'd gone to bed that she would be ready to get back to it this evening, but of course Dot had been right – there was no way that her body would be able to cope with it, let alone her mind. As much as she wanted to distract her thoughts by keeping busy, she had to accept that she needed some time off. She definitely needed to stretch her legs, though.

She decided to wander over to check in on Mrs Martin. Viv's friends would be out at work and Peggy didn't like the thought of the older lady sitting around their place on her own after the shock she'd had. If she got there before the next raid, she might even be able to convince her to go to the crypt with her to shelter. Peggy got herself washed again – the wash before bed had got most of the dust and muck off but she still felt as if she was covered in it.

She had just finished getting dressed when she heard a knock on the door. Viv hadn't mentioned expecting anybody, but there hadn't really been time to catch up when they came in earlier in the day. Peggy decided to take a message from whoever was at the door on her way out. But she was taken aback when she opened it and saw an RAF uniform. Taking in the gentleman's blonde hair and blue eyes, her first feeling was excitement that this might be William, come to track down Viv and ask her to marry him again. She had only very briefly seen a photograph of the man, but this chap at the door certainly looked familiar.

'Good afternoon. I'm Johnny Warner. I'm looking for Vivian Howe?' he said timidly, looking at Peggy nervously.

Her heart dropped. 'You've got the right address, but I'm afraid she's not here right now.'

'Oh. Will she be back soon? It's very important that I speak to her.'

'I'm sorry, but I don't know when she'll be back.' His face crumpled and Peggy felt terrible. He had obviously come a long way with significant news, which was more than likely related to William, and she couldn't be any help at all. 'I'm so sorry. I had a bit of a night of it, and Viv has put me up. I think she probably went out to give me some time to sleep off what I've been through.' Peggy wasn't sure why she was babbling to this stranger, but she felt as if she owed him an explanation and reassurance that she wasn't trying to fob him off or waste his time. 'Can I take a message?' she tried.

'This is really something I ought to tell her in person,' he replied, looking sombre.

Peggy suddenly felt overcome with feelings of sadness for her friend. This had to be about William. And she didn't think one of his friends would turn up on Viv's doorstep with *good* news . . .

'Is there any chance I could come in and wait for her? I know she will want to hear what I have to tell her.'

Peggy stood aside and gestured for him to come in. She couldn't very well leave him in the flat to wait alone, and there was no question of her sending him away. If Viv didn't come back before her shift started, then she would send him over to the ambulance station to find her there. She silently hoped that Viv was enjoying her final moments of happiness before her life was shattered into pieces.

35

Viv and Dot stood by the office door while Jim told Victor all about how Stan had been coming to him to offload items he had stolen from bomb sites. Victor hadn't said a word throughout the whole speech, and Viv was beginning to worry that he was going to call Jim a liar and send them all on their way. Jim finally finished talking, and the room fell silent. Victor, who had been sitting at his desk while Jim stood in front of him talking, rubbed his eyebrows, a pained expression on his face. Eventually, he looked over at Dot and let out a long sigh.

'This is going to make life very difficult for me, so I hope your friend here isn't offended when I ask you the following question,' he said slowly. 'But, can we trust this fella? You're asking a lot of me to believe some crook who's just walked in here off the street over my own family.' He looked up at Jim and held both hands up before adding, 'No offence, mate.'

'Oh, none taken,' Jim exclaimed, shaking his head and holding his own hands up. 'You gotta be careful who you trust these days.'

'I saw him taking stuff from dead bodies with my own eyes, Victor,' Dot replied quietly.

'I had no idea about all that. I wouldn't buy stuff lifted from corpses,' Jim jumped in.

Dot ignored the interruption and reached into her coat pocket. 'I saw him take this from Charles's body at the crypt,' she said, stepping forward and holding out the pocket watch that had started everything. 'I didn't realise at the time – I was watching from a distance and so I could only make out him taking things from the bodies. But when I came across the watch again, I put two and two together and we tracked down who Stan had sold it on to and, well, here we are.'

The colour drained from Victor's face. He took the watch carefully from Dot and ran his fingers gently over it. Viv breathed a sigh of relief. She had started to worry this had been a wasted trip.

'Charles's lucky charm,' he croaked. 'I looked for this afterwards.' He had tears in his eyes, and he coughed to clear his throat before continuing. 'He'd asked me to give it to his daughter if anything happened to him. I couldn't understand where it had gone – I knew he always kept it on him.' His voice brightened now. 'The silly sod was always telling that story about how it saved his life during the Great War.' Dot laughed along with him fondly. 'I must have heard that story more than a hundred times,' he added, smiling sadly. Suddenly, he got to his feet. 'To think that Stan ripped it from him before his body was even cold.' He was shaking his head now, his voice growing louder and angrier. 'After all the chances I've given that good-for-nothing excuse for a man! I should never have let him anywhere near my poor sister!'

'Dot didn't want to come and tell you until she had somebody to back up what she was saying,' Viv explained for her friend, who seemed too shocked by her boss's outburst to speak. Dot had told her Victor was always calm and collected, and they'd been counting on him dealing with Stan discreetly and peacefully, so as to avoid any backlash on anybody. The interruption seemed to snap Victor out of his rage. He sat down again.

'I'm glad you came to me,' he said to Dot. 'I know it must have been difficult. I understand how intimidating my brother-in-law can be. I'm sure you've already had run-ins with him you haven't told me about. I know he takes pleasure in taunting Peggy. He likes to throw his weight around.' Dot looked nervously to the ground. 'But, rest assured, you won't have to worry about him any longer.'

'Won't have to worry about who?' boomed a voice from behind them.

Viv spun round and her heart dropped to her feet when she saw Stan standing in the hallway just behind her. 'This looks cosy,' he said with a laugh, nudging past her into the room and looking around. But the smile quickly left his face when his eyes landed on Jim. Jim looked terrified.

'Just the man I need to see,' Victor said evenly. 'I need a quiet word with you, Stan.'

Viv could not see this ending well. If Victor confronted Stan about his stealing now, he would know exactly who had told him about it. Even if Victor waited, Stan had seen them all in the office, so he was sure to put two and two together. 'Would you mind leaving us to it?' Victor asked the rest of them. Jim darted for the door, but Stan stepped to his right to block his path.

'Hang on a minute,' he said. 'I wanna know what this lot are doing here. Especially this one,' he added, jabbing a finger at Jim's chest. Jim flinched and Stan laughed. Then he looked round at Victor, and his eyes settled on Charles's pocket watch.

'You can't prove that came from me,' he said.

'I think you've just done that yourself,' Victor replied.

'Why, you little . . .' Stan roared, launching himself at Jim, who flew backwards from the force of Stan's huge bulk and stumbled to the floor. Stan stepped forward towards him, but Victor jumped out of his chair and grabbed him just in time. Viv was frozen to the spot as she watched the two men grappling in the middle of the room with Dot on the other side of them.

'You lot'll regret this!' Stan shouted as Victor struggled to restrain him. Dot was kneeling next to Jim now, checking he was all right, and Viv was terrified Stan was going to lash out at them. Then, Victor leaned in and whispered into Stan's ear.

'What did you say?' Stan replied, shock running over his face. He suddenly stopped thrashing about and trying to fight off his brother-in-law and stood still. Victor took a step back and straightened out his clothes. There was silence as they all waited for him to repeat whatever it was he had just said to get such a reaction from Stan.

'I said,' Victor replied slowly and firmly, 'that if you do anything to any of these good people, then I'll tell my sister exactly where you got her eternity ring from.' The colour drained from Stan's face. 'And then I'll go with her to show the police.' Stan stared at Victor in silence. 'I knew I recognised it when she showed me, but I thought it must have been my eyes playing tricks on me. Or maybe it had ended up in a pawn shop and you'd picked it up for a good price. I didn't think you'd stoop so low as to steal from your own friends. But you were there when they pulled

Jack and Carol out of the rubble. You were there and you lifted her ring from her finger. You're a disgusting excuse for a man.'

Stan didn't even try to defend himself. 'You wouldn't,' he whispered. 'You'd break her heart.'

'That's the only reason I'm not going straight to her now. That and the fact that I need some insurance to keep these three safe. I mean it, Stan – you go anywhere near them, at any time, and I'll tell her everything.' Stan nodded slowly. 'If anything untoward happens to any of them, it will come back on you. So don't go asking any of your mates to do your dirty work for you. And it goes without saying that I won't be expecting you on duty any longer.'

Stan's head whipped up. 'What will I tell everyone?'

'I don't know.' He paused. 'I really don't care. But I'll work something out. For my sister's sake – not for yours. Now, I think you need to leave, before I change my mind.'

Stan glared over at Jim, who cowered in the corner. Viv held her breath, waiting for Stan to lash out again, but he walked past her calmly without saying a word and left the office.

'Well, at least that's over and done with,' Victor said, collapsing into his chair with a huge sigh. He reached over and picked up the pocket watch again. He turned it over in his hands as they all waited in silence.

'Are you all right, Victor?' Dot asked, walking over to her boss.

'I'm just disappointed. But I'm relieved to be able to give this to Charles's daughter. Thank you for coming to me; I know that must have been difficult.'

Dot sighed. 'I was worried, what with Stan being your brother-in-law. But I knew you would do the right thing.'

Victor smiled up at her before turning his attention back to the pocket watch.

'We'd best get back and check on Peggy and then get ready for our shifts,' Viv offered. It seemed as if Victor needed some time on his own. She looked over at Jim, who was still sitting on the floor. 'Let's help him up,' she suggested, walking over to him. Viv and Dot took hold of an arm each and heaved Jim to his feet.

'Sorry, ladies, that was all a bit much. I saw my life flash before my eyes,' he whispered. Viv and Dot exchanged a look and smirked at each other. Outside in the fresh air, they walked side by side with Jim trailing behind them.

'I can see why Beryl likes him,' Dot whispered. 'He's a bit dramatic, just like her. Also, a little bit pathetic – somebody for her to look after.'

Viv couldn't help but laugh along with her friend. When they reached the point where they were to bid Jim farewell, he pulled them both into an embrace.

'Thank you for getting me out of there,' he exclaimed.

'Thank you for your help, Jim. Stan has been getting away with too much for too long, and we couldn't have brought him down without your help,' Dot replied.

'Yes, you were very brave,' Viv added genuinely.

Jim smiled, put his hand over his heart and then hugged them both tightly again before suddenly letting them go and rushing off down the street.

'Definitely dramatic.' Viv giggled.

Walking up the path to her building, Viv was excited to fill Peggy in on the afternoon's dramas. 'It will be a good distraction for her,' she mused as she opened the front door.

But when she walked into the living room, her heart caught in her chest when she saw Peggy sitting on the sofa with Johnny. They stared at each other for what felt like an eternity.

'Why don't you sit down?' Johnny offered.

'William's dead, isn't he?' Viv blurted. 'I'm right this time. Just get it over with and tell me.' She just needed to know.

'He's not dead.'

'Oh, thank goodness!' she exclaimed, falling to her knees and putting her head in her hands. She felt Dot's arms around her immediately and she leaned into her support. Relief flooded through her body. She'd spent so long trying to keep positive while a little voice in the back of her head had taunted her, convinced she had lost William forever – lost her one chance at true love and happiness. But he'd made it out alive! 'Wait,' she said suddenly, looking up at Johnny. 'You said before that his plane was shot down – and he's been missing quite a while. Is he in a bad way?'

'He's . . . suffered some injuries.' Johnny fiddled with his jacket, refusing to look her in the eye. 'But he's alive, Viv, and he's been asking for you.'

The fact Johnny had avoided answering her question properly was not lost on Viv. But she decided to cling on to the good news here – William was alive. And he was asking for her. She slowly got to her feet and brushed away the hair that had fallen over her face.

'Well, it looks like I'm travelling back to Sussex with you,' she declared. 'I won't leave him waiting a minute longer.' She went to her room to pack a bag, with Peggy and Dot trailing behind her.

'We're coming with you,' Peggy said. Dot stood beside her, nodding her head in agreement.

'I'll be fine. William's alive! It's all I've been hoping for!' She was trying to keep her voice cheery, but she could feel it shaking.

'It's okay to be scared,' Dot said, stepping forward to put her hand on Viv's arm.

Viv nodded, her lips trembling. She was terrified of what state she might find William in. Johnny had been very careful not to give too much away – and he certainly hadn't seemed excited to give her the news that his friend had survived. She had no idea what she was walking into – he could be at death's door for all she knew.

'But you're needed here,' she whispered.

'They certainly won't be expecting me back for a few days,' Peggy replied. 'And I insist that Dot stays with me to help me through the shock of what I've been through,' she added with a wink.

'You're really going to drop everything to come with me?'

'Of course we are. We're your friends and, as much as you don't like to admit it, you need us. We wouldn't dream of leaving you to face this on your own.'

'I can admit it,' Viv replied as a sob escaped her mouth. She didn't have the energy to fight it back anymore. She was so overwhelmed to have the unwavering support of Dot and Peggy that she let down her defences in front of them and allowed them to see how vulnerable she was feeling. She fell into their open arms and wept tears of joy, relief, fear, love and pain. She let it all out. When she finally broke away and gathered herself, Peggy reached over to the chest of drawers and picked something up.

'Time for action,' she declared, taking the lid off the gold tube. 'Lipstick on and bag packed. We're off to reunite you with your man.'

Viv took the make-up gratefully and applied it with relish. With her warpaint on and her two best friends by her side, she knew she could get through this and stay strong for William. No matter what they had to face, they'd face it together.

ARP Recruitment Poster

When I came across this ARP recruitment poster online, I thought it would be the perfect propaganda for Dot to come across and get her thinking again about joining up. It is so simple and straightforward, but the images are so powerful – I think it would be difficult for any woman at the time to pass by it without thinking about doing their bit.

The Blitz Operations Manual

This book, written by Chris McNab, was invaluable while I was researching *The Blitz Girls*. I learned everything about how best to survive the Blitz – from how to build an Anderson Shelter to how to splint a fractured arm using a newspaper – which Dot also picked up during her training!

Ken 'Snakehips' Johnson

When I read about Londoners spending air raids beneath the ground at the Café de Paris, it was the perfect favourite haunt for fun-loving Viv. Learning about the resident band, the West Indian Dance Orchestra, I could picture Viv dancing away her troubles and fears to their music. I love how fun and carefree the band's leader, Ken Johnson, always looked in photos.

After the Raid

This image stopped me in my tracks. The poor woman had lost everything apart from what she had managed to cram into the pram. And she was one of the lucky ones; so many people lost everything. I hope the ARP warden directed her to a rest centre and that she got the help she needed.

ARP Warden and Baby

This photo of an ARP warden rescuing a baby from her bombed-out home in 1940 really brought home to me the true devastation of the Blitz; families ripped apart and lives ruined. I hope that little girl's family made it out of the wreckage alive, too, and that she lived to tell her grandchildren the tale of how they were all rescued by such brave people. Image from *My War: ARP Volunteer* by Stewart Ross

Acknowledgements

First and foremost, I would like to thank you, the reader, for buying or borrowing or downloading this book. I hope you enjoyed reading it as much as I enjoyed writing it and I hope you'll stick with me and The Blitz Girls for the rest of our journey together.

I must thank Naomi Clifford for *Under Fire* and Frances Faviell for *A Chelsea Concerto*; both books provided an invaluable insight into life for women volunteers during World War II. I would have been lost without Chris McNab's *The Blitz Operations Manual*, so a huge thanks to him, too.

Thank you, as ever, to my agent Kate Burke at Blake Friedmann, for your constant support, advice, and, most importantly, headlice chat!

I also owe huge gratitude to my wonderful editor, Olivia Barber, for trusting me with your Blitz girls. It means a lot that you chose me for this project, and I hope that I've done Viv, Dot, and Peggy justice.

Warm thanks, too, to the whole team at Hodder & Stoughton, but especially to copyeditor Suzanne Clarke and her eagle-eye!

Finally, I'd like to thank my family and friends for their encouragement and support while I wrote *The Blitz Girls*. The research was upsetting at times, and I'm grateful to my girls for putting a smile back on my face every time I stepped away from it all.